2010

BEST

Gay

LOVE

STORIES

2010

BEST

Gay

LOVE

STORIES

edited by

BRAD NICHOLS

ALYSONbooks

Best Gay Love Stories 2010
Edited by Brad Nichols

Published by Alyson Books
245 West 17th Street, Suite 1200, New York, NY 10011

ISBN-13: 978-1-61523-378-6

Library of Congress Cataloging-in-Publication data are on file.

Cover design by Victor Mingovits

Printed in the United States of America
Distributed by Consortium Book Sales and Distribution
Distribution in the United Kingdom by Turnaround Publisher Services Ltd

CONTENTS

INTRODUCTION vii

A PAIR OF ACES BY CHARLIE FISH 1

BEST BIRTHDAY BY D. E. LEFEVER 15

THE GAYEST AMERICAN HERO BY STEVEN BEREZNAI 29

HELLO GORGEOUS BY REX LANDRY 43

THE LAST GOOD-BYE BY WILLIAM HOLDEN 53

CRYSTAL BALL BY STEPHEN OSBORNE 61

CITY OF FOUNTAINS BY ROSS M. LEVINE 75

THE GALAXY IS OUR PLAYGROUND BY THOMAS HERMAN 91

HOME BY DEAN REYNOLDS 103

FIREBALL BY TOM MENDICINO 123

THE BENCH BY PETER CONTRERAS 141

PYRAMIDS IN ROME BY DERRICK DELLA GIORGIA 151

THE TRICK BY SAM HAWK 161

POOR RICHARD'S BAZAAR BY RYAN FIELD 177

OUT-ISLAND CRUISING BY DAVID HOLLY 195

A CLADDAGH DESTINY BY STEPHEN DEE 213

SOARING WITH A HAWK BY KENN DAHLL 235

INTRODUCTION

I BELIEVE IN wide-eyed love. However, let me make myself clear. I'm not talking about orange skies melting into a red sun as it sets over our kingdom. I mean actual love—the smoke-in-your-heart, cigarette-burned kind of love that can give you moments of extreme clarity, and moments of madness. The problem with this kind of love is that it doesn't stay this crazy too long. That clarity you receive—even the madness—slips away and evolves. You're left with something completely different, something you didn't mean to create but somehow molded in the process, and it puts your pink-inked love letters into perspective. You find yourself standing in front of a product of your love. You have a relationship.

For me, that's what love at first sight evolves into if you're lucky to make it past the glittering euphoric. But this isn't a bad thing. That first sight of love is the spark that started the fire. Those awkward nights on the phone when you're first getting to know each other to stepping on each other's worn shoes during your first slow dance. But I don't buy into the white picket fence and dog that come with the happy marriage syndrome. Every relationship has its flaws and challenges to overcome. The perfect relationship isn't that valentine on your desk or found in some old musky poem; it's in the bleeding heart, the trial and error you endure while making your relationship work. That's what makes love, relationship, soul mates, etcetera, so revolutionary. The sacrifice that comes with it makes it memorable and worthy of having its story told.

In this anthology, you'll find all sorts of love: cuddle love, end-of-the-world love, superficial love. Whether it is letting go of love in William Holden's "The Last Good-Bye," or discovering love during war in D. E. LeFever's "Best Birthday," the stories in this anthology show the depths of love and the various meanings it gives to our lives.

Yours,
Brad Nichols

A PAIR OF ACES

CHARLIE FISH

WHAT DO PLAYING cards and my love life have in common? Well, there are fifty-two cards in a deck, for one, and there are just as many names in my romance Rolodex. Now, before you get all judgy on me, that number doesn't mean I've "gone all the way" with the whole lot. (That number is much, much smaller: just shy of using up both hands.) But it does mean I've been dealt, so to speak, some real jokers and jackasses in my day. On the other hand, I've also been fortunate enough to win the jackpot. On two different occasions I called Cupid's bluff and walked away a richer man.

Incidentally, I almost never met Luca seven years ago because I kept eyeing Cameron, the tall blond with a swimmer's build. It was in a nightclub, and I shyly danced around Cameron while trying to muster up enough courage to mumble-stutter a few words at him. "What's your name?" I asked, just barely missing his ear and speaking, instead, into his neck. He quickly excused himself from the dance floor and was never to be seen again. I hung around in the club for a little longer, hoping not to have to sing the "How Soon Is Now" blues. Just when I was about to give up on trying to hook up, Luca and I spotted each other. This being an '80s-themed night, "What I Like

About You" by the Romantics was spinning on the turntables. As Luca and I circled around the floor, sizing each other up like cardsharps in a bidding frenzy, I thought it'd be cute if I pointed at him every time the lyrics called for it. Poker face intact, he either remained oblivious or was decidedly not impressed by my lip-synching and pointing. Inevitably, his friends forced us to bump into each other and names were exchanged. "Luca? That's a foreign-sounding name. Where're ya from? Oh, you're Italian? And you're only here for two more days until you go back to Europe? Of course you are! No, no, I believe you. It's my incredibly bad *luck* I don't believe."

Later, we sat at the bar and answered questions over ice waters. (We had originally asked for beers, but then the bartender asked for IDs.) His family, he told me, alternated between Italy and Miami; he was studying in Cambridge, England; he went wherever his parents called "home" during breaks. Right away I could tell he was a real charmer when he pointed at a tattoo on my forearm and, with a smile, said, "That's tacky." "That's not the best way to get into my pants," I replied. Half an hour later we were driving around Miami trying to find the best spot where I could show him more than my tattoos. On the roof level of the Baptist Hospital parking garage, Luca and I eagerly explored each other's foreign bodies. Afterward, he held me as we sat on the hood of his car and counted the stars in the 3:00 a.m. sky. We were nineteen.

Even though he was leaving in forty-eight hours, he asked me if he could see me again the following day. Our second "date" went better than the first, with any weirdness or tension being replaced with interest and attention. The hours slipped away and we both knew he'd be London bound come sunup. Right before he left he asked for my e-mail address and promised to write. Then he looked at me and said, "You know, I feel like I'm already falling in love with you." I smiled, unsure of what to say.

The next few months were spent e-mailing and placing long-distance calls and, before I knew it, I had fallen in love with him. Completely. I loved his handsome face and his eyes, his thick hair and his toned body; I loved hearing his British/Italian accent and his goofy laughter. Mostly, I loved simply being around him.

We made it a point to see one another during his semester breaks. To afford the trip to Europe, I took out student loans. We celebrated our one-year in England, where we slept on his twin-size mattress in his prestigious college dorm. Later in the week, we flew to Italy, where we stayed in his family's villa near Venice. For someone who grew up lower-to-middle class, drove a twelve-year-old Toyota Camry, and attended the local university, it was as sweeping and picturesque as it all sounds. So this was what my knight looked like? A worldly traveler—a member of the upper crust—who racked up Virgin Atlantic miles to sweep me off my feet? But he and the relationship were not without their faults.

From the beginning, I was always aware that I came second to just about everything else in his life. He put school, his mom, and his needs above all else, leaving me at a distant fourth. There'd be days without any communication, especially infuriating because he would tell me what day and time he intended to call, and then miss the mark by a week or so. His usual response when I angrily confronted him? "I was working on a project, and figured I'd call you eventually." Eventually? Anyone in his right mind would assume he had lovers on the side and—under usual circumstances—they'd probably be right. But infidelity was the farthest thing from my mind for one very simple, albeit challenging, reason: the man had the libido of an eighty-year-old.

Whenever we saw each other, usually for seven to ten days' length, we'd spend day and night together, but have sex only once or twice. At first I avoided bringing up the topic, thinking he was suffering from extreme jet lag. Then, after the normal self-esteem issues that would plague anyone (whose lover didn't seem interested in sex?) started to boil at a maximum, I asked him what the deal was. Could I do anything different? Was he not attracted? Did he want to bring in a third party? He reassured me that he was very much attracted to me, but then couldn't give an answer as to why he lacked a sex drive. Eventually, I formed my own thoroughly unscientific hypothesis. Given that he suffered from frequent bouts of asthma, I figured not enough oxygen flowed to his pleasure center in the brain. And thus I coped with not copulating with the man I loved.

(I have to stress here for anyone thinking that I'm an idiot for having fallen in love with a man who didn't live in the same continent as I did, placed me second in his life, and was rarely horny that I get it. I do. He wasn't "textbook" boyfriend material. But I was already waist high in murky love and had no intentions of turning back.)

The long-distance aspect of the relationship lasted eighteen months, until he graduated from college. Despite the odds stacked against us, there was a payoff in sight, a promise for better times ahead. Our plan was as follows: I would fly to England to see his bizarre British graduation ceremony (involving clutching a man's finger as a symbol of knowledge osmosis), his parents would lend us their

Audi (non-automatic, which proved troublesome for yours truly; there was an accident) and give us some extra spending cash, and we would embark on a road trip throughout Western Europe for the remainder of the summer. It would cost me more student loans (which I'm *still* paying off today), but I figured it was well worth the adventure and the time spent with my boyfriend.

That summer, as planned, we loaded up his parents' car with our luggage and bare essentials and drove from Cambridge to the chalk-lined hills of Dover, England, where we boarded a ferryboat to France. Paris and Normandy followed, along with the western French countryside. We explored Spain in a counterclockwise motion, seeing modern Bilbao and countless small towns that all seemed to serve *cava* and *pulpo gallego*. Barcelona was next, where he sketched *La Sagrada Familia* and other Gaudi greats. A few more hours by car and we were back in the south of France, resting in Montpellier for a bit but whizzing by Nice and Cannes. Longing for a real bed and a home-cooked meal, we drove the rest of the way to his Venetian villa, where we unpacked for the rest of the summer. Occasional day trips to nearby towns, and exploring his family's acres in Umbria, rounded out our traveling adventure. At the height of the summer sun, *Ferragosto*, we caught a flight to Miami and moved into a condo on North Miami Beach, only a main street separating us from the ocean waves. Talk about a payoff!

When we moved into our apartment, a housewarming party and countless dinner get-togethers ensued. For a while, I was happy. What I hadn't anticipated was that the problems in our relationship that seemed alleviated by the distance would be put under a giant microscope once we moved in together. Call me naïve. We built a life and a home together for a year, both of us knowing it was borrowed time. There was never an option for him to remain in America, as his mother had already decided what three schools in England she wanted him to apply to for a master's program. Unable to simply pack up my bags and legally live in the UK, I wanted to pursue my dreams and move to New York after my own graduation. Knowing this in advance worked against us, as we were unable to achieve complete and total relationship intimacy for fear of the impending "deadline."

Not that the other kind of "intimacy" was any better. After spilling all my relationship woes onto my best friend, he asked me when did I last have sex with Luca. I realized it had been over two months. That was the beginning of the end, in retrospect. In a desperate bid to shock him into a sex life, I asked him if I could sleep with other people. (The idea being that he'd snap out of his sexual slump at the thought of me being polygamous.) He said no. My eyes reddened and I replied with an insane rant, likening our sex life to a poor person scavenging for half-eaten french fries in the Dumpster. In my sex-starved mind, that homeless person and I were one and the same. Who's to say that if a hot piece of man-meat looked my way, I wouldn't jump on him like a hobo on a hot dog? "It will be hard," I told him, "to remain faithful."

As our borrowed time came to a close, I asked him to spend the summer with me in San Francisco before he moved back to Europe and I headed to New York. I didn't think much of it, as the only other option would be that he'd remain in our empty apartment, counting down the days until his own move. His response: "My mom isn't going to be very happy about that." Fed up with his inability to compromise, and with his lack of understanding what it means to be someone's partner, I called his bluff. "We're as good as over if you don't spend the summer with me. Tell your mother to stick it somewhere dark and damp," I challenged. Fights occurred, bitter words were spat, and something within me unhinged. My tie to San Francisco ended up being severed, relieving him from having to upset his dear, omnipotent mother. But from that argument onward, I started to fall out of love with Luca a little more each day.

Within weeks I was living in New York City. I understood that when I moved to New York, eventually, he and I would come to an end. We talked on the phone and e-mailed again, but this time around, I wasn't angry when he'd forget to call. I made up for lost time, bedroom-wise; we both dated other people over the course of a year. I met some good guys and some guys who sent me to the rail. Even though I was able to start having strong feelings toward other men, a small part of my heart still had Luca's name on it. Over time, my feelings toward Luca became cordial and warm, but the burning love I had felt for him was mostly gone.

With Luca being nearly 90 percent out of the picture, I decided to book a trip to London to see him. Part of me wanted to know if we could fan old flames. The selfish part wanted something familiar after a string of bad dates and other romance horror stories. One night, about two weeks before heading out to London, I sent a MySpace message to a guy I thought was hot. His MySpace handle was Nate Dawgy. He was shirtless in the picture, with a baseball cap and steely blue eyes. He was looking right into the camera, right at me, it seemed.

"You're fuckin' hot" was the message. (I had been using the social networking site to find potential late-night suitors.) To my complete surprise, Mr. Dawgy responded.

We e-mailed a lot, and I kept pressing for us to meet in person. But he would find reasons why he couldn't: The flu. Work. Working with the flu. I gave up on trying to bone Mr. Dawgy and headed to London for a week.

Seeing Luca again did stir up feelings, though they were mostly confused ones. One day over lunch he told me how much I had hurt him toward the end of our time living together. I was shocked into silence, a rare occasion unto itself. Luca was not the type of guy who spoke a lot about feelings and emotions, opting instead to stay quiet during our drawn-out discussions and heated arguments (all initiated and dominated by me, of course). Hearing him say that I had been hurtful, that I had lashed out, and that I was generally a bitter person to be around when in Miami left me still further speechless. When he finally asked me to say something, I burst into tears over our pizza.

I cried because you can't undo hurt; you can't take back words. I cried because he really did love me, and I no longer had him alone to blame. I cried because there was a way we could've prevented the end, but at this point, I no longer felt the same. And I cried because when we had sex the night before, I knew it meant more to him than it did to me. Was there a part of him that wanted to get back together? I didn't want to know. I cried because I flew to London to see if I was capable of rekindling a romance, and discovered that Luca still felt protective of me; he was still in love with me. He still thought of me and missed me, regardless of the strange ways he showed it. Or didn't. But I wasn't in love with him anymore. So mostly I cried because it meant the end. We lasted three years.

With just two days left before I would fly home, he told me he and his best friend were going to New York in a few weeks and asked if they could stay in my apartment. How could I refuse when he'd just let me stay with him? The day I left London, I was checking e-mails when my inbox showed a new MySpace message. It was Mr. Dawgy. He wanted to know when we would meet in person. "Whenever you want," I said, and a date was set.

As fate would have it, I almost never met Nathan in person because he almost canceled our date. He had been at a friend's house party in Brooklyn, and apparently Bombay Sapphire was sponsoring said party. A slightly drunk Nathan called me and said, "Hey, I know we're supposed to meet at the bar on North Tenth, but there's this awesome party going on and all my friends are here. And there's free gin! You wanna come over?" Sensing his apprehension to come meet me, and more than slightly annoyed at his last-minute change of plans, I icily replied, "I don't drink gin." Twenty minutes later we stood in front of each other outside the bar. He shook my hand and smiled. His friends, he later told me, made him take a cab to honor his date.

Nathan in person looks nothing like he does in pictures. Nathan in photographs looks more oafish, like some big muscle man with giant genitalia and a pea for a brain. It didn't help that his e-mails were full of grammatical errors and misspelled words. I was looking forward to sleeping with him, then not returning his phone calls. Luckily for me, he was not an oaf. He was slim and alternative looking, like a geeky skater (but better dressed). His grayish-blue eyes glimmered with sincerity and a healthy dose of mischief. He carried himself well, seemed highly intelligent, and was a total history buff. He was not at all what I expected. Trying to reconcile the two versions of Nathan in my mind, I made a comment about his e-mails. He laughed it off and said he'd gotten so used to writing IMs that he'd given up on cyberpenning formalities. Then he spilled his gin and tonic all over himself. But I didn't care. I sensed I'd hit it big this time.

Here's what I learned that night: he trained at the country's leading culinary academy, meaning he could cook a mean dinner any night of the week and would most likely serve more than one course. Plus dessert. Yet, he retained the same build he had since he was a swimmer in high school. He was a baseball fanatic, and the only time he'd sung karaoke was when the Red Sox won the 2004 World Series. His song of choice? "We Are the Champions." He had lived nearly everywhere in the United States and even spent eight years in Costa Rica. (I liked this last part because that meant he spoke fluent Spanish and thus was accustomed to my Latin culture.) And even though he watched *Star Trek* and *Lord of the Rings* on repeat, his favorite clothing store was G-Star and he had a penchant for tattoos. Best of all, he was a genuinely nice guy, and was unskilled in the ways of a player. This last trait was made evident when, at 2:55 a.m., rather than saying, "So, you wanna go back to my place?" he asked, in a nervous manner, "Do you like movies?"

Did I like movies? That's like asking if I drank water, or masturbated. "Who doesn't?" I asked. "Well, 'cause I was thinking that maybe we could go watch a movie. Now. At, uh, my place. I have a whole collection of DVDs," he said. Sure. Let's go watch these "movies" you speak of in the middle of the night in your bedroom, Nathan.

As we left the bar, the season's first snow had already blanketed the streets and the hoods of the parallel-parked cars lining Bedford Avenue. We spent the night together, falling asleep some time after exploring each other's naked bodies and watching Jack Nicholson kidnap Kim Basinger in *Batman.*

The next few weeks were spent "playing it cool." Generally speaking, if I like a guy, I want to spend as much time with him as is possible before getting sick of him. That way, if it was meant to be a brief, fiery fling, it would burn out soon enough without much damage done to either party. Nathan, however, was very independent and liked to space our dates apart. So at first I gave him his distance, though all I wanted to do was text him to come over. Slowly he allowed himself to spend more time with me and devote more time to "us." Just as I was getting comfortable at the prospect of a normal, functioning relationship, there was a knock at my door.

Luca and his best friend arrived just in time for New Year's Eve. As they dragged their luggage into the apartment, I decided I would tell Luca about my new relationship, which at this stage was still in its infancy. "We can't sleep in the same bed, Luca. You're gonna have to shack up with your buddy on the futon. *Buon Anno!*"

I told Luca about Nathan, and he seemed okay with it. "We're moving on, right?" he asked. We were. We had both been dating other people for a while. "I mean, it's still pretty new, but I want to see where this might go." Then, on New Year's Eve, I had one of the dumbest ideas I'd had in a while. Luca and I—having mutual friends—had been invited to a loft party. Knowing Nathan had no plans for the night other than to watch TV, I decided it might be a good idea for me to invite him. "Would it be too weird for you if I bring Nathan?" I asked Luca. I don't know if it was out of sheer curiosity or a lapse in better judgment on both our parts, but he seemed up for it. Yes, my ex-boyfriend of three years and the guy I'd been seeing for three weeks met on December 31. I have the (awkward) picture to prove it: Nathan to my right and Luca to my left, both forcing a smile and staring intently at the camera. And lest you write me off as some unfeeling jerk, you should know Luca hooked up with a Swedish model that night. That's okay. I had sex with Nathan in the bathroom of the loft while an unknowing Luca was in the kitchen eating mini corn dogs.

The following night, Luca asked if we could talk. Turns out, he wasn't as comfortable seeing me make googly eyes at Nathan. Understandable. We made small talk for a while before he asked me: "If I were to move to New York, do you think we could give it another try? A real try?"

Silence again, on my behalf. Then, "Uh, well, Luca, I mean . . . there's a *lot* that would need fixing. And then there's 'I have a boyfriend.'" But Luca wouldn't hear it. He told me he wanted to get back together, that he would leave his friends and family in London, find a job in New York, move into his own apartment, and we could give our love story another chance, a real go, from the beginning. Like a redraw of sorts. He'd see a sexual therapist to work on his libido, he would put our relationship first, and he would change anything about himself that I didn't like. I responded with a blank stare. "Well, think it over. But I have to know in a few days. I'll give you three days," he said. "I'll call you to find out your answer."

The next day, he boarded a plane and headed back to London, leaving me more than a little restless. Luca was, after all, my first true love. There was history with Luca. For all his errors and missteps in our relationship, I was equally to blame for its demise. So didn't I owe the man that had been in my life for the last three years another shot? In hindsight, I was able to see that all his dedication to his education was so that he could become a better man in the future. A future that, in his mind, included me.

But Nathan was the definition of a great guy. He was detail minded when it came to our relationship, leaving romantic notes scattered around my room for me to find and making me laugh with his boyish playfulness. He was the antithesis of Luca. Didn't I also owe it to myself to try something new and fresh after having had three years of instability and disappointment? Besides, I really liked the guy and wouldn't have had an easy time getting over him.

So that's how I found myself in a position most screen-writers would kill for. To choose the familiar, dashing Italian and my first love? Or to choose a budding relationship, the chef, and the symbol of hope for the future? If I chose Luca, would I have spent the rest of my life wondering if it would've worked with Nathan? Conversely, if I chose Nathan, would I have been able to fully move on and never look back?

Three days later Luca called me. It was the first time in a long time he kept his word about when he'd call. "So?" he asked. Without a hint of uncertainty, I replied, "I don't think you should move here. At least, not for me." You have to know who to hold and when to fold.

✦

DESPITE MINOR SETBACKS, like accusing Nathan of having Munchausen syndrome, or our two epic battles (which Nathan calls World Wars I and II, fittingly), we recently celebrated our three-year anniversary. Early in the relationship, we bought a Boston Terrier named Willow. The three of us have a quaint home and do boring things like stay in and watch movies while my friends party until morning. Not too long ago I would've been jealous of their exciting lives. Loving Nathan means I don't have to anymore.

No relationship is without its faults, and true love means learning how to deal with them. Our sources of arguments are as follows: he's defensive, stubborn, and a noncommunicator. I'm "a diva" (his words, not mine) who suffered from depression and can't properly manage money. Oh, and I'm lazy when it comes to house chores. Still, we manage. Because there's genuine love and respect for each other. Because I've learned to stop comparing our sex life to that of single gay men and my prior relationships. Because he makes me laugh on a regular basis, and he's willing to "talk it out" whenever we encounter hiccups. And, oh yeah, he's fuckin' hot.

It seems Lady Luck has been on my side twice. Both men I've loved have taught me different ways of loving and learning, and I would not have been the same person if I'd never met them. I don't blame Luca for our failed relationship. In fact, I honor that part of him that owned my heart because he was, and forever will be, my first love. Nathan remains the man I've loved most in my life, and the man that has loved me unconditionally. A real pair of aces, the two of them are. As clichéd and trite as it may sound, love truly is a gamble. You risk your heart (and mental stability) every time someone new enters your life. Sometimes you have to keep shuffling the deck, learn to never settle for less, and all that good stuff. Nathan was number 52. I hope never to keep counting.

BEST BIRTHDAY

D. E. LEFEVER

MARCH 20, 2006. It was the third anniversary of Operation Iraqi Freedom, the date on which a multinational force had invaded Iraq for its possession and active development of weapons of mass destruction. The Iraqis, at least according to high U.S. government officials, had violated a 1991 agreement to give them up. It was my twenty-third birthday.

In peak physical shape, I knew I looked handsome, even confident, in military fatigues. I gave every appearance of the poster soldier. There was no hint of the occasional pounding in my chest. I wiped my moist palms on my pant legs, aware the desert camouflage defied soiling. Bouncing along on a crowded bus to the airport, I absorbed the artificial chatter and shrill laughter that permeated the air around me. It was the way I held uncertainty at bay. It overwhelmed any thoughts of my birthday.

I recalled the first Gulf War, nicknamed the Persian Gulf War. It was the late fall of 1991. I was fifteen years old at the time. CNN occupied the airwaves in round-the-clock coverage that, at times, gave all the appearance of a made-for-television war. It seemed a less-than-real event. My father, a career military man, told my mom: "We're there to kick some ass."

The night skies lit up over Baghdad like the Fourth of July. The reporting of Bernard Shaw and Peter Arnett, in upbeat voices, was in my mind barely distinguishable from the United States making another down, just inches from the ten-yard line. The first Gulf War was all over in forty-three days. I knew little of war at the time, already desensitized by too much TV violence. As reality TV, the war didn't even fill out the season.

My enduring memory of the first Gulf War was Arthur Kent, the Canadian journalist who spiraled to notoriety as CNN's budding young reporter. Dark and handsome, usually sporting a black leather jacket, he was nicknamed "The Scud Stud," becoming an internationally recognized correspondent by war's end. A large poster showing Kent in the midst of Baghdad's destruction hung from my bedroom wall for years afterward. I sensed my father took some pride in the seeming evidence of my patriotism, ignorant of the real reason the handsome young journalist was taped to the plaster. It was not unlike the Superman of my father's generation, a secret fantasy in floundering for idols as those like me sorted out who we were.

Deployment to Iraq was something I never envisioned growing up. It made the long plane ride surreal as I conjured up vague images of the 1991 made-for-TV drama. Glancing around the plane, I studied the faces of my soon-to-be fraternity of comrades. Conversations blended in a muddle of noise as hands and heads moved like in mime. Looking to my right over my shoulder, I caught the eye of someone else, equally detached and seated two rows back, across the aisle. I judged him to be five or six years older than my twenty-three years. His face was every bit as good or better than any on *People* magazine's ten or fifty most beautiful, however many it is. The lingering shadow of his beard and coal black hair messed up by the wind gave him a rugged look.

The remainder of the flight, I was preoccupied with thoughts of the passenger who had unexpectedly caught my attention. Repeatedly turning my head and searching about the plane, my glance invariably drifted across the aisle as I shifted uncomfortably in my seat. My movements became almost mechanical, a product of restlessness coupled with the compulsive need to etch another man's image into my mind. It was as though checking over my shoulder was an involuntary response over which I had no control. Aware that I was noticed, I was beginning to feel awkward. I made a conscious effort to keep my focus toward the forward cabin until our arrival at Balad Airbase, some sixty-eight kilometers north of Baghdad.

Deplaning on arrival in the heat of the desert, I walked with slow deliberation across the tarmac in the direction of my unit's designated point of assembly. Turning my head to avoid a gust of blowing sand, I saw someone wave, jogging purposefully in my direction.

"Welcome to hell. I'm Jason Aldrich." He extended his hand.

"Marsh Breaton," I answered, feeling a little embarrassed, wondering if he was actually aware of my earlier attentive glances.

"Your first deployment here, right?"

"Yeah. It's that obvious? Most members of my unit have been to Iraq before . . . me, it's my first."

"Just got that sense. I couldn't help but notice you were damn restless from the moment we were airborne."

I struggled to respond, suddenly feeling a bit self-conscious knowing my behavior on the plane had not gone unnoticed. I wanted to change the subject. "You? You been here before, I gather."

"This is my fourth trip . . . once in Afghanistan, the others here."

"You don't appear to be military. Why be here if you think it's such hell?"

"It's what I do. I'm a journalist—one of those free-lancers. But I prefer being embedded with the troops. It's a lot safer than heading out on my own; at least being with the military offers some protection. Besides, we've been given unprecedented access so it's a chance for some great stories." He paused. "How'd you end up here? Saw you looking my way on the plane . . . thought I'd try to get some background on a few guys soon as we hit ground."

"National Guard. I trained at Fort Drum, then went on to Fort Sill, Oklahoma. I never expected this to be part of the gig. It was my way of appeasing my dad—career military. I'm part of an old family military tradition," I said, forcing a grin.

"What's your assignment making old dad proud?" Jason returned the grin.

"Black Hawk helicopter, firing a machine gun."

"You scared?"

"I guess . . ." I hesitated, a puzzled look on my face. "I suppose you want an honest answer. . . . Yes. Damn right, I'm scared. But that's not for print, at least not attached to my name."

"Sorry. I was about to say I guess that's a dumb question. I think that every time I ask it, but I almost always ask anyhow. It just goes with the territory. Usually, I get some macho response. But I like your up-front honesty . . .

you anxious about being up there? Not sure flying is your thing."

"I like to think it'll be safer up in the air. I've heard too many stories of IEDs, seen the photos, stuff I'd rather not think or talk about right now." I paused. "But then, I guess, once a Black Hawk gets nailed, it's pretty much over. Like a sitting duck up there. It's the kind of big game the Iraqis must like to pick off; usually garners bolder headlines than a Humvee taken out by some roadside bomb."

Jason abruptly changed the subject. "Before all this, what'd you do? Married? Children? Job?"

"No to all the above. I just finished college a couple months ago." Now more relaxed, I watched the deplaning passengers shuffle to a staging area of the base while some VIPs were escorted on an inspection tour amid heavier-than-usual security. As we waited idly, I was discovering just how attractive Jason was as he continued to pepper me with questions.

"Age?"

"Twenty-three . . . today." I blushed momentarily, feeling the blood rising in my face.

"Congratulations. I'm sure this isn't what you had in mind for a birthday celebration."

Our conversation was interrupted all too soon as some five-hundred-plus soldiers were called to their assigned units.

"Hey . . . thanks for your time," Jason said. He reached out his hand. I returned the gesture as Jason placed his free hand on my shoulder. "Be safe." He said it in a tone that sounded more like an order.

"You, too," I said, turning to walk away, feeling a strange sense of disappointment. As I glanced back, I saw Jason wink, tentatively raising his hand as though to say something more.

I returned a smile and continued on my way.

✦

JASON ALDRICH, UNATTACHED to any unit, found the bathroom. It was often the one place a reporter could hope for some undisturbed time in rushing a story for the wire service.

Hundreds of soldiers landed at Balad Airbase today, their mission to help transport troops, supplies, and VIPs to Baghdad and around Iraq. While some were first-timers, for many it was their third or fourth deployment. One of them, part of a battalion of a New York Guard, here on his first mission, seemed eager to begin, his name unimportant for this story. He epitomizes so many here. He's young—most are. Boots hitting the ground, they share a conviction to banish the enemy—voices reminiscent of the sounds emanating from the crowd as the home team takes the field.

A two-sport athlete and recent graduate of the University of Ohio, he hopes someday to complete his education to become a teacher. On the outside, his confidence and demeanor did not betray the jitters he expressed about his job as a machine gunner on board a Black Hawk helicopter. With steel blue eyes, hair cropped close, a strong jawline, and only the slightest hint of dimples, he bore the look of a soldier's soldier. With a disarming smile that, for a moment, spread [cont. on next page]

✦

Ten months later, I ran into Jason Aldrich again as my Black Hawk returned from the village of Turki, in the Diyala Province, northeast of Baghdad near the Iranian border, where we were sent to recover wounded soldiers of the 82nd Airborne Division who were engaged in heated skirmishes with insurgents holed up in a network of trenches and reed-strewn canals in the remote farmland. The extended wager, which ended by air strikes, netted a cache of weapons and numerous injured.

"Didn't think I'd see you again," I said, spotting Jason on the ground as we landed in the twilight. "How'd you get here?"

"Wasn't all that difficult," Jason said. "I knew your name, your unit, your assignment. All I had to do was a bit of begging. Get to tag along tomorrow. I've never been up in one of these things before."

Jason hesitated to catch his breath. "Hey, I'm sure glad to see you're all right. You look great." We shook hands. Jason's grip was firm. It was one of those handshakes where letting go was something I didn't want to do. I sensed that he shared that reluctance.

"It looks like you press types don't use razors," I joked.

"Wait a minute. I scrambled like anything to catch up with your unit." Jason grinned. "I shaved less than twenty-four hours ago."

"Only kidding. You look good." I smiled. "It's good to see you, too." My words echoed in my head, aware that Jason Aldrich was someone I had met only once. Yet, I experienced for an instant the sensation of reuniting with someone I had known from childhood.

"I'm told you're off in the morning on a short mission to keep an eye on some VIP trek," Jason said. "I asked the brass to do a follow-up story with you. Been embedded with the 101st Airborne Division for a couple months. I wanted another perspective before I head home."

"Okay. I'll see you in the morning." I wanted to hang around—catch up. But I needed to move out. This was the military. "Don't miss the flight," I joked. "We take off at dawn, you know."

In the darkness and desolation, Jason leaned into me, his hand clutching my arm by the elbow. My nostrils momentarily caught his musky scent—a smell of perspiration, desert dust, and natural body oils that gave me chills. He let go with an awkward kiss. "See you then," he said in a throaty almost-whisper. It all happened so fast, I wasn't sure it had happened at all.

Jason Aldrich was not "The Scud Stud." He wasn't attired in a leather jacket. As far as I knew, he had no international prominence or name recognition. But he was dark and handsome in a lightweight jacket that hung open to his black crewneck T-shirt that fit tightly to the contour of his abs. His face, with its one-day growth, looked every bit the model from a Neiman Marcus catalog. It was the image that stuck with me as he turned to walk away.

Morning light barely cracked on the horizon and everyone was back aboard the Black Hawk as we embarked on the somewhat more benign, though still risky, mission of escorting a VIP tour from Baghdad to nearby Karbala. It was Aldrich's only opportunity for a wrap-up interview with his unidentified soldier, a story that was previously picked up in U.S. dailies running Iraqi human interest features. It was facilitated by someone who recognized the chance for more positive press at a time when war reporting was becoming increasingly critical of the military effort.

Jason took notes. We chatted easily, both a little more distant, unsure of what occurred between us the previous night. I watched Jason write. His fingers were long, somewhat slender, with fine black hair that fanned across the top of his hand and extended up his wrist, where it disappeared beneath his shirt sleeve. He feigned interest in the 7.62 mm machine guns mounted on the cabin windows and was fascinated by my explanation that the Black Hawk, carrying out Army tradition, was named after a Native American.

The noise and vibration from the rotors made it seem like we were the only two aboard the aircraft. The three-member crew was busily engaged in the mission while the only other occupant intently focused on the sky and ground around us. Huddled together for the interview, I could, at times, feel the heat from Jason's face, feel the warmth of his breath, or catch his scent as he leaned into my ear to ask a question. Realizing his reason in being there made his conduct seem necessary for the purpose, he overplayed the role at every opportunity, somewhat teasingly cupping his hand to my ear, or lingering as he leaned into me.

It was early afternoon when we landed safely back in Baghdad. Jason was hooking up with a convoy headed toward Kuwait. At that moment I hated Iraq more than ever. Maybe I was falling in love, or maybe, I thought, it was only Iraq that made me feel that way. Jason was someone I had only gotten to know in broken sound bites, no meaningful conversation, no dinners together, no movies. Maybe, I realized, that it was only my intense desire go to bed with him that I felt earlier that morning—the wishing that he had moved his hand up my leg as he rested it on my knee to maintain his balance when the pilot maneuvered to change direction.

"In a little less than five months from now, you'll be back in the U.S.," Jason said. "I'll be stateside in a couple more weeks myself." He paused, waiting for the crew members to disperse on their return from the mission. He handed me a page from his notebook, his phone number and address scrawled in bold characters. "I call Cape Cod home. . . . It's a small place on Cape Cod Bay, overlooks Pilgrim Lake in North Truro, just before Provincetown. It's a stone's throw from Route 6. Maybe you'd like to come spend a couple weeks when you get back. It'll be the beginning of summer. By then I'll be ready for a break—some company. Between now and then I plan to become a recluse . . . writing a book on my experiences covering the war, the good and bad of being an embedded journalist."

"I think I'd like that. I'll need some time to clear my head, figure out what I'm going to do with the rest of my life. If you're sure it wouldn't be any imposition?"

"No . . . really. You don't think I've ripped a page out of my notebook for every good-looking soldier I've run across." Jason laughed.

✦

MOTHER'S DAY. IT was moderately breezy with bright sunshine and a forecast of seventy degrees by afternoon. At a few minutes before twelve, I stood on the small front porch of Jason Aldrich's cottage, staring out at Pilgrim Lake, watching an occasional gull sweep out of nowhere. This early in the year, the neighborhood appeared almost abandoned. Here and there a solitary car was parked at one of the gray cedar-shingled houses that lined the main street passing through the town, parallel to Route 6.

There had been no communication between us since Iraq. It was out of character for me to arrive anywhere unexpectedly. Before even knocking, I was certain Jason wasn't home, feeling a surge of relief when my solid attempt to arouse someone produced no response. About to get into my car for the long drive back to Long Island, I was caught off guard when Jason pulled alongside me in the driveway.

"What a surprise," Jason said as he circled around his car and reached out to shake hands, a big smile spreading across his face.

"Sorry," I said. "I should have called first."

"That's okay." His tone was genuine. "You're here now. . . . Have you had any lunch?" Jason asked.

"No."

"Hop in . . . we'll run into Provincetown and get something to eat. I just got back from dropping my mother at Logan. She was here a few days but had to catch a flight to get back for work. . . . How'd you end up here?"

"When I got up this morning, it was still dark. . . . I dressed and headed to McDonald's for a cup of coffee. I felt really restless after a week of cold wet weather. It was like I suddenly developed spring fever and needed some time to think. After a couple hours of mindless driving, I found myself on I-95 near the Rhode Island border . . . so I just kept driving. The destination just sorta unfolded as I went. I know that probably sounds stupid."

"Sounds great by me." Jason laughed, abruptly stopping the car. "We're here."

We devoured a bowl of clam chowder and shared a sandwich at the Lobster Pot along Commercial Street. Looking out across Provincetown harbor as we ate, lunchtime conversation

rehashed common ground. Exchanging stories, we resur-
rected moments in Iraq that would have been better forgotten.
Once back on Route 6, we headed eastward, away from Truro,
toward Herring Cove. Riding in silence was welcome. At the
restaurant there seemed a need for something more urgent
about our conversation, a nervous energy between relative
strangers diving head-on into one another, not wanting to mis-
step. Getting Iraq in the past was a needed exercise for more
serious topics.

Arriving at Herring Cove, the sparsely populated, sandy
beach stretched for what seemed miles. Jason parked less
than two hundred feet from water's edge. The pristine sand
sloped gently toward the waves that came in little ripples on
shore. Removing our shoes, socks, and shirts, tossing them
through the open window onto the backseat of Jason's car,
we rolled our pant legs high. We found an elevated spot on
a ridge of sand where the beach sloped more steeply
toward the water. It was midafternoon; the early spring sun
felt hot against our backs.

Taking turns, we nearly assaulted one another with
questions—all the small details there was no time for in
Iraq—siblings, college, family, sports. As the sun disappeared below the horizon, its final late-day rays glistening
in the expanse of ocean, a cool evening breeze brought
us to our feet. Jason's upper chest brushed against me as
he reached through the open car window for our shirts.
Each of us, I was certain, felt the chemistry igniting
between us.

"I'll find us something at home for dinner," Jason said.
"Mom did a lot of cooking in a few days. I'm sure there are
all sorts of leftovers hiding in the refrigerator. You can
bring your bag in and we'll get you settled."

"I don't have one," I said. "Remember, I didn't plan this trip . . . and I sure didn't plan to stay."

"Well, like I said before, you're here now." He punched me lightly on the shoulder and laughed. "An inch or two shorter or taller, not more than a few pounds weight difference . . . you don't really need a bag; I have lots of clothes . . . remember this is the beach, and it's summer, or almost," Jason said. "I'd like you to stay . . . just don't want you to do something you really don't want to do."

"Ever since I saw you on that plane to Balad . . . I fantasized about a time like this. . . ." I stumbled over my words. "When you leaned into me as we were leaving the beach . . ."

Jason pulled to the berm, and shifted into park. He leaned over the center console. "I think you know how I feel. Once I caught your glances on that flight, I knew I was willing to chase you across Iraq. For ten months, until I saw you again in Baghdad, I regretted not pushing you for more information, exchanging phone numbers, addresses, when we first talked."

Jason pulled back onto the highway heading toward home. "I was never someone to believe in love at first sight. Besides, that place plays games with the head. Maybe you were straight, just my mind playing tricks, or maybe thinking about you was my way of getting through. But I've dated a lot of guys, and I met some terrific ones while reporting on the war. Standing on the tarmac in Balad, talking with you, I knew I wanted to spend the rest of my life with you. I was hoping you'd maybe feel the same."

"I need to call my folks . . . tell them I'm visiting a friend for a few days."

"Gotta warn you, though . . ." Jason said. "There's one thing we'll both have to do without."

"What's that?" I asked.

"I don't own any pajamas." He grinned. "And oh," he added, "there's only one bed . . . in case that makes any difference about your decision to stay."

"Guess that's okay . . . I've never owned any pajamas, either."

THE GAYEST AMERICAN HERO

STEVEN BEREZNAI

"WHAT DO YOU think about Ritchie?" I asked my room-mate Kevin. He was busy curling his Afro into baby dreads. I tried to be nonchalant, but there was something about Ritchie, those lips, the weird braids he'd sometimes put his blond hair into, and he lived in a house in that exotic land known as "off campus."

"Ritchie? He's kind of scrawny for you, isn't he?" Kevin replied.

I shrugged. As a pseudo-closeted, nineteen-year-old vir-gin who'd never even kissed a guy, I knew I had to be flexible.

"Besides, he's straight," Kevin added.

"I hear he's bisexual."

"*Really?*" Kevin demanded, scooping more hair wax onto his finger.

"He's very open about it," I said. "I think he looks at me sometimes."

"I thought he was dating Ira."

"No, no," I pshawed, "Ira and Jason have been together *forever.*"

"They broke up."

"*Really?*" I demanded. "When did that happen?"

Kevin held up his hands and scrunched his face. "All I know is Jason found Ira's journal, and she wrote in it that she was totally attracted to Ritchie."

"Housemates in love," I said unenthusiastically. Jason, Ira, and Ritchie lived together, in the House, as all the freshmen in our dorm called it with reverence, along with one of Ritchie's ex-girlfriends and one of Jason's future girlfriends. The reverence would later take on a "wow, that's fucked" tone.

"It's going to be an interesting party," I said, little knowing the full extent of what lay ahead.

Kevin sighed. "I suppose it always is." And then he gave a loud chuckle, asking, "So do you know what you're going to wear?"

"Do I ever!"

Several hours later, Kevin stared me up and down.

"You're kidding, right?" His arms were folded in front of him and one hand gripped his chin. "This isn't Halloween, you know."

"Come on! It's an eighties party. This is *perfect*."

Kevin covered his mouth, speaking through his fingers. "I don't even know what to say."

I turned around, looking into the mirror and adjusting my dark blue Speedo. They sat overtop a pair of red tights (queen-size, of course), my blond leg hairs poking out. My torso was covered in a red turtleneck with an emblem made out of felt glued onto it, and hanging from my shoulders was my pillow case—now an improvised cape. I was *The Greatest American Hero*, of cheesy '80s TV fame.

"People *love* this costume," I insisted. *But would Ritchie?*

I pulled out the elastic band holding back my ponytail and gave my thick hair a shake, letting it settle to my shoulders.

"Vodka shot?" I asked Kevin, who was already unscrewing the cap on the plastic bottle of Russian Prince, the cheapest vodka we could find. He handed me a shot, and after a quick toast we knocked 'em back, liquid fire burning down my throat. I glanced at my outfit once more.

Please let Ritchie think this is cool.

There was a knock at the door, and Kevin opened it just as I threw a housecoat over my costume. I felt the need for another shot as I saw who was there.

"Oh my god you look awesome!" screeched Maxine, or Maxie Pad, as we liked to call her behind her back. Her face looked a bit like melted wax, framed by long greasy hair. Kevin and I looked at each other unenthusiastically.

"Thanks," I said.

"I came by earlier," she said, "but you weren't here." She smiled, making her braces glint like razors.

"I guess I was at class."

"No, you were between classes," she said, no longer smiling.

"Uh . . . well, then I guess I was studying."

"With who?"

"By myself, I imagine."

"Oh," she laughed, tossing her stringy hair. "So what were you studying?"

"Maxie, we have to finish getting ready," I said. "I'll see you later."

"You're going to love my costume!" she said in an off-key pitch as the door closed in her face.

"Wow," Kevin said once it clicked shut, pouring us more vodka.

I reached for my wardrobe and tore off my class schedule that was taped there, hiding it inside my Day-Timer.

"She's already got it memorized," Kevin said.

At least I knew someone was interested.

◆

AS THE DOOR opened to the House, I felt like a girl on her period going to the prom—terrified. "Girls Just Want to Have Fun" blared from the living room, and we were ushered in by a flurry of big hair, padded shoulders, and acid-wash jeans. I stripped off my jacket and pants, revealing my costume to squeals and claps of delight. Oh thank god! I basked in the sound, my vodka-soaked veins pounding to the rhythm.

And yet as much as I felt the rush of peer approval, it all fell to the background as I stepped from the dimmed hallway into the multicolor swirl of disco lights in the living room. The crowd parted like the Red Sea, and there was my Moses.

Ritchie's blond hair was crimped into a frizzy pyramid, and he was wearing a red vest with a diagonal foldover panel. Lipstick brought out his sensual lips, while eyeliner and mascara framed his haunting blue eyes.

"Girls Just Want to Have Fun" gave way to "99 Red Balloons."

He put his arm around my shoulder. I chugged from my bottle of cheap white wine (Domaine D'Or, for the one I adore!) and forced myself to imitate him, movement for movement, my arm robotically sliding up his back and around his neck. He began kneading my shoulder. I did the same to him.

Were people noticing? They were all rather alternative, many of them misfits in high school, into bands or doing sketch comedy or writing poetry. Displays of straight male physical affection were not uncommon among this lot. Sometimes they made *me* uncomfortable.

"Ritchie, where are the rest of the chips?" Ira called from the kitchen. She was a vision of Boy-Georgeness, a total complement to Ritchie's ode to Platinum Blonde.

He pulled away from me to deal with the Pringles crisis, but not before staring me in the eye and giving my arm a final squeeze.

Will he be back? I wondered. *Should I follow? Do I play it cool? How do I make myself look busy so if he returns I'm not just standing here waiting for him?*

I drank more wine, hoping that courage could indeed come in liquid form. I looked for Kevin, but he was nowhere to be found.

I swayed to "Papa Don't Preach," sliding amid the tween bodies of the other partygoers, including a Mr. T and someone dressed as David Hasselhoff from his *Baywatch* days.

I saw Ritchie emerge from the kitchen with a bowl of chips. He glanced my way, but didn't come over. My chest tightened, but I nodded to myself. It was cool. No worries. I took several more gulps of wine.

An hour later, my wine bottle was empty and so were my hopes for my first homosexual experience. A hand touched my ass from behind and I turned excitedly to stare into the glittering braces of Maxine. She was dressed as Julia Sugarbaker from *Designing Women*.

"Wanna dance?" she slurred.

I pulled at the collar of my turtleneck. My red tights and blue Speedo had started to chafe.

"I need to get a drink," I replied, stumbling toward the kitchen, intent on drinking nothing stronger than a glass of water. Vodka shots and a bottle of wine seemed to be my limit. I could barely stand. The de facto DJ mixed to a new song and an excited cheer rose up from the crowd.

I paid no mind until the people in the kitchen doorway formed a wall and blocked my way. I tried to squeeze past them, but they ganged up on me, pushing me back into the living room. Hands came at me from every direction as those in the living room joined in the attack, latching onto my arms and legs.

What the fuck was wrong with them? This is NOT cool!

I was dizzy and breathing hard, flailing my limbs in a panic, trying to disentangle myself, fearful that this was some plot on the part of Maxie Pad. *What is that conniving bitch up to?* My legs were swept out from under me.

I waited to hit the ground, but that would not come 'til much later.

Hands held me. They lifted me, above their shoulders, over their heads, ignoring my struggles.

And only then, horizontal, about a foot from the ceiling, did I realize they were playing my song. . . . *The Greatest American Hero* theme blared loud and proud.

As the lyrics ". . . walking on air . . ." belted out, my fellow partygoers "flew" me around the living room. I was euphoric. I was the teen who ate his lunch alone in high school. I was the kid in grade school who stayed inside during recess to help the teacher staple together test sheets because I had no friends. I was the loser who finally forced himself in grade twelve to join the swim team despite the acne scars covering his back—nearly drowning as a swim stud tried to teach me the butterfly stroke. I, who had ever stood on the outside, the watcher, the witness, the observer, was for this moment at the center. Not a two-bit player with three lines, but a star bathed in the limelight.

They flew me around the living room one more time, then into the hallway. ". . . feel so free . . ." blared from the speakers. Up the stairs we went. I kept my hands pressed against the sloping ceiling of the stairwell to keep from getting squished. We reached the narrow landing on the second floor.

Now what? I thought, as the lyrics, ". . . flying away . . ." echoed from below.

"Throw him on my bed!" Ritchie's voice commanded, rising above the throng.

Oh god! I panicked, suddenly realizing this wasn't Maxine's plot at all.

It was his!

Conflicting voices battled inside my head.

No!

Yes!

NO!!

YES!!!

His door creaked open, and I flew, for just a moment I FLEW . . .

. . . out of their arms and into the air. And then gravity . . . I fell onto his mattress.

I landed like a cat, on all fours, ready to jump off, ready to run, ready to not let this happen. It's what I wanted, but it was too soon, not like this, not at all, maybe never, never would be fine! But before the panic could send me hiding, a voice spoke in my head.

Stay.

I froze at that word.

I watched Ritchie sit down next to me on the mattress, leaning his back against the wall. I heard the tail end of *The Greatest American Hero* theme song give way to *Laverne and*

Shirley's anthem, the words ". . . no stopping uuuuussss!" drifting upward, greeted by cheers from below. A few people lingered in Ritchie's room, a Madonna in her "Like a Virgin" regalia and a female Max Headroom. Ritchie leaned over the side of his bed and pulled out a shoe carton. Rummaging inside, he slid out an old photograph of the Greatest American Hero.

"You got the insignia wrong," he said.

He reached over and pushed back my long blond hair, slipping his hand behind my head to rub my scalp. I closed my eyes, heart pounding, letting him gently guide my head to rest on his lap, the rest of my body collapsing in slow motion into a lying position. I felt the mattress give way under the weight of straight dorm-mates settling onto the bed, their legs arching over my own as they leaned against the wall. Ritchie kept massaging my scalp with one hand, his other fingers lightly brushing my cheek. His touch arched over my cheekbone and slid down to my chin, curling back upward around my ears to my eyebrows, gliding back and forth over them before slipping down the bridge of my nose, and finally stroking my parted lips.

I wanted to give something back, but I didn't want anyone to see, so I slipped my hand beneath his thigh, gently kneading the underside of his leg. I felt a swelling inside my Speedo, and I curled my knees toward me to hide it. He leaned in, lips tickling my ears. "Don't worry," he whispered, "we're going to take care of that." My grip tightened on his leg.

The mattress squeaked as one by one people left, until it was just me, Ritchie, and a religious girl who lived in the room next to mine. Finally even she departed. I rolled onto my back, staring up into his eyes.

This was it. Almost.

A knock at the open door broke the spell. I turned my body toward the wall to hide my erection once more. From the corner of my eye I caught sight of Ira—Ritchie's alleged girlfriend—standing in the doorway.

"Are you coming back down to the party?" she asked.

"I think I'll stay up here for a bit," Ritchie replied. His words filled my body with warmth. *He wants to stay with me.*

There was a pause before Ira answered.

"Okay," she said.

Clearly they weren't dating after all, or so I told myself. I thought it was so cool that he had roommates who knew and didn't mind that he was into guys. It was one of the advantages of hanging with arts students, women's studies majors, and latter-day hippies.

"Ira!" Ritchie cried as she turned away.

"Yes?" she asked. Was there something faintly expectant in her tone?

"Could you close the door behind you?" Ritchie asked.

She said nothing in return, the creak of hinges and the click of the knob settling into place answering for her.

His weight shifted under me, and he guided my body to flip around so that my head rested on a pillow. He lay down next to me, and I knew that he was going to kiss me. For the first time, a guy was going to kiss me.

His mouth pressed into mine, so very different than the one time I'd made out with a girl, whose lips had been huge and soft and wet. His were a graceful combination of tender and firm, the feel of our sandpaper stubble scratching against one another making my fingers dig into his back and push his body into mine. He was an expert with his tongue, which explored my mouth like Jacques Cousteau on an ocean dive. Just as his hands massaged my body, Ritchie's tongue massaged my gums, and for a moment I was the proverbial starfish, arms and legs splayed out, completely overwhelmed by the swelling in my chest. It was like a dormant seed, long desiccated and seemingly beyond life, but which was suddenly drenched in water and was bursting inside my body, filling my chest cavity and pressing out on my lungs and rib cage, threatening to tear them open.

It was so hard to breathe, and yet I did, and I eagerly imitated him, probing his mouth with my tongue. He pressed a finger to my lip, and I was shocked at how hot it was to take it into my mouth and suck up and down its length.

There was so much relief in that instant.

This is me. This is so right. I really am gay!

Confirmation, oh blessed confirmation!

And I was so, so grateful I didn't run. I stayed. I *stayed*. For once I would not be the one going to bed early and listening to other people's conquests of the night before. And this felt so right. This was what I was supposed to be doing. For six years I'd known I was gay and done nothing about it. Those days were over. I was having my first gay kiss.

I was *living*. I was having a life!

So of course I began to crash. The Russian Prince and the Domaine D'Or churned in my stomach. My head began to spin and my extremities grew numb. I wanted to keep going, but my kisses grew softer and softer, my grip on his back sometimes forgetting what it was doing there and slumping uselessly. Every now and again I felt myself nod off.

"Are you okay?" he asked.

"I think I need to rest for a bit."

He kissed me some more, oh so tenderly.

"Okay," he whispered, stubble brushing against my ear. "You stay here. I'll be back in a bit."

Within minutes I was alone, lying on his bed, drifting in and out of my sexually charged alcoholic buzz, overwhelmed by my actual participation in teenage life, in *gay* life. And of course there was the uncertainty. How soon before he came back? Was I going to spend the night? And then?

I pulled his comforter overtop of me, shivering in a swirl of alcohol and afterglow, thanking my drunkenness for helping me get this far, but cursing it as well for crippling me from going further. As I started to pass out I heard the door open, and I smiled at the thought of him wrapping his arms around me, cuddling and kissing, and falling asleep together.

"Hey, Steven," a woman's voice said.

My eyes popped open, and my head flipped around. Silhouetted by the hallway light, Maxie Pad stood there, swaying from side to side in an exaggerated manner, putting the back of one hand dramatically to her head. "I am sooooooo drunk. I think I need to lie down, too."

She walked deftly toward the bed, one foot in front of the other, like a stalking cat. The single mattress had somehow been just the right size for a horny teen's first man-on-man tryst, but frightfully too small for this. I jumped up immediately.

"I'm feeling a lot better now, but you go ahead," I said, pushing her toward the bed. She landed with a flop and I rushed for the door, closing it quickly behind me. I stood alone in the hallway for a moment, trying to get my bearings. The sound of someone flushing a toilet to the left of me made my head hurt. I glanced over my shoulder, at the closed door to the room that was supposed to be *my* room for the night, thinking of the bed that was to be *my* maiden voyage, presumably in the morning once I'd sobered up.

Why, god? Why are you such a fucking bitch? I cursed.

I stumbled down the stairs and half tripped on the landing. Kevin caught me, Kevin, my roommate, emerging finally from whatever corner he'd been tucked into, debating politics and pop culture. He was dressed as a thin Aretha Franklin—with baby dreads—and totally pulling it off. I hugged him drunkenly.

"Are you okay?" he asked.

"Can we go soon?" I begged, finally overwhelmed.

"Now, actually."

"I need to say good-bye first," I said, "and then we need to talk."

He looked at my grinning face.

"You didn't!"

"Kind of." I blushed proudly.

"With . . ."

"Yup."

"So why are you leaving?"

"Because I need to."

He took one look at the way I was leaning on the handrail and laughed in his loud huh-huh-huh way and said, "We'll talk."

I meandered through the crowd and spotted my stud sitting on an armchair. He was flanked on one side by Clara, a slender redhead dressed as Annie Lennox; on the other there was Robert, a curly-haired, flute-playing, Beatnik-inspired wrestler in cutoff acid-wash jeans. He had amazing biceps. Both were from my residence, and both lounged in the crook of Ritchie's arms.

I wanted to kiss him good-bye, but I didn't want anybody to notice.

You know what to do, the voice that had ordered me to "stay" when I'd been thrown onto Ritchie's bed now said, and it spoke true.

I walked forward, not even remembering that I was dressed in tights and a Speedo, leaned, and gave Clara a kiss good-bye on the mouth. Then I moved onto Ritchie, as he sat next to her. I intended to just give him a quick peck and was pleasantly surprised by the nibble he worked in, chewing my lip slightly. There was a spark as our eyes met, and with my lips still feeling the heat of his against mine, I moved onto Robert. I was teetering from the booze—and Ritchie—and as I kissed Robert good-bye, I didn't even realize that like a parakeet I was still in imitation mode, and I gave him a little nibble, just as Ritchie had done for me.

A pleased "hmmmm" sound vibrated from his throat, making me realize my teeth were gently clasping his lower lip.

I released, pulled back, blushed, locked eyes with Ritchie one more time, and said, "I'm really drunk. Gotta head."

Ira watched us uncomfortably.

"We'll see you again soon," he replied.

And he was right.

HELLO GORGEOUS

REX LANDRY

"PLEASE FASTEN YOUR seat belts, lock your trays, and return your seats to the upright position. We are approaching Managua, Nicaragua, and will be landing in five minutes. It is a clear day and the temperature is eighty-five degrees. Hope you enjoy . . ."

Ruben Martinez, the attorney I hired in San Antonio, shook my arm. "You okay, Chuck? You look a mess. It's all right to breathe, you know. You've already paid me the money and everything is arranged. Jose will be freed as soon as I give them the five thousand dollars. Jose is a lucky guy to have such a good friend as you. You know he was facing life in that hellhole."

A million thoughts raced rampant through my mind. *What if he was just using me? What if he didn't really love me? What if he thought I was too old, too poor, or just too plain and ugly? What if he didn't find me attractive?* I had all these thoughts right from the beginning of our relationship. And it was Jose who always made contact with me. Never had he mentioned my age or how much money I had. No, in fact he never asked for a dime and it had been almost two years.

I had logged on to Studs 4U out of curiosity, not knowing what to expect. I had read a short article in a magazine that accompanied a hot nude male centerfold, where the gorgeous stud mentioned that the site was where he was discovered. I have owned a computer for years but never logged on to any webcam sex sites before. My computer was too old and too slow, I thought.

When I logged on to Studs 4U, I looked through hundreds of profiles of hot guys. I was shocked. There for the whole world to see were photos and short profiles of thousands of gorgeous studs from all over the world in various states of dress. I clicked on a few and stared in disbelief at the hotties completely nude, dicks erect, legs spread wide, and asses wide open. Some had pictures of them having oral sex, inserting dildos, and even anal sex, not to mention the pictures of come-covered faces and asses. I searched the database of men and decided to make a profile for myself. I took a few pictures of myself—some with my shirt on and others completely naked. I didn't have to worry about getting hard; the thought of men all over the world seeing me naked gave me a raging hard-on. I selected five of the pictures and uploaded them to the website. I kept my face as a private picture. I needed a name; no one used their real names. I chose the name Dallass—joining the name of a city I once lived in and the word *ass*. I chose the picture of me facedown and bubble-ass up as my main picture.

I continued to surf Studs 4U nightly for almost two months when I realized there was a button on the right-hand side that said "webcam." I know—I'm a little slow. I clicked on the button and waited. The hourglass indicated I needed to continue waiting. After a full minute, a new window popped up. On the right-hand side was a list of names and on the left was a large open window. On the bottom were five boxes; one of them had my name, Dallass, below it.

I looked over the list on the left. Apparently the names in red had their cams on and all I had to do was double-click on the name to see them on the bottom. Below the five boxes I noticed guys were chatting with one another.

I read the chats and then clicked on the name of *topstud*. His picture appeared in the right-hand box. He was in his midtwenties and was naked, stroking his large cock. He didn't show his face, but it didn't matter; he was hot. I clicked on another name and a guy was standing, bent over with his ass and his pucker-hole wide open. I quickly filled the four boxes on the screen.

A new guy entered the site. His name was *Lucifer*. Everyone wanted to talk with him. I was intrigued. Who was this guy? I found his name and clicked on it. I was blown away. I had been watching hot naked guys for thirty minutes, but this guy was in a league all his own. He was naked just like the rest of them, but he was absolutely perfect. He had a well-developed chest with well-defined pecs and hard nipples. He had rows of tight abs, six, no eight rows and deep V-cut muscles leading down to his magnificent large, perfect, uncut cock. Two large balls dangled below between his massive legs. My weakness is perfect balls. My god he was perfect—well defined but not too muscular.

I was in lust. My dick was hard, and my breathing became short and fast. Then Lucifer smiled. That was it. Never have I ever seen such a perfect sexy smile. His lips were large and moist, his teeth were white and perfect. His soul radiated through his smile. You know how people say you can see into a person's soul through their eyes—well it was like that, only with his smile. I wanted to know him. No, I *needed* to know him.

For the first time I felt compelled to write something in the chat line. "Lucifer—Oh my GOD—UR FUCKING

GORGEOUS !!!" I typed, and then hit the enter key. I waited for the message to display on the screen. Lucifer's sexy, wicked grin became a large infectious smile. He picked up a yellow ball with a smiley face on it and placed it before his cam. "Thanks, Dallass," he replied. I couldn't believe it. This god was talking to me.

"You from Texas?" he asked.

"Born there—where you from?" I answered.

"Nicaragua."

And that is how it all started. Crazy, I know, even for me. Here I was, a man of fifty, talking to a god of twenty-six— half my age. I was old enough to be his father, and yet he was for some reason interested in talking to me, a faceless older man. We chatted for twenty minutes with such ease. No one else seemed to matter to either of us. Maybe if I had a cam he would have never chatted with me and never been intrigued with me.

"Buy a cam. Please, I want to see you," Lucifer wrote.

"I will tomorrow, I promise," I replied.

What, was I crazy? He would never talk to me again if he saw me. I was middle-aged, past the prime of my life. I was not overweight, but my body could use some definition. I was balding, and what hair that was left was almost gray. But I found myself not only agreeing to buy a cam, but very excited to do so.

I typed in "I am 50 years old—do you still want to see me?" and then waited.

He was gone. He had left the site. He hadn't seen my last message. What would he think? He never asked my age; maybe he thought I was a young guy. I thought about it for two seconds and decided—what the hell—he's in Nicaragua, I'm in Texas. If he doesn't like me, maybe someone else will.

I purchased a cam the next afternoon on the way home from work. It took me thirty minutes to hook it up and install the software. I logged onto Studs 4U and entered my name and password. I went to the webcam page and waited. My hands were sweaty and my breathing erratic. I found the box with "Dallass" and clicked on the video camera option. My picture came on screen.

"Hello Dallass—my dear friend—ur handsome." A message from Lucifer appeared on screen.

For a moment I forgot I was Dallass. He called me his dear friend. Furthermore, after seeing me he called me handsome. The camera doesn't lie; he had to know I was much older than him.

"Hello, gorgeous," I responded.

"Sorry about last night—damn Internet here goes down all the time."

We chatted again with such ease. It was like I knew him all of my life. How could this be? Not only was he a god, but he was smart as hell, charming, and extremely funny. I found myself smiling more than I have in years. When he suddenly left, I felt so alone. I waited for him to come back, but he never returned that night.

Every day I found myself racing home and logging on to Studs 4U to find my Lucifer. Every day he would call me his dear friend and I would call him gorgeous. At least I was honest. Lucifer would lean back in his chair and stroke his cock. I've never seen anything like him. He was always hard. He would play with his foreskin and show off his piss-hole, but it was his perfect large balls that drove me crazy. He could make his cock move by itself and dance. And always he was smiling with his wicked, sexy grin while showing off for me.

For some strange reason, Lucifer always watched me. I could tell by the blue light beside his name. There were always so many hot guys on the site, but for some reason he always wanted to watch me.

"Do you have MSN?" he asked one day.

"No, should I?"

"Yes—download it so we can chat in private."

So I left the chat room and did as he requested. It took almost an hour on my slow computer. I entered "dallass" as my handle and then went back to the chat room. Lucifer was still there. Man, did I love to watch him play. I could watch him play and flirt with the other guys all day.

"Gorgeous—I have MSN now."

"About time—message me—my msn name is Lucifer."

Was this really happening? I opened MSN and fumbled my way over the site until I figured out how to send a message to Lucifer.

He responded. "Hello, my love, how are you doing?"

Did he just say *my love*? My head was dizzy, my heart pounding. I responded: "Hello, gorgeous, my love."

"I love this . . . Funny I don't know your name. My name is Chuck. What is yours?" I typed.

"Jose, my name is Jose—so nice to meet you."

We chatted for over an hour. I found out he worked in the embassy as a translator. No wonder his English was nearly perfect. He loved cars and in fact once raced cars. He worked out every day at home and was on a strict high-protein diet. He talked about his family and, yes, they knew he was gay. We talked about his beautiful country. Then he sent me several nude pictures of him. And then he sent me a song—Etta James singing "At Last."

His picture kept freezing on screen, so I went out and bought some more memory for my computer. I installed it wrong and my computer died. I ran out and bought a new one. I couldn't be a day without contact. The new computer was bad. I took it back and bought a more expensive model. I signed up for high-speed Internet. When my modem came I was so excited; finally I could see and chat to Jose like normal humans do. The best part was being able to see him live without the screen freezing up.

I was falling in love. Each day I raced home to see Jose on Studs 4U and hoped that we would chat privately. It was months before we chatted again in private. All the while I grew fonder and fonder of him. We joked online and didn't care if anyone else got it. I'd never been as happy in my entire life as I was when I chatted with Jose. I wanted to know all about him. I checked online for airplane tickets to Nicaragua. I read all the news each day that I could about his country.

Six months later I sent him a message on Studs 4U. He responded, "You are the only one that truly loves me."

I responded, "I guess I really love you."

Then he sent me a message on MSN. We chatted for over an hour. The next morning I was online to check my e-mails. Jose sent me a message. And that was the way it was. Every morning and every evening we chatted, about everything and about nothing. Every time we chatted, my cheeks hurt from smiling so much. Every night I went to sleep thinking about Jose. Sometimes at work I made mistakes because I was thinking about him.

Funny, in the beginning it was pure lust. I just couldn't get enough of his naked body. I even told him it should be against the law for him to wear clothes. But now, it was Jose I was in love with. Everything about him was perfect. He was so kind and caring. My heart ached to be with him. I wanted to make sure of his feelings, so I always let him be the one to contact me. I had fallen in love with Jose on a purely spiritual level. I just wanted to hold him in my arms and make sure he was real. I wouldn't let my mind even think about how great it would be to make love to him.

Then one day there was no contact. Two more days went by. I was going crazy. Then I got an e-mail. It was in Spanish. I couldn't read anything except *amigo de Jose*. I printed the e-mail and took it to work with me. Raul, a coworker, translated it for me.

"Chuck, please help. Jose has been arrested for possession of a gun and found with protest posters. They are charging him with attempting to assassinate the president. Jose is innocent—he wouldn't hurt a flea. Please help my friend Jose. Please reply. Jose's friend Camacho."

I was floored. How could this happen? What was happening to Jose? I've heard about all those terrible prison rapes. I was devastated. I took off work and went straight to find an attorney, one who had experience with other governments. I checked with four law firms, and three all gave me the name of Ruben Martinez. I found his office and asked to see him.

"The earliest I have an opening for a new appointment is Friday next week," the receptionist told me.

Then it happened. I went to pieces, sobbing uncontrollably. I sat in the chair and cried for at least thirty minutes. All I could say was, "Jose, my poor dear Jose."

Ruben came out to see what the problem was. He took me into a conference room and sat me down. I was still unable to talk, so I handed him the e-mail.

"This is serious, very serious. Other countries don't play around. Your friend is in serious shit. Sit here while I make a few phone calls. I have a friend down in Managua."

I sat for two hours and filled out payment guarantees. Seven thousand for Mr. Martinez's fee plus his airfare, and that didn't include whatever legal fees or payoffs down in Nicaragua.

"We need to move fast. Things can get real nasty down there. My guy says he can get charges dropped, but because he had a gun, this will cost you."

"How much?" I asked. It really didn't matter. The thought of Jose in jail, maybe for life, was more than I could bear. I would sell myself if that's what it took. I'm not a rich man, but anything I had I would use to help Jose.

I went to the post office and paid the hundred fifty dollars to get a passport expedited to me in five days. I emptied my savings account, sold my old truck, and got a personal loan at the bank for five thousand dollars. I bought a cashier's check to pay Mr. Martinez. I bought two round-trip tickets to Nicaragua: one for Mr. Martinez and one for me. I packed a suitcase and took ten thousand in cash and a pocket full of credit cards with me to the airport.

I had first heard of Jose's problem six days earlier. Jose had been in jail for at least eight days. I was a total wreck. I hadn't eaten or slept in days. Now I sat with my seat upright and my seat belt tight. My hands were sweaty, and my eyes were red and misty. I held Ruben's arm tight, rested my head on his shoulder, and began to cry.

"Chuck, get a hold of yourself. You don't want Jose to see you this way. You need to be strong for him. I'm not gay, but I wish I had a guy like you, someone who loved me as much as you love Jose."

We went through customs and then headed to meet Ruben's friend. After five hours and countless meetings and much arguing in Spanish, I was told everything had been arranged. I was almost twenty-five thousand dollars poorer, but Jose was to be freed in just two hours. Some judge was willing to take fifteen thousand dollars in exchange for my Jose's freedom and a passport—so much for justice.

When Jose walked out of jail, I held my arms open wide for him. He ran to me and hugged me. We cried in each other's arms for fifteen minutes. I kissed him on the cheeks and held him out so I could see him. My god, he was even more beautiful in person.

"What now, Chuck?" Jose asked.

"Fly home with me for a month. Then we will figure it out, my love."

THE LAST GOOD-BYE

WILLIAM HOLDEN

I NEVER THOUGHT I'd be standing here without you by my side. I feel empty, helpless, and all alone. I try to look ahead to the days, weeks, and months that loom in the distance. All I see is darkness. There is no sun, no light, no smiles or laughter. I walk into that darkness. My arms are outstretched. I feel my way through as if I'm blind. I reach into the void, hoping to find your hand to hold onto, to guide me back to the life that I once knew with you next to me—and the love that we shared.

We were good together. We stood side by side regardless of what life threw at us. Our friends, family, and ex-lovers said we would never make it, that we were too young and that the odds were against us. We beat the odds and proved them wrong. Tomorrow we would have celebrated twenty-nine years together. Twenty-nine years of tears, laughter, and unconditional love.

We were the Dynamic Duo, the Lone Ranger and Tonto, Laurel and Hardy, and Ozzie and Harriet all rolled into one life—one love. That's why your leaving has thrown my life into a tailspin. We were supposed to be together forever; isn't that what we promised each other? I know this sounds corny, but I had always imagined that we would walk off into the sunset together hand in hand, but we won't realize that dream now, will we? That dream has been shattered into a million pieces. I want to pick up the sharp, jagged fragments of our life and somehow put it all back together, but I can't. The edges burn as they cut into me. I bleed from the pain and sorrow your departure has left. All I have now are the memories of what we once had.

I remember the day we first met as if it were yesterday. The visions and flashes of the life we once had are now flooding me, drowning my mind and my heart with sadness and unending pain. You were twenty-five and I was twenty-two. We were on break from history class. You were digging through your pockets for some change to get a cup of coffee from the vending machine. You had a cigarette in your mouth. The embers smoldered as you searched your pockets. I had been watching you throughout the semester. Your dirty-blond hair was kept long. It fell down around your face and shoulders. You were always unshaven and had thin, dark whiskers. You wore the bad-boy look perfectly. Your body was strong. The muscles in your arms stretched the fabric of your shirts. You always wore black. Black shirts, black pants, even black socks. I often wondered if your underwear was black as well. It was. When others would mention you they always just referred to you as "the guy in black." I don't think anyone knew your name. Your ice blue eyes seemed to pierce everything. We were complete opposites. That was the reason I never talked to you: you scared me and thrilled me at the same time. I was the preppy one. The one with perfectly groomed black hair. I was always clean-shaven with a hint of Old Spice aftershave. My wardrobe consisted of dress shirts and sweaters, black dress slacks, and dress shoes. I wasn't scrawny but wasn't by any means well toned. Someone would have had to look really hard to find a noticeable muscle on my body. You must have felt me staring at you that day, because for the first time you spoke to me. You asked me if I had a dime. I walked over and handed it to you. Our fingers touched. Our eyes locked. It was in that moment, that split second, that I fell in love with you.

We stood there without speaking, holding on to our respective side of the dime. We were lost in the moment. You smiled at me, that beautiful, brilliant smile that I had grown to love and to count on. It was in that smile that I always found hope and happiness. It was all that I needed, that and your embrace to help me through even the roughest of times. I asked you if you still wanted the dime, as you hadn't taken it from me. You laughed. Your face reddened from embarrassment as you slipped the dime into the slot. The coffee poured down out of the machine; the cup followed. We laughed so hard, I thought we would burst. You hit the coin return in frustration, and the dime appeared. You never did get that cup of coffee. It was then that I found out that your name was Frank. From that moment on, we were never apart.

I don't think that I ever told you, but I still have that dime. I've carried it with me every day since we met. I was afraid to let the dime go, fearing that you would go with it. I'm holding it right now, rubbing it between my thumb and forefinger. I feel the cold, faded surface as if it somehow has become a symbol of the life that we once shared. I'm not sure when or why I started rubbing the coin; perhaps somewhere deep inside of me I was hoping it would be my genie in the bottle—that if I rubbed it long enough, you'd come back to me.

Your mom called me last night. She wanted to make sure that I was okay. She apologized for things she didn't need to, for not wanting her son to waste his time with someone like me. She expressed her regret for the things she said to me when you first brought me home. She said that she had grown to love me as if I were her own son. She told me that I would always be a part of the family and that I am always welcome in their home. The conversation was odd and uncomfortable. I wasn't sure what to say to her. What could I say? That I was angry that her son left me? That her beloved son left a hole in me that will never heal? We did our best to carry on a conversation, but after a while it was easier to say good-bye than to struggle trying to find hollow words with little emotions or feelings. After all, they were just words to fill the emptiness of the dead space between us.

She's a sweet woman and I do love her, but I kept hearing your voice in hers. Every word she spoke, every change in her tone, came to me as if you were on the other end of the phone. I know it was my imagination, but I couldn't bear to hear your voice coming to me in that way. The same voice I woke up to every morning and fell asleep to every night for the past twenty-nine years.

Last night, the first night without you, was hell. I would close my eyes and pretend you were there next to me. At times I could feel your breath against my neck as your body pushed up against me, spooning me like we always did as we fell asleep. I'd reach behind me to pull you even closer to me, but your side of the bed was empty. I curled up with your pillows. Your scent is still on them. I buried my face in them, trying to get closer to you. I inhaled that warm, sweet musky scent of your body that has become a part of the fabric. I ended up crying into the pillow for most of the night. I don't know when I've cried so hard. The despair and pain fell upon me without warning, as if my defenses had finally crumbled. I feel like crying now, but the tears won't fall. I can feel the pressure building inside of me. It wants to be released. I worry what will happen to the grief if I'm no longer able to cry. Will I just explode? Will it consume me until I'm an empty shell? I know I'll have to wash the sheets at some point, but for now your scent is all that I have left of you. I can't wash that away—not when the pain of your departure still cuts like a knife. I need your scent to survive these lonely nights.

Last night, as I curled up with your pillows, I remembered the first time we made love. We were both so nervous, not from inexperience, but from wanting to make sure we got everything right between us. We were both sweating before we even had our clothes off. Neither of us knew what the other liked or didn't like in the bedroom. It was like the blind leading the blind, but somehow we managed to get undressed. Your body was a gift from the heavens. It was covered in the softest blond hair that I had ever seen. It was damp with your sweat. I reached out and ran my hand down your body. I could feel you tremble under my touch.

We leaned into each other and kissed. It wasn't our first kiss—that came after the botched coffee break—but it was a kiss that I will always feel lingering upon my lips. Your lips were thin, warm, and wet. I could taste the tequila you had been drinking—I can almost taste it now as I'm standing here. As your tongue slipped into my mouth I reached down and felt your cock for the first time. It was thin, but long. It was warm and felt at home in my hand. We fell into the bed, eager to explore each other's body. As the passion grew that night, so did our love. Our bodies became one. It was like we had been made for each other, by each other. There were no missed moments, no awkwardness, no pauses or worries. We blended perfectly. The sweat from our sex soaked the bedding. The scent of our desire hung heavily in the air. We could still smell it the next morning.

It's starting to snow now. The first snow of the year was always your favorite. The gusts of wind whip my face. My ears and cheeks are cold, like my heart. I wonder if you remember our first winter together. It was over Christmas break, and the first winter storm dumped over a foot of snow on Christmas Eve. We ran outside to greet the crystalline white flakes. We tried to catch them on our tongues and in our opened mouths. We became dizzy. We fell into the snow. Our mouths met. We rolled in the white blanket of winter as we kissed. We didn't give a fuck who saw us, or what they thought. It was our time, and that's all that had mattered. We ended up making snow angels. Those angels didn't last long with the heavy snow. I wonder now if that had been an omen—a foreshadowing of a life that we were not meant to live out. We made snowmen as the day progressed. They looked naked, so we took our clothes off down to our underwear and dressed them to look like each other. We ran into the house we were renting and curled up in bed together. We made love the rest of the day while the snow continued to fall outside.

We woke up on Christmas morning. You leaned over and kissed me. Sometime during the night you had slipped a small box under my pillow. I opened it with trembling fingers. It was a ring. You told me that you loved me and that nothing or no one would ever change that. I promised you then that I would never take it off. As you know, I still wear that ring. Over the years as we grew older, I had to keep switching it to a different finger. It's still on my pinky where you placed it last year on our anniversary. I will take this ring to the grave with me and keep that promise to you.

I know you would be angry with me, but I brought with me this morning a single red rose. You always hated it when I gave you flowers. You said it was sweet but a waste of money because the flowers always died too quickly. That's why I'm giving it to you now, because you died too quickly. You shouldn't have left me. It shouldn't have been your time. We had so much more to give each other, so much more to do. We had plans for the rest of our lives, and now they will go undone. All I have now are the long dark days ahead of me. I can't see past tomorrow for fear of all the loneliness I'll be facing. You will always be the light of my life, my one and only true love. Rest now; you deserve it. Please don't forget me, wherever you are, as I will never forget you.

I think you should have this. It's the dime that I gave you twenty-nine years ago. I don't need it now.

The sun is starting to break through the clouds. The rays of light feel good against my cold skin. Perhaps it's you looking down on me. Warming me and trying to comfort me like you did when you were alive. It's time for me to go. The sun is setting, and I would like to take one final walk with you into the sunset.

CRYSTAL BALL

STEPHEN OSBORNE

"LET'S DO THE Tilt-A-Whirl," Ron said, pulling on my sleeve. "We haven't done that yet."

I made a face. "There's a reason for that. It's a crap ride. It just spins you around until you want to throw up. Thanks, but I can just stick my finger down my throat and get the same thrill, and it won't cost me a ride ticket that I paid a dollar for."

In truth, I was losing my carnival spirit. Ron and I had been there since morning, and now that the sun was setting I was finding that my legs really weren't up to standing in a long line for a ride that lasted all of a minute. I would have suggested we call it a day and head back to the car, but Ron was still full of energy and, besides, we still had tickets left to use. I knew that Ron, frugal soul that he was, would never depart until each and every ticket had been used.

Ron continued tugging. "You won't get sick, Theo. If you could stand the Rocket to the Moon ride, you can do the Tilt-A-Whirl."

I refused to move. "I barely survived the Rocket to the Moon. Ten more seconds of that thing and you'd have had my lunch in your lap."

Ron and I have been friends forever, but we couldn't be more different. He's straight and works construction. I'm a retail fag. He's got a huge chest and boxes for fun and recreation. I'm thin, and my only workout consists of running around the block with my dog, Cheshire. His hairline is beginning to recede (something I would never call attention to—did I mention he's a boxer?), and my own mop is still growing thick and full. True, there are a few gray hairs at the temples, but I can live with that. Also, I'm single, and he's got a girlfriend. A girlfriend who, despite his protests, I know doesn't like me. I can tell by the way she looks at me. It's written all over her face. She thinks that when she's not around, Ron and I are fucking. I know that's what she thinks, and it's the stupidest idea ever. For one thing, Ron is just about the straightest straight guy I've ever known. For another, he's not my type. Don't get me wrong, I love him like a brother. I just don't *love* him. Not even slightly.

Penny (that's the bitch's name) will make little jokes every now and then that really aren't jokes but not-very-subtle accusations. "I'm going to the grocery store. Theo, do you think you can keep your mouth off his cock while I'm gone?" Ron insists that she says things like that to show how cool she is with him being friends with a fag. Love can make you so delusional.

Her animosity toward me has increased to the point that this morning when Ron suggested we go to the carnival, she suddenly developed a headache. I'm sure she thought Ron would decide to stay at home with her, but he shocked her by saying, "That's cool. Theo and I haven't had a day to ourselves in a while."

He totally didn't pick up on her aggravated mood. I foresee a breakup in their future.

Anyway, Ron was trying to guide me over to the Tilt-A-Whirl of Death, and I wasn't budging. It was then that I saw the Madame Olga's Fortune Telling tent. I don't know how I'd missed it before, since it was close to the corn-dog stand where we'd had lunch, but there it was, nestled a little behind the Whac-A-Mole booth. There was nothing flashy about Madame Olga's. Every other booth or display at the carnival had flashy neon signs. Not Madame Olga's. Her dark tent just had a wooden sign above the entrance, telling passersby that here was Olga, Fortune Teller. In the fading sunlight, it was hard to even read the sign. Olga desperately needed some bling to advertise her business.

I went to tug on Ron's shirt, but he wears his T-shirts so tight that there wasn't enough material to grab, so I ended up just pinching his arm. "Let's go over there instead."

He looked. "A fortune teller?"

"It'll be cool," I insisted. "I bet she looks like Maria Ouspenskaya in *The Wolf Man*. Let's go. I want to know if there's love in my future."

"Maria Ouspen . . . what?"

I quoted in my best gypsy voice, "Even a man who is pure in heart and says his prayers by night may become a wolf when the wolfbane blooms . . . and the autumn moon is bright."

He blinked at me uncomprehendingly. I really have to get him to watch more movies.

We approached the tent, and I swear it seemed like we were walking into some sort of weird *Twilight Zone* dimension. The noise of the carnival seemed to fade away, and the air got colder. The sun had completely vanished, and the shadows cast by the trees around the little tent gave the area a creepy feel. Ron pulled back the flap covering the entrance, and we went inside.

We found Madame Olga seated at a small table in the center of the tent. I had expected that she'd look like a regional theater version of a gypsy, but old Olga had taken things even further. She had the whole gypsy costume going, with puffy sleeves, rings on every finger, and huge dangling earrings, sure, but to top this off she had apparently used several bottles of fake tanning product that, instead of giving her a swarthy look, made her look jaundiced. She wore a bad Cher wig that just didn't suit her wrinkled face. By the way Ron stopped suddenly right next to me, I know he was as shocked as I was. I didn't know whether to laugh or to pretend we'd walked in by accident and graciously back out of the tent.

"You young men want your fortune told?" Olga asked. The gypsy accent was as thick as it was fake.

"I don't know," Ron said in a fairly quiet voice. For a construction worker who likes to box, he can be pretty shy around people he doesn't know. He held up some of our ride tickets. "Do you take these?"

Olga gave out a hollow laugh. "Do I look like a midway ride? Olga takes only cash. No tickets. No credit cards."

Ron smiled weakly. "We don't have that much cash on us. Sorry to have bothered you. We'd better just . . ."

Madame Olga ignored Ron and stared into my face. "You want to know about the love of your life," she said simply.

I gulped. Something about her gaze made me forget the tacky wig and the theatrical accent. Somehow I knew that this woman just might be able to see into one's future. "How much?" I asked her.

She shrugged. "That depends on whether you want me to read your palm, if you want a tarot reading, or if you want me to use the crystal ball."

"How much to read a palm?" Ron asked. I knew whatever sum she said would make him balk.

"For you," she said steadily, "I make a special price. Ten dollars."

Ron's eyes bulged. "Ten bucks just to . . ."

I held up a hand and pulled out my wallet. "I'll pay for it."

Olga took the bill with a smile, and Ron and I sat down in two rickety chairs opposite her. She took Ron's right hand in hers and examined it. "You are very strong," she said, "and you take great pride in your strength."

That wasn't such a stretch, considering Ron's bulging muscles and the tightness of his T-shirt. I could see a smirk beginning to form on his lips. Her next words wiped it away.

"You have a great secret. You have been cheating on your loved one."

Ron gasped, and I could see the color drain from his face. Madame Olga had struck a nerve. Ron looked at his own hand as if expecting to see the word *cheater* written there. "What else do you see?" he asked, a little desperation showing in his voice.

Olga ran a finger over his hand and nodded. "She knows. Your girlfriend knows that you've been seeing someone else. She plans to break off your relationship."

Ron looked at me and then back at his palm. "Holy shit," he muttered.

I didn't know what to think. On one hand, I was hoping Madame Olga was right, because that meant that I'd be free of his bitch girlfriend, but I was also annoyed that Ron was seeing someone and that he hadn't confided in me.

When had he planned on telling me? Hell, I kept nothing back when telling Ron about my relationships. Well, that is, back in the days when I actually *had* relationships. Lately there hadn't been much to discuss.

When Olga finished his reading, Ron slumped back into his chair, obviously drained. She turned to me with a little half smile on her face. "Would you like me to read your palm as well?"

I had my eye on the large crystal ball in the center of the table. Crystal balls, at least from what I'd seen in movies and on television, saw into the future, and it was the future I wanted to know about. "What does a crystal ball reading cost?"

Her eyebrows arched. "Twenty-five."

I fished my wallet back out and handed her the bills. She stuffed them into a seemingly invisible pocket on her puffy shirt and then hunched over the crystal ball. She gazed intently for several moments before saying, "You have already met the love of your life. You met him several years ago, but then fate tore you apart. You will never have another love as strong as the one you felt for him."

My heart sank. I had hoped she would spout out some good news, like I would be meeting someone tall, dark, and handsome soon who would sweep me off my feet. I knew deep down, however, that what she was saying was true. I would never find someone like Greg again. I leaned forward and looked into the crystal ball, trying to see what she was seeing. It just looked like a glass ball to me.

Olga went on, "You will be reunited with him, very soon. You will rekindle your romance, and you will be very happy together for many years to come."

She continued to talk, but I wasn't hearing what she was saying. Something about work and money, but it meant

nothing to me. I could only think about Greg and her pre-
diction that we'd meet up again. I knew it was impossible,
but part of me hoped to the heavens that she was right. As I
looked into the crystal, I thought I saw a tiny black shadow
forming in the center of the glass. I peered at it, hoping it
would take some sort of form.

✦

GREG HAD BEEN twenty when we met, fourteen years
younger than me. We met at a party thrown by my friend
Renata, and I'd be lying if I said it was love at first sight.
Quite the opposite, actually. Oh, he made it plain from the
first that he was interested in me. He just wasn't my type,
and I really didn't want to start seeing someone who wasn't
even old enough to get into a bar legally.

The first time I saw him was in Renata's kitchen when I
was trying to see if there was something other than beer to
drink. I found a cooler with cans of soft drinks floating
around in icy water and was pulling out a Diet Pepsi when
someone else plunged his hand in and somehow managed
to grab hold of the same can. I looked up to see a thin
young man with long brown hair and a cute face smiling at
me. "Sorry," he said, releasing the can. He flashed me a
grin and stuck out his hand for me to shake. "I'm Greg," he
said. The hand was dripping icy droplets. I shook it quickly
and told him my name was Theo.

Yeah, he was cute, but too young. I thought that his
slightly bucked teeth made him more attractive—you know,
an imperfection that somehow is endearing—but after he
pulled out a different can and walked away I didn't give
him another thought. I snapped open the tab on the soda

and began to roam back through the crowd looking for Ron and the Queen Bitch . . . I mean, Penny.

I found them in the living room, where most of the throng seemed to have gathered. I forced my way through the crowd and finally managed to get next to Ron. As I came up, I saw a faint look of distrust and dislike cross Penny's face before she put on her fake smile.

"You should like this party," she said, speaking loudly to be heard over the music. "There are lots of fags here."

Some people can say *fags* and not mean it as an insult. Penny wasn't one of them.

"Maybe you'll meet someone," offered Ron with a smile.

"I doubt it," I said, turning to him and ignoring the fact that Penny was standing next to him. It was pretty easy to ignore her. "The only one I've met so far was some kid out in the kitchen. He was skinny, had long straight hair, stick-out ears, and an overbite. I think he was an elf."

Ron laughed. "Don't knock it. You know what they say. Once you go elf . . ."

As the night went on, I noticed that every time I moved into a different room, Greg would soon follow. Then he began to try to make eye contact with me. You know, the gay-bar little stare and nod that shows you're interested. I would nod back politely and then immerse myself in some conversation with anyone around me. It didn't work. Greg tired of the subtle approach and went for a more direct line. He came right up to me.

"Has anyone ever told you that you're hot?" he said.

I chuckled uneasily. "It doesn't really come up all that often, actually." I don't know what I meant by that, but it seemed like I had to make some reply. Greg had picked his moment well. Ron was off getting another beer, and Penny

was . . . well, I assumed she was in the bathroom or something. Frankly, I didn't really care where she was as long as
it wasn't around me.

Greg tapped his soda can against mine. "I see you don't
drink, either. Alcohol, I mean."

I shrugged. "Occasionally I do. I'm designated driver
tonight."

He grinned. He really did have a sweet smile. "I'm not
really legal to drink yet. I don't turn twenty-one until June."
He moved a little closer to me.

"Yeah," I said slowly, "when I became legal to drink, you
probably hadn't even hit puberty yet."

Now it was his turn to shrug. "So?" he asked. How does
one argue with "So"? After a pause he went on. "Are you
busy this weekend? I thought it might be nice to go out to
dinner and a movie. There's this movie I've been wanting
to see, and I hate going alone, and . . ."

I cut him off. "Look," I said as gently as I could, considering that I had to speak loudly to be heard over the music
and the crowd, "you're really sweet and cute and all that,
but you're out of my age bracket. I make it a point not to
date anyone who could, in a theoretical sense, be young
enough to be my son."

Greg nodded sagely. "Oh. So you're an ageist."

I didn't like the sound of that. An "ist" is never good.
Communist. Fascist. Republican-ist. "No, it's just that I . . ."

"You don't think we'll have enough in common to make
a good couple," he finished for me.

"Well, yeah."

"Wouldn't it make more sense, if you aren't an ageist, to
go out with me and find out for sure rather than just assuming I'm like other guys my age?"

He had me there. Of course, part of me wanted him to convince me to go out with him because he really was cute as hell. The other part of me knew I'd feel a little like a dirty old man going out with a bit of eye candy. Decisions, decisions.

While I was trying to figure out how to answer, he suddenly leaned his face up to mine. His hands went behind my neck and he pulled my head down a few inches to meet his. Our lips locked.

Fuck, what a kiss. It was one of those that made your toes tingle. His face seemed to melt into mine. It was like our lips, our tongues, were made to be together. If the music hadn't been so damn loud, I'm sure I would have heard bells ring.

When we finally came up for air, I muttered, "Dinner and a movie sounds good."

Hey, it was a really good kiss.

✦

I HAD TO endure the obvious jokes from Ron, of course. Cradle robber. Did I have to help him out with his homework? Was it hard to burp him after he ate? Things like that. As the weeks went by and I saw more and more of Greg, the jokes ceased to bother me. Hell, I added some in myself. We had to take my car when we went out on dates since Greg's was a bumper car. I referred to myself as Woody Allen's gay cousin. That, I guess, was my way of dealing with the age difference. Not to ignore it, but to embrace it and have fun with it.

Greg and I had three official dates before we went to bed together. It just happened. We had planned to go out to a movie, but then we started kissing and one thing led to another. He surprised me when we got to my bedroom by pushing me onto the bed and leaping on me. God, he was wiry. With an evil grin he said, "Let's wrestle for top."

I thought he was kidding at first. I mean, I had thirty pounds and four inches of height on him. I soon learned he wasn't kidding. I could tell from the effort that he put into the wrestling that he really wanted to win. Who'd have thought, with his elfin features, that he'd be a top? Guess that's what you get when you assume things.

I let him win.

The first time we fucked, it was all passion and fury. I swear they must have heard us several states away. After a short breather, we went at it again, this time all sweet and tender. Greg's face was so beautiful when he came. He looked like he was listening to the singing of angels.

✦

AFTER SIX MONTHS we began to talk about him moving in with me. It made sense, since we spent all our free time at my place anyway and his apartment was tiny, cramped, and infested with cockroaches. Even Ron was supportive of the relationship, despite the kidding. Penny wasn't, of course, but fuck her anyway.

Then disaster struck. I'd known, of course, that somewhere in town was Greg's father. Greg didn't talk about family much, but I gathered he and his dad didn't get along. Greg's mother, I had learned, had died in a car crash years ago. So his dad was a known entity, but I had sort of assumed he was out of the picture. I found out I was wrong when he knocked on my door one evening.

He was of a slight build like Greg, but that's where the similarities ended. He wasn't a particularly attractive man, and the permanent scowl he seemed to wear didn't help matters any. He introduced himself and practically shoved his way into my apartment.

"We need to talk," he said stiffly.

By talk, he apparently meant that he'd talk and I should just listen, for whenever I tried to speak up he talked right over me like Ann Coulter on a talk show. He accused me of "enticing" his son, of breaking up their family, and of consorting with the devil. He didn't actually say that last one, but he was thinking it, I could tell. I tried to explain the situation, but Greg Sr. already had his mind made up. He had decided that the thing to do was to ship Greg out to join the navy. That, he was sure, would make a man out of his son. During Greg's two-year stint we were to have no contact whatsoever. When he paused for breath, I finally got a word in.

"Greg is of legal age," I reminded him. "You can't make him join the navy or anything for that matter. And you certainly can't tell me that I can't have any contact with your son."

The man glared at me, and I thought for a moment he was going to haul off and slug me. Finally he just curled his lip and stormed to the door. "We'll see," he said, slamming the door behind him.

I didn't see Greg until the next night, when he came to my apartment just a mass of long hair and tears. I held him as he cried. Just when I thought he'd cried himself out, a new flood would start. We went to bed, where I just held him close.

Finally he got to where he could speak. "I've got to do what my dad says," he sputtered in a choked voice. "He says he'll disown me if I don't do this."

I didn't think that would be a bad thing, but I kept quiet.

The tears started again. Greg held me fiercely, gasping in between sobs. "I don't know what to do. I love my dad, but I love you, too."

I felt like a heel. I could see how it must look through Greg's father's eyes. Here was this older guy having an affair with his son. Hell, I was closer to his dad's age than I was to Greg's. I didn't know what to say, so I just held Greg until he finally sobbed himself to sleep.

In the end, of course, his dad won out. Greg insisted that after his two-year stint he'd come back and we'd take up where we left off, but I knew it wouldn't happen. Before he left, we had one last kiss. It was as sweet and tender and electric as the first had been.

◆

MADAME OLGA WAS still speaking, but I was still reminiscing about Greg. Then she asked me something that shifted my attention back to her. "The young man you love, he has recently contacted you, yes?"

My heart sank. I had been hoping that despite the trappings that maybe this bewigged woman actually knew something of the future. Apparently not. "No. Haven't heard from him in over two years," I told her numbly.

Olga looked slightly confused but covered with, "Then he had tried to contact you. You will hear from him soon."

That didn't seem likely.

The reading was obviously over, so Ron and I made our way back out into the night. The carnival throng was quickly dispersing, everyone making their way back to the parking area. As we ambled along, Ron said, "So, was she right? Have you heard from the elf?"

"No," I said. "I would have told you if I had. Unlike you, I don't keep secrets! How long have you been having an affair, and with whom?"

Even in the moonlight I could tell he turned bright crimson. "I was going to tell you. After all, things are pretty much over between Penny and I anyway."

"Who's the new love?"

Ron beamed with the pride of new romance. "Her name is Rachel. You'll love her. I've already told her all about you. Actually, I should call her. I was supposed to go over to her place tonight, and I didn't think we'd be out this late. Can I borrow your cell phone?"

I pulled it out of my pocket and handed it to him. We stopped walking so that Ron would be able to dial. I love him like a brother, but walking and dialing a phone at the same time is beyond his abilities. As he looked at the phone, a wide grin spread over his face.

"You've got several missed calls," he told me. "And a text message." He shoved the phone in my face.

The message was short. Just the words *I'm back* followed by a familiar name. . . .

CITY OF FOUNTAINS

ROSS M. LEVINE

I COULDN'T BELIEVE what I had done—or hadn't done.

There was Garth Rodriguez sprawled atop the hotel bed in nothing but his white briefs, his arms stretched out like Christ's on the cross, his beautiful Aztec chest heaving quietly like the power source of a mythical planet—and me just sitting there in the room, almost too guilty under the self-imposed circumstances to even let my *eyes* caress him. After all, he had a wife and child back home, and even if he did look at me sometimes with those burnt-umber orbs like he wanted nothing more than to, yes, do what he'd just done, only moments before, throwing his arms around me, drawing his lips toward mine . . .

And what did I do? *I stopped him.* I said, "Garth, it can't just be the alcohol. It has to be—real. . . ."

Real? What does *real* mean? It should have been either, "Garth, stop it—you know this is totally wrong," or . . .

As if to silence me, he called me by a nickname one of the professors had given me at work—he softly slurred it, in his drunkenness, and with a heart-piercing tone of affection that left me dumbfounded.

"I mean, tomorrow," I said, "what will you think?" He

looked up at me as if he didn't know who I was. "Garth, I'm crazy about you . . . you have no idea. . . ."

But he was already slipping into unconsciousness. I suppose his tolerance for liquor was less than mine, or maybe he'd just had a lot more than me—I'd lost track. I laid his head down gently on the bed. He'd already removed his shoes, his tie, unbuttoned his red-checked cotton shirt and extracted one arm from its sleeve—I simply guided his other arm out, repositioning him higher on the mattress so his feet weren't hanging over the edge, and, yes, in doing so, after cupping my hands under his arms, moving him forward, and then releasing my grip, I allowed my fingertips to slide down the smooth surface of his hairless chest, felt his dark nipples, the relaxed flesh of his stomach, before I put my hands to less furtive use, sliding off his pants and socks, covering him up. As the room was fairly warm, he himself, without opening his eyes, slipped the blanket back down just past his navel.

What could I do now but retreat to my own bed? We needed to be at the airport very early—the conference was over—we both agreed it had been a waste of time, figured we might as well get plastered the last night—like one of those sex dates I enjoyed in my roaring, pre-"plague" twenties—it was even Garth's idea, though that didn't mean I wasn't in some measure responsible for the aftermath.

Tears invading my eyes, I rose dramatically to peer out the hotel window. A large chunk of moon was drifting high across the sky, reminding me that every inch of earth was subject to the same physical constraints. I tried to discern something in the dark landscape that said Kansas City and nowhere else, and true, it wasn't Southern California, no spindly palms reaching toward the heavens, but otherwise,

I could see nothing distinctive. Lomas and I had been here nearly twenty years ago, on a trip across the country, and discovered that Kansas City, which we'd always imagined a landlocked slaughterhouse, was also the "City of Fountains," with some of the most elaborate waterworks we'd ever seen outside Europe. But Garth and I had witnessed none of that, just the airport, hotel, conference center, and hotel bar, of course, which made it seem even less advisable to torch our friendship, and the classified nature of my infatuation, in such quotidian surroundings.

✦

TURNING FROM THE window, looking over at Garth again, I experienced that white-hot stab of desire so powerful in those with "n-erotic" tendencies. But it was too late—now it would be like raping him. Perhaps in the morning he would remember it all, and profess his love for me in a state of stark light and sobriety. If not, at least I'd finally seen and, albeit quickly (like a reluctant looter snatching merchandise from an already besieged store), caressed his naked body—so far beyond the one or two embraces I'd managed to pilfer over the years. There was a certain dark blue sweater he was wont to wear on those half days before the Thanksgiving or Christmas breaks, a garment that showed off his well-tended torso much more than the formal dress shirts our jobs normally required. The sweater accentuated the developed contours of his chest that, ably bridging his wide shoulders to his slender abdomen, had many times driven me to distraction.

One year, right before a long holiday interlude, I situated myself near the back door of our office building at the moment I'd estimated he'd be on his way out with his bicycle. Sure enough, I ambushed him, and in saying good-bye, "spontaneously" put my arms around him. He not only went along with this transparent maneuver, but reciprocated, and, for hours afterward, I was schoolgirl-giddy, as if I'd actually obliterated a barrier between us, when all I'd done was further animate my own impossible longing.

✦

AND ONCE I helped him move a piece of furniture—a small but heavy dresser with two drawers. He'd driven his wife's weather-beaten Maxima into work that day and parked it on a street off campus. We took the dresser there atop a dolly, and, loading the piece in the backseat, my hand, as we tugged at it, landed on his, and I noted with astonishment that he didn't yank his away like any self-respecting straight guy would. This was all the more surprising given his somewhat obsessive contempt for germs; Garth hated shaking hands or touching the knobs or handles of well-trafficked doors. Perhaps he hadn't noticed, I thought—but he must have, and, in my case, was either so secure in his invulnerability, or maybe . . . well, I certainly acknowledged the possibility, but then told myself I was just being presumptive the way so many gay men are, picking up Geiger-counter spikes of desire in every pair of pants they're attracted to.

✦

I WALKED OVER to my bed and started to undress. It's not that Garth had never spoken about girls—he often did—and his taste seemed pedestrian enough—blonde cheerleader types, far from the women of his own ethnic lineage, and far from his brunette wife, Daria, who I had often dismissed as physically unequal to her husband's charms, though over the years, she'd proven herself nice enough. She had a high-pitched voice I knew Garth had to find grating, but they'd been together for years—since college—and Garth was approaching forty now, though he hardly showed it. Except for one or two silver strands, his hair was jet black, his scalp yet undepleted, and he kept himself in shape, riding nearly fifteen miles each way to the office on his seven-year-old French derailleur, lifting weights at the university gym many mornings before work, surfing in summertime, and running year-round; he once described a winter jog he took along a Northern California beach, the rocks, the churning gray sea, the soaring pelicans comically nose-diving for fish, and he barefoot, in sweatpants and sweatshirt braving the blustery cold—the image caused me a few restless nights. Somehow I always imagined the two of us in tropical Hawai'i, a place I'd never been—yes, terribly banal, but still—sun, palms, sand, ocean, cabana, playful exercise, and finally, the full-blown volcano. . . .

✦

BUT BACK TO "girls," his word—he was adorably primitive that way, never using "women." A few years back, before Garth became a father—and who drove him home that fateful day but yours truly?—a young lady named Janet had joined the staff—married, unable to have children, as she explained to all who might or might not want to listen, because she was born with one kidney and, as I gathered, other anatomical deficiencies. Thin and fit, she had short

brown hair and brown eyes set into a round, elfin face liber-
ally punctuated with freckles. She took to Garth like an
oxpecker to a bull, and for a period, the two were inseparable. Because she lived out his way, she tried biking to work
with him a few days, but soon abandoned the enterprise,
acknowledging it was too hard to keep up. She and Garth,
however, along with another young woman at work, registered for a triathlon as a relay team—Garth would bike,
Janet would run, and the other female would brave the
swimming portion. For perhaps two months, Janet and
Garth were at the university track during lunch break two
or three times a week, with Garth purportedly "training"
her. It was all so obvious; I couldn't fathom how Garth
could be so blatant about it—either he was utterly naïve or
completely secure in his state of male privilege. I contem-
plated calling his wife or leaving her an anonymous message, but faced with the hypocrisy of such a step, couldn't
bring myself to do it. Instead, I simply watched through the
sealed window of my second-floor office as Garth and Janet
would head off toward the track, or, at the end of the day,
depart for home, Garth walking his bike, a diffident air
about him, like a teenager held captive by a crush, and she
shamelessly rapacious for all the world to see.

That wasn't the first time I'd played omniscient voyeur
with Garth. I parked my car in a multistory structure, and
could, if I timed it right (since, upon leaving the office,
Garth had to first stop at the gym to change into his biking
gear), be atop the roof looking down at the boulevard as
Garth set off for home. On more than one occasion I
watched him—dressed in his bike gear, including helmet
and oversized goggles, his dark calves, thin but muscular,
exposed—dart fearlessly into the stream of boulevard traffic

so he could get over to the left-turn lane, taking his place there among the waiting cars. Then, when the arrow went green, he'd take off like a jackrabbit, executing his left turn at a near 45-degree angle before disappearing behind a row of buildings. What purpose I had in watching him this way was hard to discern—it only made the chasm between us seem that much wider. Still, it gave me the sense that in some way (known only to a collective mind infinitely greater than my own), I was connecting to him; that by observing him, I was imprinting his essence on my heart, like recording a video I might play back later on.

✦

BUT RETURNING TO Garth and Janet—the intensity of my jealousy mortified me—so pathetically human after all!—like the evil queen in her tower, hatching deformed and vengeful thoughts of toxic fruit.

✦

FORTUNATELY, THEIR LITTLE "affair" finally cul-minated at the office holiday party at the end of that year. The party took place at night in a family restaurant at an outdoor mall. On the ground floor, at the restaurant bar, a lot of drinking unfolded before we headed to one of the upstairs banquet rooms for dinner. Garth, whose wife that year had been unable to attend, had had a few, and so had Janet, who was there with her husband, Ryan, a downright pretty Asian guy of about thirty. Once we sat down, I found myself not quite directly across the small round table from Garth (it was the best I could do)—Janet at his right, Ryan at her right, and then me. I chatted with Ryan as Janet, seemingly oblivious to his presence, shamelessly flirted with Garth. I was expecting a scene, for Ryan to drag his treacherous mate away from the table and out to their car, but it never came. Instead, the painful dinner ebbed on, an air (at least from my perspective) of strained conviviality hanging over us, the cloying Garth and Janet Show, Ryan obviously upset but too—timid? uxorious?—to speak his peace, the tension building in me, knotting my stomach, narrowing my throat. At last, as everyone got up to head downstairs, I had yet another shock to my apparently Victorian sensibilities—Garth escorting Janet down the stairs with his hand placed squarely at the small of her back—did Ryan not see? Was he an utter eunuch? And then the crescendo: as part of some kind of plan, Ryan's parents were having dinner at another restaurant in the same mall, and were set to drive him and Janet home. But Janet, who apparently wasn't done partying, arranged with Ryan to remain with Garth and two female workmates so they could have a few more drinks, after which one of the women would drive them home. Incredibly, Ryan acquiesced to this betrayal and was soon gone, leaving Garth and Janet to their further mischief. It was painfully obvious to me that I was not to be part of this hastily arranged foursome, so I said good night to Garth and tore myself away into the brisk night air. I had had a bit of wine myself and needed to walk off its lingering effects. Given my mood, the people parading about outside seemed especially grotesque, and once I'd completed a full circle around the mall, I briefly considered returning to the restaurant to see if Garth was still there. But even *my* masochism has its limits, so I just headed to my car and drove home.

✦

I NEVER SPOKE to Garth about that night, but did notice that soon afterward, the rapport between him and Janet had precipitously cooled. In fact, before long, it positively congealed. The triathlon got nixed, and Garth began to describe Janet in my presence as "stupid," much to my unspoken delight, but part of me—well, it seemed dangerously telling that his affections could reverse so quickly. I later found out—without asking—from one of the two female witnesses, that he and Janet had made out in the backseat of her Explorer on the way to their respective domiciles. It shocked me that Garth could be so blatantly unfaithful to his wife, for I couldn't imagine myself (too accustomed to self-denial, perhaps) succumbing to temptation in front of such a garrulous onlooker. But there it was—the liquor factor, I suppose—so that tonight, with enough of it in him, he had seemed willing to navigate the same course with the likes of me. Had I allowed it, surely he would have despised me the morning after, with our "relationship," whatever it was, destroyed—"Janetized"—forever.

Even with what had actually occurred, or not occurred, I feared the worst. After all, Janet eventually got another job and vanished from all but memory, with Garth bringing her up only on rare occasion, and usually to deride her incompetence. Every time he did, I wondered why he never acknowledged my awareness of (if not the scene in the Explorer) all the coaching, bicycling, and other contact he'd had with her—his brown hand with its patches of flaking dry skin against the one-kidney small of her back just like in high school days. The image of it reminded me of when I myself dated women I wanted nothing to do with, hoping it might awaken in me some latent normality, when in fact the effect was quite opposite; the whole charade turned me against decorum and societal ritual—symptoms of an atrophied soul—and made me the type never able to fully belong anywhere.

Soon after Janet disappeared, I came across a *National Geographic* article that attempted to scientifically delineate the difference between volatile and enduring love. It seemed to clarify my whole conundrum, my long-term affiliation with Lomas, my compulsively passionate obsession with Garth. Explained it, decriminalized it, yet there was only so much longer I could continue to stoke such an all-consuming fantasy. By the time of our trip to Kansas City, my Garth fixation had not exactly faded, but had been softened by time and circumstance so that I no longer spun tales at night of our scandalous assignations. That is, unless he looked at me that certain way during the workday, in which case I might once again be inspired to drum up something.

As I sat on my bed in that generic hotel room, I still couldn't fathom what had happened and how I had reacted. Yes, I did stop him, but perhaps not quite the way I initially described. When Garth put his lips to mine, I did not pull away immediately, but for a brief moment, yes, allowed my own mouth to sink into his, as if releasing myself on a bungee cord into a dark but sublime chasm. Then, guilt-wracked sort that I am, with that day a few years back unfolding in my head, I pulled back. That was the day Garth, nothing visibly unsettled about his demeanor, stepped into my office and said he needed a ride home. Figuring he meant at the end of the day, I said sure, and asked him why.

"I have to drive Daria to the hospital."

"Oh, you mean—*now*—right—of course, no problem, let's go!" I said, apparently more nervous than the expectant father. "What about your bike?" I asked foolishly.

He smiled with a hint of sarcasm. "I can pick it up later."

We headed toward the parking structure and up the three flights of stairs to where I'd parked. It was the first time I'd had Garth in my car, an eighteen-year-old Cressida afflicted with a long list of ailments: no A/C, capricious power windows, scratchy radio, a moribund right wiper, etcetera. Garth, appearing to enjoy my car's imperfections, directed me to the freeway, which, given the car's spotty health, I preferred not to drive—what if we broke down and he missed his son's birth? Would he ever forgive me? It was a convoluted route to his house, a total of four freeways in all, and seemed to take forever, me driving faster than I thought prudent in that car, and Garth perched uncomfortably (and dangerously) at the front of his seat because if he leaned back, the broken seat would collapse. It was an unaccustomed intimacy to have him so close to me, the two of us "alone" together amid the threatening, violent roar of traffic, and me wishing I could just reach over and stroke his leg with no social or biological barriers to stop me. When we finally arrived at his house and I pulled into his driveway, Daria, climactically pregnant, came out and greeted us, then she and Garth got into discussing the business at hand. Of course, I felt like the consummate outsider, and knew it was my role to depart as soon as possible, though I would have preferred to linger, to fully cement my presence in Garth's life, a context in which my existence seemed to have actual meaning, thanks to whatever esteem issues had brought me to this juncture. Garth graciously thanked me for the ride and gave me directions to return to work on surface streets, while Daria, understandably pre-occupied, did not say good-bye as I climbed back into my car. I came to the paranoid conclusion that she "knew," that wives know such things, no matter the sex of the third party—that they have an innate sense of a threat from any quarter, whereas even their husbands might not suspect. A woman Garth and I once worked with, a longtime lesbian who was finally set to marry a guy (if not for him, she said unequivocally, she surely would have ended up with a woman), once looked me straight in the eye and asked, "What's going on in the office these days? I bet you spend the whole day lusting after Garth."

"No," I said, like an embezzler caught with the funds. "What makes you say so?"

"Everybody lusts after Garth," she said.

Her perspicacity, however random, disturbed me greatly. To think that I was just another one of Garth's admirers, that my sacred faith was nothing more than a dime-store religion available to all—I knew then the whole business was pointless, yet there I was, driving back to work from Garth's house, still believing there was something behind his eyes at certain moments that only I could see.

✦

AT LAST, I had gotten myself into the hotel bed and underneath the covers. The nearly six years I had known Garth rolled through my mind as if I were plotting out a way to legitimize my getting up, joining him in his bed, and con-summating our inevitable destiny. There was the day we met, when, according to his recollection of it, he mispronounced

my last name and I snottily corrected him. Our first work holiday party, in a depressingly windowless room at a downtown
club, where I initially met Daria and noticed how attractive
Garth looked in a suit and tie. The day of his accident, when,
not far from the school, he ran a red light and the rear of his
bike was broadsided by a car, throwing him to the ground and
knocking him momentarily unconscious; someone from
work who just happened to be at the intersection saw the
whole thing and went to his aid. That evening, Lomas and I
visited Garth at the hospital where they were holding him for
observation (as it turned out, he was fine). Then there were
the times Lomas and I dogsat for Montezuma, Garth's aging
Doberman, whom he'd had even before he met Daria, and
who I felt represented his life before the responsibilities of
marriage and children. It was the perfect ploy for insinuating
Garth into my life on a weekend, without any sneaking
around behind Lomas's back. And then there were the times
Garth and I screwed up at work and were jointly chewed out
by our boss, bestowing upon us a certain camaraderie in
adversity. And finally the day—can't recall exactly what trig-
gered it—I felt so overcome by my hunger that I printed a
photo of him I'd stashed away in my computer and tried to
draw his portrait, as if somehow achieving his likeness on
paper—transferring him, so to speak, from flesh to art—
would in some measure relieve me of my need. But no matter
how many times I tried, I could not capture him the way I
wanted to, turning the project into a futile exercise that only
heightened the absurdity of my predicament without in any
way making it better.

Having ultimately fallen asleep in the midst of this
reverie, I suddenly found myself responding to the hotel
wakeup call. To my surprise, Garth was already up and

dressed. I could tell almost instantly that his demeanor had turned businesslike, that whatever he remembered from the night before, he had decided to cover it up with an impenetrable coolness that cut into me like a knife. Suppose we had awakened in the same bed—what would he have done? Leaped away in disgust? Accused me of some unauthorized personal trespass? Beaten me up?

All I could think was I had missed my chance, one I would surely never have again, that given his current reaction, I might as well have taken full advantage of the situation and, like an unremorseful vampire, drunk my fill. Had *he* shown any compunction at all about making out with Janet? It was only *after* the fact that he had put things "right" again, ejecting Janet from his life, then making it seem as if he'd never messed with her at all. I could have done the same—brought this nonaffair to its appropriate conclusion—that by finally giving in to the once near unimaginable, I would destroy it, obliterate years of worthless emotional meandering, be done with my Garth Rodriguez "blue period" at last.

And then suddenly I wondered if that was indeed what I had done. That maybe he hadn't come on to me after all, but was simply too drunk to resist, and that I had translated his lack of resistance into an invitation for me to make love to him, following which I had blocked it all out—the irony of it, after all the anticipation—because it was too hard for me to reveal, to let anyone know, especially myself, that my supposed love for Garth was nothing more—absolutely nothing more—than the same rapacious desire that had overcome Janet when she first met him. That all the emotional turmoil was just the polluting by-product of what was just a sexual urge frustrated by fear and rotten luck. So much for my pretentious claim that decorum and societal ritual did not rule my life. My soul had indeed atrophied, and the cool look in Garth's eyes—the hostility—was more than ample proof.

In the back of the hotel shuttle, we rode to the airport in oppressive silence. Was it really over with Garth, I wondered. How would I live without this unauthorized love to nurture and cultivate? It was a talent I'd fostered since my first stirrings of consciousness, and as I felt Garth's tense, tempestuous presence in the seat in front of me, I knew beyond a doubt that I would surely find a way to love hopelessly again.

THE GALAXY IS OUR PLAYGROUND

THOMAS HERMAN

I GUESS I was being slightly unreasonably cranky; after all, I did accept the promotion that put all this bullshit in my lap. I'm a farmer, and I might add a damn good one. I have lived on this station since I was seven, and I have had a pretty good life. When Earth was finally abandoned and humanity moved to the stars, my grandfather and I made a home here, on Central Station. The clever name is because we are centrally located in the middle of a colonized galaxy, on top of good ole Earth. We utilize the gravitational pull to create day and night, which helps the plants have a more natural light source.

We are almost exclusively a farming station, with the exception of the top four floors. They host a large communications grid and traffic centers. When my grandfather passed away a year ago I took over his harvest, and I made some moderate improvements some reporter thought were just wonderful. He exposed me as some space-farming wiz, and now, thanks to that grossly negligent writing, I am a wanted man.

The mayor of the station invited me for dinner, which she had not done since Grandpa died. Mmm, she must be up to something. "Greg, you know how much we love you and how proud we are that the article has brought so much attention to our station." She was such an attention whore, as if being the mayor of Central Station wasn't enough; she milked my story dry. I smiled my best fake smile; I wasn't in the mood. "Another interview?" I asked flatly. "No! You must think I'm such an attention whore!" she said, laughing loudly. That got an actual smile out of me. "Yeah, I do, but that makes you good at what you do." She laughed more. "Yeah so, that hot sex kitten of a diplomat Josh Perez wants to borrow you. I kind of told him you wouldn't mind as far as I knew, but that you had the final word." Borrow me, like I was a book or an essay to download. "What am I borrowed out for?" She passed me another martini, took a big bite of salad, and smiled awkwardly as she chewed. Last time she stalled this much, she dropped a whole class of children on me for a day to see how the mechanics of farming really worked.

"Well, as you know, the station to the far east is a bit chopped off from the rest of us. Josh wants to convert the bottom three floors to farming levels, and he thinks you are just the man to make it happen smoothly. You have grown up farming in space, and the adjustments you made after . . . The modifications you have made have just been great. Think of it as a vacation; I'm sure you'll be in the lap of luxury for the four days it takes to get there." She smiled and gulped a big sip of her martini. I'm sure she was preparing herself for my rebuttal. I simply said, "Okay." She looked confused. "Okay? That's it?" I shook my head no. "Yolanda needs to watch my floor while I am gone. I know she'll say no; make her say yes—she can split her time between her precious coffee trees and my little simple low-maintenance floor."

She smiled her big fake smile. "He arrives day after tomorrow, and he wants a tour and private dinner with you." Unknown to the mayor, I thought Josh Perez was totally fucking hot. He was a bit of a flake, the son of one of the members of the board of United Nations who felt the need to be a full-time humanitarian. If he stayed with one cause and seemed less self-important, I would probably have liked his public image more. With that said, four days alone with him would be interesting if nothing else.

So Josh arrived early, and he seemed surprisingly low-key. I didn't know what I expected, but more somehow. Don't get me wrong: he was gorgeous and kind. He had no security, no big entrance, no press; he was even dressed in casual attire. His ship was sporty, but nowhere near the level of pretension he could certainly get. He was, after all, the son of a wealthy man on the highest board of government in the Milky Way.

He smiled at me shyly and introduced himself. "I asked the mayor to forgo all the greetings and let me get to work. I hope you don't mind." "Not at all, the sooner we get started the sooner I get back to my crops." He nodded. "Fair enough. You mind if we grab a bite to eat before the tour?" I smiled. "You read my mind. Do you like Italian?" "Only if you have wine to go with it," he said with a wink. "Well, not normally, but I'm sure I can find some for a diplomat," I said with a smirk. "I doubt that; your profile says you like reds." I laughed. "You do your research, huh?" He nodded. "So some red with our red sauce?"

Lunch was fun; it was slightly odd at first. That new-person oddness, but it soon became a fun, flowing conversation. He was charming and, pardon the pun, down to Earth. I kept watching him eat, like a total perv. I think he liked it, but said nothing to indicate any interest. His skin was light caramel, and his eyes dark blue. His hair, like his ethnicity itself, was a mix of light and dark hues. My skin was a couple shades lighter than his, and my eyes are light brown.

"I can give you a tour of my ship before you show me your crops; that way you can look to see how much you want to pack. I have a lot of music and books in the memory, but we could lose links during the middle part of the voyage." "Fair enough, let's check out where we will be for four days."

It was not the glory I would have expected for him. It was nice and modern and warm. It was also very small. We had a pilot and copilot seat in the front with various controls. The two beds were directly behind those seats, with cute little windows above them that followed the length of the beds. Behind the beds were support bulkheads, and just beyond that the bathroom and a small set of drawers.

"Nice and small," I said, looking around. He laughed. "Bigger isn't always better," he said with a smirk. "It has a lot of hidden features; the window shutters roll down and become a viewing screen. The beds are adjustable, and there are monitors in the roofs above the beds as well. I would rather have lots of fun in a tight space than room to roam and nothing to do," he explained. "Can't argue with that logic." I so wanted to be pervy but didn't; I showed restraint. "Okay, I showed you mine," he said, gesturing for us to exit. "Actually, you didn't," I said with a laugh. "I'm offended at the suggestion! I'm a gentleman!"

"I'm so sorry! I didn't mean to offend you; I was just . . ." He busted out laughing. "You won't see it either if you're not good on this trip!" he said with a wink. "Now show me all the tricks we are going to use to sustain a good farming base for the people in the east." We made our way through the small access hatch and back to my station. Show him I did; we went through in great detail the boring mechanics of farming. He seemed really intrigued. "I hope to God this works; I have put a lot at stake for this. An attempt was made a couple years back, with limited funds. It had limited success, but not enough to really help the region." He seemed like he really did care; maybe he wasn't such a flake after all.

Soon our day was over, and Josh saw the sun setting for the first time in his life as we slowly tilted away from Earth. "It's amazing! You see this every day?" I laughed at his child-like exuberance. "Yup, there is a Greek restaurant above the Italian one we ate at earlier with a crazy view—no wine, though." He laughed and gazed into my eyes, and for the first time I felt he might like me too. "Maybe when we get back, as a reward for our hard work."

I didn't sleep much that night; my mind kept wandering and chasing itself around a few different thoughts. I wondered if the couple of moments of flirting and gazing at each other could mean anything. Maybe he flirted with everyone. I was also worried about a long trip—truth be told, the last time I was on one, it was to come live here. Grandpa didn't like to travel. I always wondered when I was little why he didn't take more chances, have more fun. As an adult I can see now it was because he felt safe here on Central Station. I decided to see my crops one last time; I found the solace of my empty floor comforting.

My floor wasn't so empty. "What about getting some sleep?" I asked as I approached Josh. He seemed surprised, but glad to see me. "Easier said than done. What brings you here so late?" I smiled, a little embarrassed at myself. "To say good-bye, to feel the soil in my fingers. I find it soothing." "When is the last time you were off the station?" I shrugged.

"When we left Earth." We sat there and talked about nothing and everything for a couple of hours. He seemed more trapped by his surname than enabled by it, which I found surprising. He was amazed at the normalcy of my life, and I thought about it for the first time, that I was lucky. I went back to bed for a couple of hours and actually slept.

We were off bright and early the next day. I was nervous and didn't know why. My anxiety seemed not at all warranted as the journey began. Josh had cleared out a drawer for my stuff if I needed it, and after we left the busier traffic of surrounding ships, he put us on autopilot. "Want to watch a movie?" he asked. "Sure, what you got?" He laughed. "Access the library." I did, and he had many titles I liked, and a few I loved. "You don't have *The Galaxy Is Our Playground*, do you?" He looked at me in shock. "Um, yeah. It was awesome, still is! It made me feel empowered at a time when I didn't."

I couldn't imagine a time when this sexy, confident man didn't see endless options. I guess there was one, though. He smiled and continued. "I was young and my family had my whole life planned. Marry a nice girl; become a politician. Nah," he laughed out loud, "I was not into marrying a girl, or being a politician. I guess I've become a politician of sorts; trying to get the red tape bulldozed for those that really need it. I meet with them, and get funding, etcetera. . . . It is funny how fate works out, huh?" I nodded in agreement, and we started the movie. We sat on one bed opposite the closed window, and the cabin became our own mini-theater.

The movie was, and still is, my all-time favorite. It is about hope and rebellion, of youth and love. The main character risks it all for the chance to go exploring beyond known space, and he finds love along the way. It seemed an oddly appropriate way to start our journey, as our hands bumped on occasion and our eyes met at our favorite parts of the movie. "It seemed different this time," he said, and my only response was to move in and kiss him. It was sweet and gentle, not anything at all like my earlier pervy thought of making him a notch in my belt.

We pulled away gently and looked at each other. "Well, um, have you ever flown?" "No. I farm." We laughed and he got up, grabbing my hand as well. "Come on, you need to know basic survival skills." "I'm sure driving your little sports car wouldn't fall under that umbrella." "Maybe not, but the basics are the same." I sat in the pilot chair, and he beside me in the copilot chair. I did feel oddly powerful, this fast sporty coupe's capabilities in fingers' reach. Space was a slow-moving, large, and bulky event most of the time. Now I felt like I was from my movie, that I had an infinite stretch of adventure in front of me. His hand cupped mine as he showed me the tracking, speeds, and environmental controls. "I'm glad we met," he whispered as his hand guided mine on top of the information monitors. I was happy and annoyed all at once. I was glad too, but where could this really lead to? "Me too," I finally responded, and rested my head on his shoulder.

The next two days were all work and no play. We mapped out what we needed to do upon arrival to the station, which was a lot. Power grids, water flow, and oxygen supply all had to be modified. I worked on a training manual for the potential farmers on the station and previewed applicants' requests and experience. Josh crunched numbers for the supplies that we had to order now so they would be there a day or two after us. "As requested, this is your notification that you are thirty-six hours from your destination and on time with your flight plan," the computer announced through the speakers. "Let's eat," Josh said, rubbing his eyes. He was so cute, his sexiness shining even through his tiredness. Dinner was wraps, and they were good. I was ready for a full meal, but couldn't complain I was hungry at all. We had a fun casual dinner, and I requested we watch another movie.

We cuddled up on a bed and started watching a light romantic comedy. Our snuggled bliss didn't last long at all, though. The lights came up, and the movie paused. "Incoming emergency bulletin: pilot requested at helm," the computer voice announced. "Proceed with emergency message," Josh said loudly as he popped up. "Mr. Perez, Samantha here at Central Station. The eel anomaly has flared up suddenly without notice. Increase speed to maximum, staying on your current path, for the next ten minutes. At that time shut down all systems except vital life support. You should have ten minutes at most until the storm makes contact with your hull." "Roger that, thanks." He ended transmission and disengaged autopilot. "Get buckled in, now!" I threw myself in the copilot seat, and we were off. "Computer, maintain current course. Do not give me verbal warnings about velocity or engine status." The computer made a beeping noise in acknowledgment. I had never moved so fast in my life; it was intense. "What's next?" I asked. He was looking at the readings on his monitor. "We rush as close to our destination as we can, then do a total power shutdown. All we will have is life support. Then we will just have to wait out the storm."

"It's been ten minutes," I said as we flew through the stars. He glanced down at the monitor that was full of various data and warning alerts flashing. "Computer, open window shutters to full open position and execute emergency security lock." The computer beeped in response, and the shutters rose behind us. "Decreasing speed; watch the engine temp right there," he said, pointing to the upper right of his screen. We bucked back and forth as the little ship decreased speed dramatically. "Computer, release internal heat burst, then commence emergency total shutdown program 'eel contingency' on my mark. Mark." The cabin got very warm, and things started powering down all around us. "The engine temp is rising," I warned, still watching the box he had told me to. He hit a couple of buttons, and the computer responded, "Shutting down engine; total engine shutdown will occur in one minute. Total power shutdown awaiting engine shutdown completion."

"Look to your right," he said, wiping sweat off his brow. "Wow, it looks kind of pretty." It was like electronically charged cotton candy, and it was closing in fast. "What is that noise?" I asked, worried as a hissing sound came from behind us. "The engine is expunging energy; when this is over, we will be going in like a retired vacation couple," he said, laughing. "Total shutdown commencing now," the computer announced, and then a slight hum led to total silence. No light at all except what the stars and the eel provided. "Hold on!" he said as the blue haze surrounded us, and I reached for his hand. Zapping noises surrounded us, and our view of the stars was replaced with a fuzzy blue fog with flashing bolts of raw energy.

"So I guess we'll have to watch that movie on the way back. Have you even been in zero gravity before?" he asked, looking at me. "Artificial gravity is not part of basic life support?" He looked at me like I should know better, which I did. "No, it'll be okay, I'll guide you." He reached over, undid my safety buckle, and ever so gently lifted himself out of his chair. "Come on! Use me or the roof as a guide to the beds." I sat up and went crashing into the window in front of his pilot seat. "Easy, you okay?" he said, reaching for me. "Oh yeah, just my pride is injured." I turned around, slowly, to see him floating and gracefully turning about in the air. "Very gently, ever so gently push off toward me." I did so, barely, but it was enough—I was gliding through the small cabin reaching for his outreached hand.

To my surprise he brought me into him and kissed me gently; we floated, entangled, and I welcomed his advance. "I've wanted this since we first talked on your farm," he said between kisses. Our kisses became more passionate, and we flew against the window above his bed. The blue haze was all I could see, and it made a romantic glow that dimly lit the cabin. He pulled at my shirt, and we floated upward to bump the roof. I looked over at my floating shirt as he threw it to the center of the room. "This could get cumbersome," I said as I bit his lower lip. "We can cuddle up under the covers; they are attached to the base of the bed," he responded as his hands explored my torso.

We did just that; we cuddled up in the comfort and constriction of the covers. It was our own little cocoon, and we made love. It was passionate, gentle, and rough; sweet and naughty. It was as if the electric outside and the attraction we had tried to not let get in the way of work were finally out and free. No work could be done right now, and no one could contact us. It was our private blue sanctuary. We lay in our afterglow, talking about how crazy and right this felt. We fell asleep holding each other. When we awoke later, still surrounded by our blue eel storm, we made love again.

Finally the blueness faded and the beauty of normal stars

took its place. Josh slid from under our covers, and I watched his perfect body float around nude. "Well, come on, we have to power up." I smiled at him and his cute nudity. "Don't you want to get dressed first?" "Nah, it's easier to get naked than dressed in zero gravity," he said, winking. We floated up to the controls up front, and to my relief, there were still no ships around us. He opened a side panel with an old actual touch button. He reached in and held it down for several seconds. Hums began and systems powered backed up.

We restored power, got dressed, and headed to the station. They had us share one room, which of course we didn't mind. The next few days of work were some of the hardest of my life, but two years later the station is thriving. Josh and I were not lucky enough to encounter another eel storm on the way home, but we always hope for one when we vacation together. We talk all the time, and between his causes and diplomatic meetings he stays with me on Central Station. I met his parents—I'm not the wife they hoped for, but they like me just the same. Josh surprised me the other day when he asked me what I thought about him making Central his permanent residence.

"Well, I have this problem you see," he continued. "Yeah, what's that?" I asked as we started setting up for dinner. "I met this wonderful guy two years ago, and every time I'm away from him, I don't seem to get as much work done because I'm always wishing he was around." "Is that so?" I asked. "Central Station is the major communications grid; I'm sure the mayor could find me a small office up there somewhere. A diplomat on board would get her even more press." I laughed and nodded in agreement. "Well, I have this guy that comes around sometimes, between causes and flights and what-not, but I'll just have to tell him I've been scooped up." He rolled his eyes and reached for my hand. "Sounds like a plan."

HOME

DEAN REYNOLDS

ON DECK, I am conscious of the sound of my own voice as I speak. What I hear is alien and disembodied, an unconvincing drone of tension. I can only hope that the two port officials who greeted my arrival and guided me into the marina hear things differently as I answer their routine questions. I give my personal details and describe my journey. I am Ray McGrath, a New Zealand national, date of birth 07–09–1965; I am just back from a six-week round trip to Teoavu; my voyage was for pleasure, a holiday combined with my brother David's wedding; my yacht is registered here in Gisborne. As I finish, the gulls that glide above our heads monitoring every event below break into a loud verse of calls and repetitive cackles. One of the officials, a large, breathless man of about fifty, disappears below to satisfy himself; all is as it should be. I tick "nothing to declare" on the imports form and hand the clipboard back to his young colleague who asks me to confirm my address. He is well over six feet and looks down at me imperiously as I speed it off and wait for his next question. When none comes, I risk offering a few innocuous facts. My parents are in their seventies and live in town; I have three sisters and a brother, who is the youngest among us; I run a cycle shop up in north Gisborne, swim each morning, and walk to work. I only stop waffling because I can find no encouragement in the almost blank expression confronting me. The guy eyes me up and down for a moment, fans my passport before his face, and puffs a gobful of air from the side of his mouth, a performance I imagine is one of any number rehearsed daily before the bathroom mirror. Then, as I wipe a few tiny bubbles of spit from my shirtsleeve, he lets me have it. "Mr. McGrath, you can drop the attitude. I recognize you and your boat, and I don't need your life story." I haven't noticed this bloke around the harbor before but resist the temptation to say so. During the following uncomfortable seconds he just stands there and stares, then squints as the sun re-emerges from behind a lone cloud. For a second the front he's been posing drops. Perhaps he is younger than I first thought. His simple uniform of white short-sleeved shirt, navy tie, and trousers is without a blemish, nor is a crease out of place. Apart from a couple of days' stubble on his chin, he looks fresh out of the box. Happy for him to go on thinking me irritated by proper procedure, I keep my mouth shut but manage a smile as the older fella suddenly emerges from below and wishes me good day. My passport and registration documents are then returned, and the two men step off the yacht onto the jetty. I can hardly believe it's all over as they walk briskly in the direction of the port offices. I also disembark, turn my back on their receding footfalls, and face the ocean. Its horizon is lost in fusion with the dark intent of a distant storm. I stand there motionless for a few minutes, listening to the gulls and watching the waves beyond the breakwater rise and topple into one another, making an effort to summon some of the calm friends tell me I possess in bucketloads. But the unease I feel does not subside. The law of the land has been broken and a few of my own principles with it. A nugget of guilt insists that some future penalty awaits me, but as there can be no certainty of its nature or forewarning of the day on which it must be paid, my rational self-reliance quickly chisels it away and I focus on the here and now. Right now the fears I have disregarded in order to get what I want must be faced. Foreboding simmers just beneath the skin of my face and forearms and churns my stomach, a combination of sensations I have not experienced for many years, but which I recognize as the prelude to something unpleasant. Even if I took a fast RIB back out there, daylight would be fading by the time I reached the spot where he slipped quietly over the side. By then the storm, which appears to be approaching the mainland, would make a one-man search downright stupid. I must keep to the plan.

✦

UNTIL DÎDE, I had not bothered to question why so much of my life revolved around those of my family. Their kids, their jobs, their values and rules. I have the bike shop and the yacht and a few mates I share a beer with now and then. But family demands have always taken precedence, and everyone has been happy for it to stay that way, including me. It was instilled in me from the earliest age that the rules of church and family came first and must be respected, that they have great value, that they guide and protect as you negotiate a way through life. After a few transgressions in my teens I left the church and the family home for good. Even so, I have lived pretty much my entire adult life safe behind the comforting picket fence of anonymous suburban respectability. I consider what my family and friends will say when I see them for the first time in almost two months. Everyone will want to know why I missed David's wedding. I wouldn't be surprised if David never speaks to me again. No excuse will be good enough, and the truth? Who knows what the truth will mean to them. I try to think of someone who will still talk to me if the truth gets out. Cath comes to mind. We were both twenty, had jobs, and were living together when I told my devout parents Cath was pregnant. They took me aside and suggested that we ought to marry, and failing that, I should persuade her to have an abortion. I was not at all surprised that the first thing that came into their heads was marriage, but was completely thrown by the suggestion of an abortion. In anger I unwisely shared the gist of the conversation with Cath, whose parents belonged to the same church as my own. Her old man began pressuring her to ditch me and have the baby adopted when it was born, but she had plans of her own. It was just a matter of time before the shit really hit the fan. Our families entered into a feud that began on the polite pews and had consequences that have never been fully resolved. Neither of us spoke to our parents for a while. In the end, we split not long after Mike was born. Cath married a Maori fella she met at work a year later. They are still together, and I have a son on the other side of town who I have watched grow up in the peculiar freeze-frame of irregular monthly visits. He's just about to start uni. And I am about to turn forty. What he would make of all this doesn't bear thinking about. My sisters and brother would be shocked. Bloody horrified, more like. My elderly parents, destroyed. I cannot, nor would I, change anything now. Whichever way I look at things, it is clear to me that the tenuous contentment defining my life till just a few weeks ago burned off like a struck match sometime during the voyage home to New Zealand. And once that contentment was consumed, nothing but Dîde and the boat were left. Something like a hangover followed; a dilute bitterness toward my family surfaced and hung around for about a week, fed entirely by regret at my acquiescence to a life that was never really my own. Maybe I even wallowed a little and sprinkled salt onto old cuts and waking pleasures. My mood swings during the first week's sailing didn't go unnoticed. Then I woke one morning after a couple of hours' rest and listened to the lines tapping against the aluminum mast in the wind. Dîde was sharing my bunk, lying on his side, his head on my chest. I had to move, get up on deck, but I couldn't do so without disturbing him and my own contentment, the first true contentment I think have ever felt. I had just begun living my life, for the sake of life.

✦

STANDING HERE WITH these thoughts and memories, I feel exposed and vulnerable before the uncertain days ahead. As late-afternoon clouds obscure the sun, for the umpteenth time in a fortnight I ask myself what it is, exactly, that I have risked for my own happiness. And whose risk is the greater, Dîde's or mine? A small boat with an outboard chugs into the crowded Gisborne marina and brings me swiftly into focus with unfolding events, events that are now beyond my own or anyone's ability to influence. I have to get a grip. My belly murmurs, and my senses blur as a pelican waddles up to see if I have anything tasty to share. The only thing on offer is the contents of my stomach, which I hurl into the clear water lapping the stern of my boat. I steady myself against a rail and wretch painfully, as if my own knotted fists were wringing out my guts. The bird is unimpressed and plods off down the jetty toward a group of fishermen loading a pickup. They saw me puke and seem to be having a joke at my expense. "You all right, mate?" one of them shouts. I wave an assurance that I'm fine, which gets a laugh, check my watch, and then prepare to move the boat to its usual berth. In an hour from now, in the fading light of a late summer's day, I will be on the beach at Twin Rocks, watching the waves and waiting.

✦

MOST DON'T KNOW it, but the sea offers good company to the lone sailor. Two weeks out of Gisborne, the first living things to notice my passing were a pod of porpoises. I counted six. They tagged my boat for several hours. At one point they came very close, just a few feet ahead of me, and I lay over the edge of the bow to watch them swim, mesmerized by the perfection of their movement through the water. They in turn seemed interested in me as I hung off the rail with a camera. The following day I woke an hour before dawn to the sound of pinging instruments. Up on deck a tiny cluster of distant lights caught my eye, and by morning, with the sun already hot on my back, I was tying off among the fishing and charter craft of a small port whose cluster of low buildings crept up from the shoreline and dispersed into densely forested hills. A modern marina stretched the length of the busy seafront. The air tasted ripe, strong with the smells of briny evaporation, marine fuel, and raw and cooking fish. All around people bought or sold the morning's catch, carried out maintenance, or stood in groups exchanging news and views. Nearby some Ozzies bartered loudly for the day hire of a powerboat, and at the far end of town a rusty launch was unloading a few crates from a ship that lay off-shore. A brief conversation with a guy selling bait revealed the island to be Pirturoa and the town its capital, Port Eliza-beth. This meant I was about twelve miles west of Teoavu, the principal island of its group and the place where my brother's beach wedding was to take place in just over a week. Family and guests wouldn't be flying in from New Zealand until the day before the ceremony. As best man, I had planned to reach Teoavu well ahead of everyone else to check out the accommodation and make a few final arrange-ments. After all that was taken care of, I would have an opportunity to chill out before the big party started. A little ahead of schedule, I grabbed a rucksack and headed into town. I spent an hour or two exploring Port Elizabeth's steep main street; bought some fruit, tea, and a few cans of beans; had coffee in one of the small bars with a view over rooftops to the bay below; then decided to head back down to the boat. If I shoved off sometime soon, I could make Teoavu by late afternoon.

✦

BACK AT THE road along the seafront, I could see that a small open ferry had just arrived. It was low in the water and listed slightly as passengers disembarked. Two women strug-gled to get off with a heavy wooden chair, and a boy jumped impatiently from the side carrying a black pig. When the boy reached the road I stopped him to ask about conditions beyond the bay. All was fine, just calm waters with nothing more than a light breeze. The crossing to Teoavu would be short and uneventful. As the boy strode purposefully into town with the pig asleep in his arms, I caught a glimpse of my boat across the marina and saw what appeared to be someone's head disappearing below. I remembered closing the cabin door, but couldn't be sure I had locked it. I ran along the road, brushing people out of the way, almost getting knocked down by a kid on a moped. Some guys rolling their nets on a boat moored opposite mine watched my approach with interest as I flew down the wooden jetty and leaped on deck. The main hatch was unlocked, the hasp hanging free, its disc-lock still on the aft deck bench where I had left it. The guys stopped what they were doing and shouted a question that I only half heard. I turned to face the men and shouted a question of my own. "Did you see anyone messing around on my boat?" They nodded and pointed at the hatch. Someone was inside. I stood in the cockpit and listened, my pulse banging in my head. A moment later two of the guys were on the aft deck offering assistance, their oil-stained shorts and eager expressions looked more like trouble than help. Both grinned brilliantly, and one stripped off his vest to reveal a toned body detailed with finely drawn blue tattoos. "Ozzie?" he asked. I frowned. "Kiwi." It sounded blunt and unfriendly, but I wanted them to think I was unfazed and in control, though in truth I felt anything but. Then I did something really stupid. "Wait here. If he comes up, grab him." Sliding back the hatch and pushing open the companionway door, I descended to the galley, grabbing the short length of hard rubber pipe I sometimes used as a jam on the way down. Once below I listened again, but there wasn't a sound. The galley appeared undisturbed, with the things I had used to make breakfast still beside the sink, washed, dry, and waiting to be put away. I crept into the saloon and again found everything exactly as I had left it. On the dining table was a single tin mug half full with cold tea and the partly disman-tled spare shower pump I had been cleaning with an old toothbrush. The book I had been reading lay on one of the sofas, open facedown to save my place. Then on the coffee table I noticed the wad of notes I had emptied from my wal-let for peace of mind before heading into town. Any intruder would have quickly spotted the money, so whoever it was had been disturbed before they had a chance to have a good look around. Above I could hear voices, low, almost whispering, then silence once more. The presence of the two lads on deck only reminded me how vulnerable I was. If I ended up with a knife in my belly, they were the only ones who would be able to help. The thought crossed my mind that the intruder had been a lure to get me below. The yacht was a valuable boat. I had heard a few stories over the years. I found myself regretting an early decision not to keep a revolver on board. Whatever was going to happen next, I had to be ready for it. My senses high on adrenaline, the length of rubber pipe became slick in my damp fist. I barely gave a thought to what I would do with it if things got nasty. Taking a few deep breaths, I began searching the boat start-ing aft with the master berth. After counting down slowly from three in my head, I crashed through the door and straight into a chair piled with the previous day's clothes. The sound of splintering wood as the chair collapsed under me was met with calls from up on deck. I had hit my head on something and scraped both knees, but felt no pain. I got up and quickly checked the wardrobes and shower, then heard someone coming down into the boat. I was back in the galley in a split second. The tattooed guy was halfway down the steps but stopped dead when he saw the pipe in my hand.

"You're bleeding, mate," he said, pointing at my head. Warm viscous liquid tickled my right eyebrow and ran down my cheek. "I said stay on deck." The guy gave me a hesitant look but did as he was told without saying another word, making me question what I must look like with a weapon in my hand and blood on my face. Emboldened slightly, I stalked through the saloon to the forward berths. All three doors were closed. I waited, searching the silence, my senses alert to movement or noise. At first all that could be heard were sounds from beyond the boat: the sea and birds, engines and voices on the marina, and the background hum of the town. Then from within the center berth came a noise like the sound of someone brushing against a panel wall. I raised the pipe to shoulder height and began an internal countdown from three. Before I got to two, the door was yanked open and the guy was out of the room. The struggle that followed did not last long. He moved so fast I couldn't tell if he was tooled up as he flung himself onto me without a sound. The force of his attack pushed me back into the open space of the saloon, his arms locked tight around my head and neck, his legs around my waist. In shock I grabbed him under the arms to pry him off, dropping the pipe. He just squeezed harder, crushing my nose against his chest, making my eyes water. The boat came alive with the sounds of my heavy foot-falls and our short breaths, which hissed with effort and fury. The strong smell of his underarm sweat stiffened the air I sucked through my teeth as I punched him hard in the ribs. He grunted in pain but managed to lift himself higher above my head, shifting all his weight forward. I grabbed the back of his shirt collar and pulled down hard, but it was already too late. I staggered as he lurched forward, once, twice, in an effort to unbalance me. Then the shirt tore in my hands and

I felt myself falling backward. Expecting a heavy impact from the unforgiving floor, I was surprised instead to feel my shoulders and lower back sink deep into one of the sofas. My feet lost contact with the floor as his body sank into mine, winding me. He now struggled to disentangle himself, but before he could free his arms and plant one on me, I gripped him tightly under the arms once more, charged my muscles, and heaved him away from my body, twisting sideways off the sofa. In a single movement I slammed him down into the floor. The resistance I had expected hadn't come, and he hit the wooden tiling hard, his head loudly drumming a single hollow beat into the bowels of the boat. And I was on him, pinning him down by the shoulders, but he no longer fought me. It had been so easy, his body so light, limp even. Panting to catch my breath, I stared down in amazement, expecting to see the face of some teenage thief staring back. What I saw was something else. When the sobbing began, it seemed to come from somewhere way down inside his guts. "Please. Please don't hurt me. Please don't." It was a man, younger than myself but not by much, his features soggy with tears and bloodied snot. He lay shaking beneath me, gripping my forearms in his hands, fingers rigid, digging in as if he expected me to pull free at any moment and bludgeon him with punches. I just stared, unsure of what to do next.

✦

LAUGHTER INTERRUPTED FROM the hatch, then a voice slow and thick with the veiled humor of thugs. "Mate, don't kill him. Let us have him. We will take him off your hands." More laughter. I made no attempt at a reply, didn't even look up. I just stared down at the guy underneath me, his wet eyes screwed shut, his lips thin shrivels of misery, exposing clenched white teeth. "We can take him to the cops. Or for twenty dollars we can teach him a lesson." "It's okay, lads. I don't need any help. I can deal with it." The voice at the hatch persisted. "Come on, mate. Twenty dollars. He won't trouble you again." It was obvious that if I let them take him they would give him a bloody good kicking before any cop got involved. I was in no mood for jokes and bargains; I wanted them gone. I turned angrily to the matching grins in the hatch. "I said I don't need any help, now get off my fucking boat before I come up there and throw you off." After a couple of standard fuck yous, a vacant silence threatened trouble, then the tattooed guy called me a dumb prick, adding that the police were already on their way; he had called them from his mobile soon after I went below. The two leering faces then retreated from sight and could be heard jumping to the jetty. Now it was just me and the thief, and I still wasn't sure what I was going to do next. Not that there was much to think about. The options were limited after all. Either hand him over to the cops when they showed up or let him go before they got here. I gave my captive a quick once-over. He appeared similar in height and build to myself. His hair was thick and shaggy, dark brown, almost black, and his eyes a striking greenish blue. It was difficult to tell if he was European or Asian. The only thing for sure was that he was filthy, as if he had been sleeping rough. His threadbare shirt, torn during our brief struggle, allowed a partial view of one shoulder, which was patched with dark ripe shapes that could have been dirt. Something made me look closer. With his fingers still embedded in my arms, I pulled his shirt open just enough to see that his upper body was mapped in bruises. The sight was unexpected, shocking even. The injuries were old, the result of a serious beating. There was no way I could have inflicted them, but even so, the sight filled me with remorse for the heavy punches I had just landed on his sides. He flinched as I raised a hand to my brow to massage my temples, something I do instinctively when stressed. He hadn't taken my money, had no way of concealing anything bigger than a spoon in the pockets of his gray joggers, and as I didn't want to sit on him all day and watch the poor bastard cry, I decided to let him go. "I'm going to let you up. Don't fight me, okay? I'm not gonna hurt you." After I released my hold and got to my feet, he just lay there, shuddering, so I held out my hand. He took it gingerly in his, and I pulled him to his feet. Now we stood and studied each other eye to eye. "If you have anything that belongs to me, I want you to hand it over now." He pointed to a polythene carrier bag on the sofa that had gone unnoticed by me till then, even though we had just fallen on it. "There are my things." He spoke English with hardly any accent. "I have not stolen from you. I am not a thief." Anger swelled up within me. I shouted, my face barely an inch from his, and he twitched as if being prodded with needles. "If you haven't taken anything, what are you doing on my fucking boat?" He trembled from head to toe and clutched his privates like a boy kicked in the balls. I felt like a bully, dissatisfied and disturbed by the power I had over another man. It was obvious the guy posed no threat. He was scared shitless, frozen to the spot. More than this, he looked crushed. Not by me, but by life. I grabbed a roll of paper towel from the galley and handed him a length of sheets. "Stop crying and wipe your face, you have a nosebleed." He screwed the sheets into a ball and pressed it into his eyes. A few drops of blood had dripped from the end of his nose and made splat marks at our feet. As a crimson rose bloomed in the paper towel, another drop threatened to fall. I tore off another handful of sheets and held them to his nose, applying a little pressure. He winced, I think more in fear than pain. We stood in the middle of the saloon for a minute or so, the principal characters in a surreal silence. Then, with his voice dulled by the slight pressure I still applied to his nose, he told me apologetically that I too had a nosebleed. Looking down, I saw that the front of my shirt was stained with blood. "Hold this." He took charge of his bleeding nose and I went to the sink to wash my face, taking care with the stinging cut above my eyebrow. As the reddish water swirling down the plughole cleared, it dawned on me that the guy had probably been looking for a place to stow away when I disturbed him. I dried myself, took off my bloodied shirt, and pulled on a cotton cagoule. Still holding the paper towel to his nose, he watched my every move around the boat over the back of his hand. I picked up his bag of stuff and sat down. "My name is Ray, what's yours?" Surprised and cautious, he hesitated for a few seconds. "My name is Dîde." Then he quietly watched as I emptied the contents of his bag onto the coffee table and held up a pair of white football shorts, a faded blue T-shirt, and a slim wallet containing photos, notes, and coins. The only other item was a passport with the words *Islamic Republic of Pakistan* embossed in gold on the front. "So where are you headed? There's no way you could have stayed hidden on this boat for more than a day, and the only place within a couple of hours' sailing from here is Teoavu. From there it's just the Pacific Ocean for two weeks solid in every direction." He studied the paper towel. The bleeding had stopped, so he allowed his arm drop to his side. "I am going home." The evasive simplicity of his statement was unnecessary, as I didn't care much where he was going. I opened the passport and found a name, Dipak Khan, and a photo, the colors a little bleached. In it a man wearing a jacket and tie, with his hair combed into a neat center parting, smiled up at me from a different life, place, and time. The name didn't tie up, but the face in the photo was definitely that of the man before me. "You said your name was Dîde." He let his eyes drift to the hatch, unsure what answer to give, or perhaps considering making a run for it. I wouldn't have stopped him. "It doesn't matter. It makes no difference to me what your name is." The interrogation over, I got up and began putting his things back in the bag. It felt the right moment to get him off the boat and cast off, but the strangeness of the situation and the alienation I felt from the normality of just ten minutes ago, when I had inquired about the weather in the street overlooking the marina, was stark and powerful. At its center was Dîde, or Dipak, or whatever his name was; the intruder, the unfamiliar presence. It permeated the air and clung to passing seconds, begging time that I found myself wanting to give and in other circumstances might be easy to give. I handed him his belongings, an unspoken dismissal. As I did so, my eyes met with the empty depths of his, dangerously stirring my pity and curiosity into something messy and open ended. After a few intense moments spent eyeballing each other, I turned my back on him and filled the electric kettle, took a mug from the rack, and spooned tea into the pot, all the while listening for the half-expected creak of the steps and the thud as he jumped to the jetty. The only thing to be heard was the gentle pop and rumble of the kettle getting hot. As the water reached boiling point, I took a second mug and placed it beside the first.

✦

THAT WAS HOW all this began. That was how I met Dîde. When the family made contact from Teoavu the day before the wedding, I was almost halfway back to New Zealand with Dîde. I made up a story about a storm-damaged mast, said I was okay but had been forced to turn for home. Dad knew my boat's position on the night before I made Port Elizabeth, so was immediately suspicious. To avoid questions that would be impossible to answer without lying, I asked to speak to David and made a brief apology I knew to be worthless, the conversation punctuated with short silences due to a time delay. I wanted to know if he was ready for the big day, but was met with one long silence. Either the signal was lost, or he ended the call.

✦

AS I DRIVE south along the deserted road from Gisborne to the cove at Twin Rocks, a local radio station gives out a storm warning. The claustrophobic tension I felt an hour ago, during my brief interview with the customs officers, returns with the taste of my own puke. I change the radio station. An old Crowded House hit opens up like a lullaby, and I can't stop thinking about the plan. It was a joint effort, but I feel responsible for the bulk of it. I brought the boat to a position a mile or so offshore from Twin Rocks. The high green peaks that stand just inland and give the place its name can be seen clearly up to five miles from shore and mark the position of the cove's long curving beach, the only safe landing on this quiet stretch of coastline. With luck Dîde could make the swim in daylight unnoticed by the Coast Guard or anyone else, but would have to swim hard against the currents and keep aiming between the peaks. We allowed two hours for the swim and timed his landing to coincide with dusk. He claimed he could easily make the distance before darkness fell. We argued about that, the sea being nothing like the rivers he learned to swim in as a boy, but in the end it was agreed. Though dangerous, it seemed the best way to get him into the country; the question of getting permission for him to stay, if that is even possible, has yet to be faced. The craziness of it all only hit me as he pushed away from the yacht wearing my wet suit, mask, and fins, using an anchor buoy as a float. If I hadn't fully understood what he meant when he told me he was going home that day in Port Elizabeth, now I do. Completely. He looked small and was soon lost from sight among dark waves. To him this leg of his journey to safety and a place where he could find home was worth every bit of the risk. An Iraqi Kurd, Dîde had been witness to his lover's murder in a packed café by a militia death squad hunting gays in the name of Allah. They came in, asked for their victim by name, and shot him where he sat across the table from Dîde. Weeks later, Dîde had crossed the border from Iraq into Pakistan. He managed to get to Karachi, where he bought a forged passport and stowed away on a container ship. He was discovered and taken off in Manila, but using the last of the American dollars he carried, was able to bribe his way onto a second ship bound for Fiji and Brisbane. While aboard this ship, more money was demanded. He could offer nothing more in payment but worthless Iraqi currency, and so they beat him to within an inch of his life and put him ashore at the first opportunity. Some in his situation are simply thrown over the side, so he considers himself blessed to have ended up stranded on Pirturoa.

✦

AT THE BEACH it is almost dark and I wait, watching the waves for any sign of him. Throughout the day I have tried to prevent the real being blemished by the unreal and the unimportant taking precedence over what really matters. It is a chaotic attraction that has brought Dîde and me together. No simple fact like I must be with him and he with me; more a complex equation that none but the two of us can know and understand. Or so it seems. It is almost dark now. A few drops of rain make impact with the warm, dry sand where I sit waiting and thinking. Maybe he has been picked up by the Coast Guard or a fishing boat, or succumbed to fatigue. If he tired, the currents would take him up the coast and away from the mainland. I am out of my mind with fear for his safety. As the rain begins to pelt the beach with drops that would fill an eggcup, I see the shape of a man rise up from the waves a few yards from where they break onto the flat expanse of sand before me. I jump to my feet and start running full pelt into the sea. In a few seconds I am pushing through waist-high water against waves that slap against my chest and face. Then Dîde throws himself onto me, knocking me from my feet. A cold, watery darkness and a sound like a boiling kettle claims my senses, then we stand and cling to each other, as if crushing our bodies together will meld them into one.

On the beach, the rain really starts to hammer as I help Dîde from my wet suit and throw it down onto the sand, where it is immediately forgotten like torn giftwrap. My own clothes join it, and we are naked together in the torrential rain that frees an earthy perfume from the sand, rocks, and brown grasses covering the dunes. We make

love, unrestrained and instinctive, though not entirely
fearless, both aware that our lives from this moment will be
governed by the unpredictable. I come, then begin to cry.
For him. For us both. I haven't cried since I was a kid.
Somehow I manage a joke. "Welcome home, Dîde," I say
stupidly. He laughs and holds me as the rain pummels our
bodies. Then we make our way to the place where I left the
car. We dress in the dry clothes I have brought and I drive
along the long, sandy track and pull out onto the road with
all our hopes and our possible futures alive in my mind.
One way or another, we will be together and we will be fine.

FIREBALL

TOM MENDICINO

I WAS NINETEEN YEARS old and terrified of my own cock the summer I met Darrell Torok. It was 1973 and being a homosexual meant Paul Lynde giggling in the center square, Lance Loud flaunting his mascara, and Malcolm, my mother's beautician, complaining about Donald the florist's latest two-day bender. The summer before college, I'd driven into Pittsburgh on a humid Fourth of July, circling the Holiday Bar (*Where Every Day's a Holiday!*) six times before summoning the courage to park the car. The bartender didn't bother to ask for ID when I ordered a Rolling Rock. He told me to help myself to dogs and kraut, compliments of Antoinette's mother and aunt, who were hunkered at the end of the bar, their Benson and Hedges 100s threatening to ignite their shellacked bouffants. I was working on my second beer, when the mother—or maybe it was the aunt—dropped the cartridge of a portable record player and the floor show began. Antoinette, a skinny dark-eyed boy wearing a one-piece woman's swimsuit covered with sequins, hopped on the bar. I bolted halfway through his baton routine to "God Bless America," barely making it to the car before I threw up on my sneakers.

I swore I'd never become one of *them*, a freak, a pariah.

I spent my freshman year at West Virginia desperately trying to make myself into the man I feared I could never be, getting drunk and stoned enough to work up the courage to fall into bed with any girl willing to offer up the furry hamster snuggling in her panties. My old man decided drastic action was in order when I stumbled home in early May with a transcript distinguished by a B– in Introduction to Astronomy and a grade point average below the threshold of academic probation. Three months of backbreaking servitude and abject humiliation would bring me to my senses. I would spend the summer as a Laborer-Class 1 in Jones and Laughlin's Aliquippa mill, working the lowest assignment in the bargaining unit. Janitor in the shithouse. By mid-June I was determined to make a new beginning. West Virginia was already in the rearview mirror. Marquette, a Jesuit sanctuary with fewer opportunities for distraction and dissipation, was willing to provide a fresh start. I registered for chemistry and calculus classes. Eight more weeks until I began my new life as a dedicated scholar.

Eight very long weeks. An eternity. The shithouse was hell on earth, my worst nightmare, every day a fresh torture. But for the rank and file, it was a quiet oasis, a place to escape the blazing inferno. They strolled in with the *Post-Gazette* and their lunch pails and hunkered down in the stalls to relax with last night's box scores and a little snack. I stood sentry with my broom and dustpan, armed and ready to sweep up the wax paper and apple cores and Twinkie wrappers they tossed at their feet.

"Un-fucking-believable. Your old man's the president of the local! You must have really pissed him off to get assigned to shithouse duty," the fellow at the sink said after a particularly toxic explosion in the stall behind us.

He was scrubbing his hands and forearms with Boraxo, slowly and carefully massaging the gritty powder between his long, tapered fingers and into his wrists. He was tall and lean as a whippet, still fresh and pressed despite the blistering heat, his crisp work shirt tucked into his narrow waist. He dried his hands and, instead of throwing the paper towel on the floor, crumpled it into a tight, wet ball and made a clean hook shot into the trash barrel across the room. He turned and flashed a row of straight, white teeth, his blue eyes twinkling in the harsh fluorescent light. He had a friendly, open smile and a boyish face despite his salt-and-pepper hair.

"Hi, Bobby. I'm Darrell Torok."

I was amazed that someone as good-looking as any television star, a dead ringer for Dr. Kiley on *Marcus Welby,* would notice me, let alone knew my name.

"I'm Bobby," I mumbled, self-conscious of my gangly frame and creaking voice, unwilling to look him in the eye. "Bobby Mastroianni."

"Yeah, I already figured that out," he laughed, extending his hand. "Your old man is always bragging about how smart you are."

I was stunned. I hadn't done anything to earn my father's pride since I was named a National Merit Scholar back in high school. The only words he wasted on me these days were threats to kick my ass into the Ohio River if I didn't shape up.

The jerk with the violent colon spasms started calling for more toilet paper.

"Knock yourself out, buddy," Darrell laughed as he grabbed a roll and flipped it into the stall. "I'm working the day shift for the duration. See you around," he said as he turned to leave, surveying the shithouse from corner to corner and nodding his approval. "I don't think I've ever seen this place so clean. I'll be sure to tell your father what a good job you're doing."

I felt the blood rushing to my face and my chest swelling with pride. From that day forward, I kept my domain spic-and-span, anticipating Darrell's arrival, regular as clockwork, precisely at eight in the morning and two in the afternoon. *Good morning, see you tomorrow* and the occasional *good job* kept my unrequited crush on life support. Industrial disinfectant was an aphrodisiac. I spit-polished the sinks and swabbed the bowls until they sparkled. Richard Nixon himself could have dropped in unannounced to take a leak.

"How's it going there, guy?" he asked as he sauntered through the door one Friday afternoon in mid-August.

"Not too bad."

"How many days until they unlock the prison door?"

"Two weeks," I said, mesmerized by the quick snap of his wrist as he ran a comb through his thick hair.

He winked at my reflection in the mirror before I could look away, blushing.

"We're gonna miss you around here come fall. This place won't ever be this clean again."

I'd get a farewell handshake, maybe a friendly slap on the back on my last day of work as he sent me off with a *best of luck, kiddo,* then he'd forget I existed. He'd never know that seeing him twice a day had sustained me through that miserable summer. But that Saturday morning, the old man hauled my sorry carcass out of bed after loading the station wagon for his annual summer vacation on Geneva-by-the-Lake.

"Darrell Torok's expecting these receipts today, and your mother and I are going to the hit the weekend traffic if we don't get on the road by seven."

Darrell was treasurer of the steelworkers' local, my father's money man, and the accounts needed to be closed at month's end.

"He's a good guy," the old man promised. "Don't worry. He won't bite you."

Good guy. That's what everyone said about Darrell Torok. One hell of a crane operator. The best in the mill. Responsible. He'd enlisted in the army right out of high school and did two tours of duty stationed in Okinawa before coming home to nurse his widowed father after he was diagnosed with colon cancer. He still lived in the house where he'd grown up, a big ramshackle heap on ten acres, out in farm country, with only his hunting dogs to keep him company. Women thought he was a sweet man, good-looking, too. But, still young at thirty-seven, no one tried fixing him up with their sisters or daughters. He was an odd duck, different, kept to himself, didn't even have a telephone. Set in his ways was the polite way to say it. It was understood he was eligible in name only. Darrell Torok was a confirmed bachelor, no questions asked, since the only reasonable explanation was the one no one dared to consider.

I drove up to the house, jittery as a cricket. The rolling front lawn was neatly manicured. A lush vegetable garden with perfect rows of towering tomato plants and sagging pole beans flourished behind the garage. A spotless Ford pickup sparkled in the sun. I wiped my already clean feet on the welcome mat and knocked on the screen door.

"It's open."

I stepped inside and was greeted by the soles of his bare feet. Darrell was on the floor, stripped to pair of blue trunks, weights strapped to his wrists and ankles, pumping out his daily push-ups.

"Just a second . . . eighty-seven, eighty-eight . . ."

Elton John was on the turntable, "Daniel," that creepy song about brothers that always made me change the station whenever it came on the radio.

"One hundred!' he yelped as he bounced to his feet. "Caught me red-handed. Damn, it's hard to stay in shape now that I'm getting to be an old man."

He grabbed a towel and dabbed the moisture under his armpits.

"What I'd give to be your age again," he laughed.

"I guess," I said, so focused on not staring at his hairless chest and well-defined abs that I was only half aware of what he was saying. The already prominent bulge in his trunks grew even more obvious when he lifted his arms to pull a T-shirt over his head.

"Have a seat, Bobby," he said. "Want something to drink?"

I sat on the sofa, fumbling with the paper bag of deposit slips and receipts I balanced on my knees.

"Your mother and dad get off okay?" he asked from the kitchen.

"Yeah, I was supposed to come over this morning, but I went back to bed," I apologized. "I hope I didn't mess up your day."

He handed me a Coke and smiled.

"Look like I'm real busy?"

"No. Yes. Maybe," I stammered, not wanting to insult him by implying he had nothing better to do on a Saturday afternoon but wait for me. "You like Elton John?" I asked, anxious to change the conversation.

"Sure. Don't you?"

He sat down across from me, resting his ankle on his right knee. He stripped off the weight and massaged his foot.

"I don't know. Not really. Isn't he a fag?"

Darrell peered between his toes as if he expected to find the answer to life's deep mysteries etched into his skin. After a long, awkward moment, he finally looked up and smiled.

"I don't know. Maybe he is," he said softly. "I like his music, though."

"I guess he's okay," I conceded, feeling like I'd just been exposed as a fraud.

"Well, thanks for bringing this stuff over. See you Monday," he said politely, clearly dismissing me.

"Hey, I read in *Rolling Stone* he's going to play the Pinball Wizard in *Tommy*," I sputtered, not wanting to leave on an awkward note, not really wanting to leave at all. "That's very cool."

His smile turned warm again.

"You play pinball?"

"Sure."

"You any good?"

"Fuck yes, I'm *very* good," I bragged, suddenly flush with confidence. "I can beat anyone's ass."

"We'll see about that," he laughed, nodding for me to follow him into what at one time had been a dining room, the table and chairs and sideboard now replaced with a magnificent new Bally Fireball. The flaming alien painted on the backglass, armed with a blazing sphere, dared me to accept the challenge.

"Okay, champ, prove it."

I paused to study the playfield, not wanting to look too cocky even though I played this game well enough to crush him. I yanked the plunger and launched the ball into play, quickly running up the score on eleven ramp shots in a row. I slapped the flippers, racking up points, the feeling of invincibility swelling as I pulled off a perfect death save.

"Impressive," he murmured over my shoulder, shattering my concentration long enough for the ball to slip past the flippers and roll down the drain.

He touched my shoulder as I stepped aside.

"Let me show you a few tricks," he said, sounding almost modest.

I stood behind him, staring at the rippling muscles of his ass as he nudged the cabinet with his hips. He was master of the playfield, in complete command of the machine, his quick reflexes controlling the movement of the ball. He skillfully juggled the flippers, smacking his targets, his score racing ahead of mine. Fireball had leaped off the backglass and possessed him!

"Not bad for an old man," he laughed after he finally tilted, the exhausted machine locking down for a well-deserved rest. "Damn, you're good," I conceded, my voice barely audible. "I'm really embarrassed."

"Come on, Bobby," he laughed. "Don't give up so easily."

We played until the sun dropped below the horizon, Darrell cheerfully humiliating me every time I stepped up to the cabinet.

"I ought to go," I finally said, totally dejected.

"Hungry?"

"A little bit." I was starved.

"I can throw a couple of steaks on the grill. Maybe some protein will help your game."

At first it felt strange, sitting at his kitchen table, not knowing what to say. Elton John was off limits.

"How's your steak?"

"Real good."

"You want to try a shot of this?" he asked, setting a bottle of golden liquid on the table.

"What is it?"

"Slivovitz," he laughed. "Made it myself. The plums are from the trees in the orchard out back."

Sweet as Mountain Dew but powerful enough to take out an ox, the first shot went down easily. He poured a second round, then a third. My knees buckled when I stood and I grabbed the edge of the table to steady myself.

"Don't tell your father I got you drunk," he laughed.

"Come on, man. I'm ready to beat your ass," I boasted.

He brought the bottle into the dining room and we played through the night, celebrating every round with a toast. Long after midnight, I unexpectedly executed a perfect bangback, despite—or maybe because of—my state of intoxication. On his next turn, he flubbed a drop stop, tilting the machine. Game over. Victory at last!

"Yes!" I whooped, losing my balance and stumbling to my knees.

"Well, Bobby, looks like we better call it a night. And don't even think about it," he said as I fumbled in my pocket for my car keys. "There's plenty of beds in this house."

I slobbered into his ear as he guided me up the stairs, telling him I thought he was really cool, calling him Fireball, all of my repressed fantasies about Darrell Torok unleashed by the slivovitz. The liquor sloshed in my stomach when I fell on the mattress. I threw my arm around his neck, pulling his face close to mine, insisting he let me be his friend, babbling, not wanting to let go, until I finally passed out, my head spinning, helpless as a pinball slipping down the drain. Strange dreams kept pushing me to the brink of consciousness. Music was playing in a distant room. "Daniel." Someone was watching me, a shadow squatting on his heels beside the bed, stripped to his skin, moaning as he furiously pounded his prick. I heard a voice whispering my name, asking me a question. I struggled to move my lips, trying to say yes, but plunged back into oblivion before I could answer.

✦

THE ROOM WAS bright as a beach on cloudless day. I squeezed my throbbing head, half expecting to find a cleaver wedged into my skull. I jumped off the mattress, relieved to find my belt still buckled and my zipper still closed. I was fully dressed except for the sneakers waiting for me, side by side, at the foot of the bed. The bedroom was tidy as a dollhouse, a boy's refuge with Pirates pennants on the wall and Clemente and Mazeroski bobbleheads on a shelf above the headboard. My booze-addled dream faded in the daylight, growing benign and harmless as it receded from the sun.

"The dead have arisen," he laughed as I shuffled into the kitchen.

"Morning," I mumbled sheepishly.

"Not anymore. It's almost one in the afternoon."

"Did you just get up?" I asked.

"I was up with the sun. Worked in the garden and been to eleven o'clock Mass. Now I'm going to make you breakfast."

"I ought to go."

"You ought to shower. I put out a fresh towel in the bathroom," he said, pointing me in the direction of the bathroom. I was slapping a splash of Old Spice on my cheeks when he knocked on the door.

"There's a clean pair of shorts on the bed if you don't want to put on your dirty clothes after your shower. Get a move on. Your breakfast is ready."

I was famished, my appetite fueled by the erotic charge of wearing only a loose pair of cutoffs and no underwear, my cock flopping in my pants every time I moved.

"Beautiful day out there," he said. "I ought to tackle that dead apple tree that fell in the storm last week. Struck by lightning. Split the trunk down to the roots."

"Want some help?" I asked through a mouthful of pancake and maple syrup.

"You know how to use a chain saw?"

"Not really."

"It's bad enough I got you drunk. Your old man would crucify me if you cut your arm off."

"I can clear away the branches," I insisted.

"Deal. Just promise not to kill yourself."

Stripped to the waist, we worked slowly in the heat and blazing sun. Darrell yanked off his work gloves and grabbed a bottle of Coppertone out of the toolbox.

"You're gonna fry out here if you don't put this on."

I rubbed the lotion on my face and chest and handed him back the bottle.

"Turn around, kiddo," he ordered. "You're getting burnt."

My shoulders stiffened, resisting his cool, wet palms as he smeared the slick cream across my back. I closed my eyes and slumped forward, swaying at the knees, finally capitulating as he slipped his hands under my armpits and touched my chest. My elbows flailed helplessly, a feeble protest, as he lightly tweaked my nipples. He reached down and squeezed the erection straining against my shorts.

"Relax," he said, unbuttoning my pants and pulling down the zipper, freeing my prick to snap to attention.

"That's beautiful," he said, dropping to his knees in front of me, staring at my cock like it was a rare and valuable work of art. "No, don't," he pleaded, as the first drops of precome dribbled from my slit. "Not yet. I want you to do it in my mouth."

The words pushed me over the edge. He grabbed my hips and pulled me toward him, forcing me to empty my load on his face. I slumped on my butt, too shocked to move as he wiped his chin with his hand and licked my come off his fingertips. He looked at me warily, anticipating the disclaimer about to be announced.

"I know you're not queer," he said, a gentle lie to absolve me of complicity, allowing me to pull up my pants and crawl back into my rabbit hole without having to acknowledge the invitation he'd felt in the tense muscles of my back. I looked at his face and couldn't deny what I was still afraid to admit.

"I don't want to be," I admitted, my voice cracking.

"The only choice you have is what you're going to do about it, Bobby. You okay about this?"

"I'm okay."

"Then let's finish up here," he said, picking up the chain saw and attacking the fallen tree. The pale skin on his back started to glow as fierce sun blotches spread across his shoulders.

"You're getting burnt, too. Want me to put some lotion on your back?" I asked, wanting to touch him like he'd touched me, to feel his slippery skin and let my hands explore his body.

He looked into the sun and squinted.

"I think I'll just put my shirt on," he said. "But thanks for offering." Maybe he was testing me, wanting to see my response, relief or disappointment, when he rejected my offer.

"Anyway, it's Miller time," he announced. "Run back to the house and grab a few beers while I finish stacking these logs."

He was sprawled on the grass when I got back, propped on his elbows, watching a summer cloudburst approach. Ominous warnings were rumbling in the atmosphere, and a strong wind whipped through the orchard, rustling the leaves of the fruit trees.

"It's really going to pour. You can smell it in the air. You get these every day in Hawaii," he said, pointing at the distant lightning on the horizon. "They roll in quickly and blow over almost as fast. You ought to go to Honolulu some day. You'd love it." He told me I reminded him of a buddy he'd met on leave in Oahu, Alan Kennedy, a navy seaman from a little town in Arkansas called Pumpkin Bend. They'd met in a dive bar, a real hole, the last stop after a long night of drinking. Alan had five bucks left in his wallet at closing time, and the cheapest flophouse in Honolulu cost ten dollars. Darrell told Alan he could crash at his motel if he didn't mind the floor. The room only had one bed.

"We were really loaded, but somehow we managed to stagger back to the motel. He was a skinny kid, like you, not a hair on his chest. He was swaying beside the bed, pants around his ankles, too shitfaced to untangle his feet. When I bent down to help him with his shoelaces, he grabbed my head and shoved his crotch in my face. He laughed when I pushed him away and said it was okay if I didn't want to go first. He'd suck me until I was hard, then I could stick it in his ass."

He woke the next morning with Alan snoring beside him on the narrow mattress. His first instinct was to shove his gear in his duffel and disappear. But he couldn't resist running a hand over his Alan's smooth ass and, next thing he knew, they were lying head to toe, their cocks in each other's mouths. They didn't leave the room for three days, ordering in beer and cigarettes and Chinese takeout. The night before Alan shipped out, they went to an off-limits bar where a fat Hawaiian drag queen lip-synched to Diana Ross and the Supremes and no one flinched when Alan kissed him on the mouth.

"He was a real character, that Alan," he laughed. "You would have liked him."

"Did you ever see him again?"

"No, but years later, right after my dad died, I got drunk one night and got his number from directory assistance. His wife answered the phone. He was real nice, didn't even seem surprised to hear from me. Told me to drop in if I was ever nearby."

He looked up and smiled when I laughed at the preposterous idea of Darrell cruising through Razorback country.

"I actually got in the car the next day and drove straight through to Pumpkin Bend. Lost my nerve when I got there. Didn't even stop for a cup of coffee."

Thunder cracked overhead, and a black curtain dropped on the sky. The deluge began without a warning drop. We bolted indoors, leaving wet footprints on the hardwood floor as we ran to the bathroom for towels.

"Let me hop in the shower first. I can start making dinner while you take yours," he said, modestly turning away as he peeled off his wet clothes and pulled the shower curtain behind him.

I heard him splashing in the water, only a thin sheet of vinyl separating us. I could slink away quietly, a coward, throwing away this last opportunity to see, touch, even taste, the thing I'd fantasized about all summer, the mystery left unsolved. I'd never know if it was long or short, thick or thin, how it would feel when I squeezed it between my fingers, if I would gag and choke if I put it in my mouth. I stepped out of my shorts, hesitating, finally summoning the courage to yank back the curtain. Darrell was bent slightly at the waist, stroking his crooked cock with his soapy palm. He grabbed my wrist and pulled me into the shower, wrapping his arms around my waist and grinding his hips against mine, his long, thin penis poking at my short, plump one. Squinting in the spray from the nozzle, he grabbed my face and forced his tongue into my mouth.

"You don't know how bad I want to fuck you," he hissed in my ear.

He wrapped me in a towel and led me to his bed, gently pushing me on my back and arching his lean, muscular body over me. He kissed my forehead, my cheeks, my mouth and chin, slowly making his way along my neck. He nuzzled my armpit with his sharp nose, nibbling my chest and belly, his mouth finally settling on the head of my cock. He grabbed my ankles and, hoisting my legs, dove to lick my balls, his tongue dipping into my asshole. I gasped when he slipped one wet finger inside me, then a second. My legs thrashed around his head as he slid his fingers in and out. Yes, I nodded, when he asked if I was ready for this. But the mind was more willing than my stubborn sphincter, which refused to yield to the stiff cock trying to crack it open.

Darrell smiled and rolled over on the bed, pulling me on top of him.

"Let's try this instead," he said, spitting in his palm.

He threw his legs over my shoulders and guided me into his tight ass.

"God, you feel good," he said, gasping a bit as I planted myself as deep as I could go.

He tossed back his head and, through gritted teeth, begged me to go deeper, faster, push harder. *Your cock is so hard inside me.* And when I couldn't hold back shooting my wad any longer, he grabbed my buttocks, forcing me to stay inside of him, refusing to let me pull out. *God, you don't know how long it's been.* After my flaccid prick finally slipped out of his wet ass, he guided my mouth to his cock. A gentleman to the end, he gave me fair warning, ignored, before blowing his load down my throat.

The storm gave no sign of subsiding as we lay on the bed, listening to the soaking rain beat down on the roof.

"So much for grilling steaks," he laughed.

"I'm not hungry anyway." He rolled back on top of me.

"You will be when I get done with you," he said, his smile shy and a bit sad. "I'm not letting you out of this bed until the alarm goes off in the morning. We've both been waiting too long for this."

◆

MY MOTHER ASSUMED I spent two weeks living on McDonald's and chocolate milk when she found the provisions she'd left in the refrigerator untouched and moldy. I'd spent every hour away from the shithouse with Darrell, falling asleep snuggled against him and waking up in his arms. The night before my parents returned, drunk again on slivovitz, I announced I'd changed my mind about Marquette. I'd keep my job at the mill, swabbing toilets and scrubbing floors; I didn't care as long as I could stay close to Darrell. It was a sweet thought, he said, rubbing a noogie on my scalp. He was going to miss me, too, but he wouldn't let me make the mistake he'd made, coming back here when he had the chance to get away.

"Now it's too late for me to do anything about it," he said. "But not for you. And I'll be here when you come home for the holidays."

I showed up at his house unannounced on Thanksgiving morning. The truck was nowhere to be seen; an unfamiliar Chrysler sedan was parked in the driveway. The tricycle on the front porch and the paper-plate turkeys displayed in the front window were signs of ominous changes. I turned and left without knocking on the door.

"What's the matter? You don't like your mother's cooking anymore?" the old man asked, pointing his fork at my barely touched plate.

"No. I mean, yes," I said, pouring my third glass of wine. "By the way," I asked, trying to sound casual and barely interested. "How's that guy Darrell Torok I met last summer?"

It was the damndest thing, the old man said.

"He walked into the mill one morning and gave his notice. Sold his house and truck and dogs and was gone by the time the leaves changed. Told me he'd be in touch. Sent a postcard from Hawaii a few weeks back. No address, no phone. Just said he'd settled in. He must have liked the job you did last summer because he said to tell you thanks," the old man laughed. "The guy was always a little strange."

THE BENCH

PETER CONTRERAS

ANTHONY AND JIM had met two years ago on a hot summer day just like this one; almost every detail was the same, sort of an anniversary ritual. The most that had changed was the boys themselves, a little older and a little wider around the middle. Anthony's once short and well-kept black hair had been let to grow wild in long, loose jet black curls that went past his ears. Mostly because he was afraid of his hereditary trait of early baldness; luckily, he had made it to the age of twenty-five with only little receding in the sides. Anthony had also given up his daily routine of healthy eating and exercising, causing him to go from his twenty-nine-inch" pants to a comfy thirty-four-inch" waist. Luckily, his charm and charisma were the most noticed of his qualities. Jim hadn't changed nearly as much as Anthony, only the usually changes with age and maturity. He was still the same six-foot hearty hunk of a man that Anthony had first fallen for two years ago. His stringy blond hair was a little darker than it used to be, but he still wore it in the same messy yet neat style.

When they met on the beach two years ago, they would never have thought they would be coming back every year to commemorate the relationship they had built thanks to that one day.

From their first date, they knew that they were soul mates, whether they got along all the time or not. They were quite in love, yes, but with *one* very strong emotion, there always seems to be *other* emotions just as strong. As much as the two boys seemed to love each other, they also seemed to get on each other's nerves. Anthony was a very playful and silly kind of guy who loved to have fun and was a total extrovert, whereas Jim was a much more serious soul who loved to be more adult about things. With a more sarcastic kind of wit, Jim was a very extreme introvert; it was the ultimate case of opposites attracting. Just the way that they met was the perfect example of just how opposite they really were.

It was an exceptionally hot day in July when Jim was sitting on a bench at the beach with his dog, reading a book. He would just sit there for hours at a time reading any one of his favorite books while his best friend, his dog, would run around and play. Today, Jim was reading a nice, short novel due to the fact that it was such a hot day, even Little Buddy was taking it easy under the hot sun, only leaving Jim's side for a good reason like to meet up with another dog for a nice little romp. After he had finished his book, he was gathering up his area and was bending over to put on Little Buddy's leash when something came crashing into him from behind.

Anthony had been rollerblading all morning long and usually, as he rode along and listened to his MP3 player, he would just kind of zone out. That was the case as he was coming up to the bench, and when he ran into Jim, it was almost more of a surprise to him than it was to Jim.

Anthony wanted to be upset about being sidetracked on his daily exercise routine, but he knew that it was actually his fault . . . even if this man had been right in the middle of the path doing nothing. After the two and the dog untangled and brushed themselves off, it was almost like they had known each other forever, the way it was so easy to go from "sorry" to a real conversation. Right away, they both sat back down on that little bench to "recover."

"I'm Anthony, by the way."

"Oh, yeah, I'm Jim, and this is Little Buddy."

Jim could tell Anthony wasn't much of a dog person, but that he petted Little Buddy just to be polite.

"So, whatcha readin'?"

"Huh? Oh, it's *Breakfast at Tiffany's*. Just finished it before you, uh, well, before our little tumble."

Right away, Anthony liked Jim, especially the way he didn't place all the blame on Anthony for the run-in. That was one thing Anthony really liked in a person, the ability to let things go easily.

"Wow, I loved that movie, never read the book, though."

"That's kinda funny, 'cause I have never seen the movie. So, do you skate by here often? Wow, that sounded like the cheesiest pickup line ever. Sorry, it's just that I read here almost every Saturday and I have never seen you before."

"Actually, yes, I do come by here every Saturday. I have never seen you, either, not that I saw you today."

It seemed as though that cute little joke was the deal-sealer for Jim.

"Well, if you'd like, we can do dinner so we'll remember each other next time."

"Well, Jim, I don't think that I could forget you if I wanted to, but I would love to do dinner. I'm free tonight."

"'Kay, how about I pick you up around seven and I'll call you for directions? Here's my number."

And with that, the two went their own ways to get ready for their date.

At dinner, Anthony realized that the two were completely opposite in almost every single aspect; he was very religious where Jim had no beliefs whatsoever; Anthony wanted a whole circus of kids where Jim was only just thinking about maybe having one. Every little sign pointed to suggest that it was just not worth even trying a second date, but everything that Anthony was feeling was telling him to just go for it. Jim may not have led the lifestyle that Anthony had hoped for in a partner, but he was everything that Anthony could have hoped for as a person; he was sweet, polite, and just had some kind of allure to him that Anthony couldn't resist. The fact that Jim would open car doors, building doors, and even pull out Anthony's chair was all that he needed to know that Jim was a truly "nice guy"! He had never met such a gentleman, let alone someone who clicked so well with him. He could tell that he must have been as new to Jim as Jim was to him, but still Jim seemed not to mind it at all. In fact, it was Jim who had proposed the idea of going out again.

✦

"SO, I HAD a really great time with you tonight and at the beach today, as painful as it was."

"Yeah? Even though you have the ugliest bruise on your calf from where my skate jabbed you?"

There it was, that cuteness that made nothing else matter to Jim other than spending time with Anthony.

"Well, then, since you are man enough to handle a bruise, I'm sure I'd love to see you again! How about tonight . . . I have quite a little bar in my kitchen."

"That sounds great!"

✦

AFTER THEY WOKE up the next morning, it was as if it were meant to be: waking up in each other's arms. What followed were quite a few dates . . . that week, as well as every single night together! As the months passed, they found themselves with each other more and more and neither one seemed to realize how they had both just kind of moved in together.

As different as they both were, not only from each other, but also totally different from the people that they had imagined themselves ending up with, they usually seemed to agree on everything. Big decisions such as where to live and how to spend and manage their finances were never an issue for them; it was all the little things that made them fight like crazy. It was little things, like attitude or being grumpy, that would throw them into a fury of mean words and bad tempers. Because of the strong bond that they had, a fight would never be allowed to be slept on, even if they had to stay up all night and fight it out. If it weren't for Anthony's temper and stubbornness, and in large part for Jim's ability to forgive and to take the blame, the fights would probably never end. Anthony would get special pleasure out of pushing his poor Jim to his limits by pushing and pushing long after Jim had apologized, always knowing that no matter how far he took an argument, his Jim would always make it better with his love. Anthony had to be weary though of how often he did this, for Jim was a very fragile person when it came to anything said and done by Anthony. Jim would never get mad at Anthony, who always seemed to get mad at Jim; he would only be sad that they were fighting at all and try to conquer any bad feelings with love. Anthony would relish all the affection and emotion he would get from Jim, but eventually seeing the man he truly loved cry would make Anthony stop and take stock of the situation, bringing the fight, and himself, around.

✦

TODAY, ON THEIR second anniversary of meeting, Anthony was in one of his grumpy moods from waking up early to catch the plane from the Norfolk airport in Virginia to the Long Beach airport. From looking and talking to the couple you would have thought that Jim hadn't made the trip with Anthony since he was cheerful, calm, and pleasant. He was happy to just get to be on the beach, on their bench, with the person whom he cared more about than anything in the world. Anthony was grumpy in the morning just because he wasn't meant to wake up before noon, let alone before 7:00 a.m. From the moment they got to the airport, everything seemed to upset Anthony, from the Starbucks not being open to the pace at which Jim was walking. Anthony always let the little things get to him. There was no question that he was madly in love with Jim; it was only that he let everything else come first.

As they sat on "their bench" it was hard for Jim to get Anthony in a sentimental mood, but when he was able to, it was pure heaven for them both. When they were in their special spot, they would talk about the past, about what was going on in their life at the moment, and about all of their plans for the future. It was as if they were in a bubble that was sheltering them from the smell of passing smokers, or the extreme heat from the California summer sun, only letting in the sound of the crashing waves. They talked about having children, or not wanting to have children. They talked about where they wanted to be when they retired, but mostly they just talked about how much they loved each other and how they wanted to be together forever.

Once Anthony had gotten over his tantrum and they had finished their chat, Anthony announced that he had a surprise for Jim. Then, he took Jim over to an area where there was a man standing by a tree with two sets of rollerblades. It was a very surprising sight for Jim, because not only did he not like rollerblades, he had never even tried them before!

"You trust me, don't you, sweetie?"

"Well, yes, of course I do, babe. I just don't trust those skates!"

"Let me teach ya, Jim. I'll always catch you when you fall."

As much as Jim dreaded it, he did it to indulge in Anthony's little surprise. After no time at all, Jim was getting the hang of it, and as long as he had his Anthony by his side, he felt a lot safer than he would in any other situation. After about fifteen minutes of actually skating around the beach pathway, they made their way back to their bench and Anthony announced that he had another surprise for Jim. When the bench was in sight, right away Jim saw what the surprise was: it was a perfect little picnic for two just behind the bench on the grass under a tree.

As much fun as Jim had skating around, he was more than relieved to be done and unharmed. As they sat down to a wonderful little buffet of all of their favorite foods, Jim noticed that there was a copy of *Breakfast at Tiffany's* there; Jim had long ago lost his copy—one of his favorites.

He couldn't help tearing up a little, for although he knew how much Anthony loved him, all of this was just more than he could have ever hoped for or expected.

Just as Jim thought that it couldn't get any better, Anthony asked him a question.

"Are you happy?"

"Yes, very!"

"Good. I love you very much, Jim, and I know I get very grumpy sometimes and don't show you how much you mean to me, but you mean the world to me . . . and I have another surprise for you, too!"

Then, Anthony stood up and started to whistle and clap his hands, and from far off they could see a little brown ball of fur running their way. It had a huge blue bow around its neck, almost as big as its own body. Eventually, its little legs ran their way over, right into Anthony's hands. It was a puppy, a golden retriever—the same breed as Little Buddy, who had just passed away the year before; this would have been their first time here without Little Buddy. As Anthony handed it over to Jim, he whispered in his ear and sat next to him.

"To new beginnings, and a start to our life together, forever."

When Jim held the little puppy, he was totally in tears, and when he saw what was attached to the bow on the puppy, he just went quiet . . . it was a ring.

Anthony took the ring off of the puppy and got on one knee.

"You are my life, my heart, my reason for living; will you marry me?"

After about a whole minute passed, Jim just started to laugh.

"Wow, I always thought that I'd be the one to ask you, but this is even better. *Of course I will!*"

"Good, but we have to do it right here; this place means too much to me now. Everything that I have ever wanted in life has been given to me right here."

✦

AFTER A YEAR'S worth of planning, there they were again, at their bench, but this time there were a lot more people there than the couple and a dog. Everything was perfect—Anthony wasn't even grumpy! It was a nice ceremony that was pretty traditional besides the fact that it was two men, and that the ring bearer was Little Buddy Jr.

PYRAMIDS IN ROME

DERRICK DELLA GIORGIA

AROUND ME, THE calm waters of the Tiber. I was attempting to cross Ponte Sisto, one of the bridges that connected Trastevere—the Roman answer to the New York's West Village—to the other side of the historical center— Spanish Steps, Colosseum, Trevi Fountain. It was a perfect night of August after four in the morning, when everybody moved slower and happier either toward home or the last open pizza/kebab/croissant place to dry up those extra fluid ounces of alcohol shaking in their stomachs. I wasn't looking for food, nor trying to reach home, because besides the waters of the Tiber I had Luqman around me. His left arm twisted all the way up my neck, his chest leaning now on my torso, now on my waist, his right arm around my waist, together making a perfect modern reproduction of a Greek statue. He was drunk and unfortunately still not exactly capable of controlling the euphoria that the amount of alcohol he had swallowed down provided him. Every three steps, his shoes were on mine and his saliva made the wet spot on my red-collared shirt bigger, wetter, and warmer. His voice, switching between an Arabic chant and moans of pain and intolerance to motion, wet my ear and my neck with every guttural sound or laugh. I even had to grab his ass a couple of times to avoid going on the floor with him: propel his butt cheeks upward and quickly pull him by the belt as I screamed. "Luqman, please! Try to stand up! We are almost there! I can't carry you, you are too heavy!"

Despite that, during those forty-five minutes of intimacy his body stopped being sexy to me. His swollen biceps around my neck, his firm chest—mostly exposed since his shirt was unbuttoned to his jeans—rubbing against every part of my body and sending up to my nose the hottest smell of male flesh and cologne, were never in my thoughts. Not even his right hand, which clumsily tried clinging on to any-thing stable—anything stable often being my belt, my fly! or my inner thighs—excited me that night. My only worry was his apartment in Campo de' Fiori: the nice one-bedroom apartment on the third floor where I would park him on his twin-size bed under the Cheops Pyramids picture and finally go home. Having sex with drunk people was like masturbat-ing to me: the excitement coming from the other person's desire for you wasn't there. Plus, I didn't even know whether he was interested in male items.

Walking back home after I left him, I wasn't alone; his arms, his smooth chest, his stomach, his fragrance, his lips on my neck, his hands all over me, his sexy Arabic words, his soft brown hair on my lips, every inch of his body stayed with me. The fear and excitement with which I had taken his pants off when he was finally in his bed trembled under my skin. The sight of his white boxers rolled up on his thighs—which the last lights in Campo de' Fiori varnished—had multiplied the butterflies in my stomach and my desire. I had met Luqman through university friends. We both attended the American University in Rome, me being an Italian studying marketing and willing to move to the States, and him being an Egyptian studying communications and wishing to live in Rome. Both in our twenties, both in transition, both very shy and profound.

✦

"HELLO?" MY VOICE rolled away in the darkness of my room.

"Fab-rizio?" Only my English-speaking friends pronounced my name that way.

"Yeah, who's this?" I was still tired and willing to go back to sleep as soon as that phone call was over.

"It's Luqman. Are you still sleeping?" His voice was deep and without having him in front of my eyes, his young body and fresh face, it felt like talking to a middle-aged man.

"Hm . . . no! You just woke me up! Don't worry. I had to anyway." I looked into the little blue screen of my cell phone and I read *Luqman*. It was him!

"Sorry. I just thought that if I was able to get up . . . you'd be up, too."

"How do you feel? Last night you were pretty dead!" I was curious to know what he remembered, how much of our twisting on the way home he was able to recall.

"I know. What a mess! I couldn't even stand straight. My head felt like a Tic Tac box. If you hadn't been there, I would have probably slept in the street. I wanted to thank you. It was very nice of you." He sounded embarrassed and uncomfortable for having been in need.

"Don't even mention it! That's what friends are for, aren't they? Really, it was no problem. Just pick the restaurant where you are gonna take me to thank me, that's all." I laughed and he laughed, too.

"Wait! Wait! You pick it! Wherever and whenever you want. That's the least I can do for you after you carried my drunk ass all the way back home."

"I was just joking. You don't have to, Luqman." I wanted to add, *It was a pleasure, to touch your hot body, to see you in your boxers, to feel your heart beat next to mine, to have your lips on my neck . . . even if you didn't mean to kiss me. You made my night!*

"I'm serious, Fab-rizio. I want to. What are you doing tonight?" He was serious most of the time, and that made me go crazy. A sweet, serious, gentle, hot guy. I was slowly falling for him.

"All right. Hm . . . tonight . . . nothing! I'm not doing anything tonight." Too bad for Andrea's birthday party, but I could always make up some story at the last minute.

"What if we go to Trattoria da Trinchese in Piazza Navona?"

"Sounds awesome." I couldn't believe he had picked one of the best—and obviously most expensive—restaurants in Rome. I mean, I knew he was rich, but he didn't have to do that! His family owned the number one clothing company in Egypt and lived in a sort of palace in Cairo. His father was pure Egyptian, and his mother was a mix of Egyptian and Italian. They wanted him to study and then go back to Egypt and take care of the company, but he didn't sound very happy about that.

"I'll book for nine. Will you meet me in front of the restaurant at five to nine?"

"I'll see you there at eight fifty-five." He was so funny sometimes. Why didn't he just say "meet me at nine"?

"Great!"

"Luqman. I was thinking, should we go to a restaurant closer to Campo de' Fiori? Just in case you need to be carried again! Hahaha." That was my hope more than a joke.

"You bastard. Watch it! Tonight, you'll be the one needing transportation!"

✦

HE LOOKED LIKE a model. I entered Piazza Navona from the opposite side where he was, hoping I would be able to look at him for a while without him knowing it. He was standing by Bernini's Fountain of the Four Rivers, matching perfectly with the baroque architecture of the buildings that claustrophobically surrounded the square. The sky was dark, and the purposely insufficient lighting swallowed everything into a sepia tone. Suddenly, my body started being sensitive to every thought, every word, every emotion that stormed inside me. My stomach ached sweetly, that pain that usually anticipated something big or new in your life. My breaths got shorter and quicker, and my hands got cold, refreshing in the heavy heat of that summer night. He was there for me, waiting to take me to a romantic restaurant and have a nice dinner. I felt something burning, and I had to calm myself down or I would have ruined everything. As I continued walking toward him, something buzzed in my pants pocket. It was my cell phone; I had received a text message. I AM HERE. Signed *Luqman* with a smiley face. It was nine-oh-five. At the same time he spotted me.

He sort of hugged me and patted my back. "What's up?" he said.

"Very hungry. I hope you brought that credit card!" Being funny was my only chance to hide all the waiting and the excitement for our date. He looked amazing. Ready for the runway. Shaven, rested, elegant. He was wearing a black-collared shirt with two pockets in the front that fell right on his pectorals and made him look somehow military-ish. A slim, dark green tie ended up right above the black belt of his gray pants. At his feet a nice pair of tuxedo shoes. His shoulders looked bigger and his brown eyes sweeter, not challenging like the night before when we had gone out with all our friends.

"Let's go."

We moved slowly—as the atmosphere required—through the rooms and the tables of the restaurant until we arrived at our table, under an antique chandelier. We sat and went through the previous night's arduous walk home again. He couldn't stop apologizing and even flushed a couple of times when I told him how he couldn't stand up and hung himself on my shirt and my pants. Before ordering our food, I picked my favorite wine—Amarone della Valpolicella—and the red nectar expedited our conversation even more. I told him about my project to move to the States for a while, to study some more over there before deciding where I wanted to live my life, and he opened up, too.

"You see. I love Egypt, and I miss it so much, too. Sometimes at night, I wake up and feel like suffocating. I run to the window and look up at the sky, hoping to hear the desert, Cairo, my pyramids. But I know I am much happier here in Rome. If I went back there, I would have to deal with every single thing my parents expect from me, and I am not ready for that right now." The combination of the wine and the discreet lighting of the room worked its way into his seriousness and secretiveness. He had never before then talked about his family in such terms. He confessed to me—his eyes almost watering—that his parents had everything planned for him, from the job he would get to the wife he would marry, the house he would live in, the political party he needed to join, and that scared him because he thought they would never ask what *he* wanted to do or liked.

"When was the last time you went back to Egypt?" My eyes were fixed on his lips, waiting for more words to come out of them. More sentences and details that would have tied me to him, brought me into his life. Into his heart.

"Two years ago now. My family has come here to visit me many times, but I never returned after I started college."

"I have an idea! A little surprise for you. To thank you for this beautiful dinner. And your amazing company!" I lifted my glass and invited him to toast us and our special night.

"What?" He made a face, something in between embarrassment for having been made the center of attention and childish curiosity for the unexpected.

"I'll show you later. When we get out of here."

✦

WHEN HE GOT out of the restaurant, his sleeves were rolled up above his elbows, his shirt had partially come out of his pants, and his ass looked like a wrapped candy in that shiny fabric. He also talked slower and was more uninhibited, but could stand straight and didn't unfortunately need my help to walk.

"Okay, come with me." I grabbed his arm and pulled him through Piazza Navona, dodging all the people, the artists and their paintings, the fountains, his questions, and all our doubts. Making him run.

"Where are we going?"

"We need a cab."

"A cab?"

" Shut up." We entered the first cab we found by the Pantheon, and I instructed the driver to take us to our special place, without letting Luqman understand what that was or where it was.

"You are crazy!" he told me in the backseat, staring at me like he had never done before. I wanted to kiss him right there, but I stopped myself.

The driver went fast, passing cars and accelerating every time there was space in front of him. The ride was only ten minutes or less, but long enough for Lugman to talk more about his Egypt and more about himself. The alcohol went to our heads: now fast, amplifying the multitude of thoughts and feelings; now slowly, together with the meter, prolonging sensations and stares.

"Let's go!" I dropped the guy my ten-euro bill and peeled Luqman off the seat. "Don't look!"

"What?" He hated it, not being in control. And when I covered his eyes with my hand, he got scared. "What is it?" I believe he couldn't take the fact that I could look at him but he couldn't look at himself, checking his pants, his hair, or his shirt. His hands performed a ballet of movements in the attempt to tame his anxiety.

"I wanted to take you back to the pyramids for a second. . . ." I freed his eyes and turned him around toward the Piramide, the awkward white monument in the Ostiense zone that was in the middle of everything.

"You're . . ." He didn't say anything. Nothing came out of his mouth. Everything decided to spill out through his eyes. A smile of surprise first, amazement right after, and finally some tears that under the moonlight sparkled as if he were wearing diamonds on his face.

"I know it is just a little pyramid, but I'm sure it feels familiar. . . ." The Piramide Cestia was the consequence of Egypt becoming a province of the Roman Empire and definitely stood out, especially at night when its white appeared to become thicker and shinier. Suddenly, I ran out of jokes and the atmosphere got serious: two guys, an August night, and the romantic noises of a Rome that was secretly active.

His chin was up in the air, and his strong neck made its way out of the shirt. He was transfixed, staring at the tip of the big triangle of bricks, mute.

"Thank you." He came close to me and repeated: "Thank you."

"How much did your creation take, o angel?" He delicately landed his lips on mine and stood immobile for a second, as if he wanted to make sure we were compatible. Then he pressed his into mine and our mouths became inseparable for the longest time.

"I promised myself I would use that verse when I found the person that would make my heart melt." His eyes locked on mine. "It is my favorite poet, Abu Nuwas . . . putting into words his love for a beautiful boy."

THE TRICK

SAM HAWK

DURING MY FIRST year in Dallas I was such a slut that I could actually hook up with guys without meaning to. That's how I met Tedd. It was at a progressive July 4 party, three parties at three different pools themed red, white, and blue. It was cleverer than it sounds. I entered the "white" pool area through billowing swaths of white fabric, and there before me were all the boys I had dated, tricked with, been in love or lust with standing around in white bikinis and square cuts (whether they could carry it off or not) sipping white grape martinis and ignoring the white cheddar canapés.

Was it only last summer that this would have been a shimmering dream for me, a sheltered, closeted soldier in some backwater army post in Alafuckingbama? Dallas was like the Emerald City to me then, and I came to find love and happiness. Life right out of the closet was full of dizzying possibilities for romance, but it wasn't long before I discovered that an army credential was a man magnet, along with an army-fit body, and I was able to get laid without much effort. If I said, "I'm a soldier, I just got out," it usually sealed the deal. Gradually, without my realizing it, my dreams of romance were pushed aside by the thrill of sex without strings. I became one of the party boys for whom hooking up without consequence is a way of life and who think relationships are for breeders. With the exception of weekly brunches with my friends, Joe and Michael, my social life revolved around the A-Gay party circuit with its endless quest for the perfect body, the perfect shoes, and the perfect lay. Now my deb year was drawing to a close, and here I was at yet another overworked theme party with the same crowd.

I sat on the concrete and dangled my feet in the pool and stared into space, unfocused. I realized with a start that a guy across the pool was meeting my eyes. *Shit*, I thought, *he thinks I'm coming on to him when I'm really just bored.* Then I saw he was kind of cute, or at least cute enough, and the first fresh face I had seen in a while, so I went with it. I gave him my most meaningful eye contact. He got up to go to the bar, and I seized the opportunity to chat him up. Up close, I realized he was a bit chubby and a lot queeny, but he seemed really into me, and there's no bigger turn-on. Besides, I had gone through every other guy at this party. I approached him as he asked the bartender for a water.

"You don't like clever theme cocktails?" I said as he turned to me.

"I don't like drinking vodka in the hot sun. I might lose control of myself."

What a tease.

"Wouldn't want that happening."

Without taking my eyes off him, I ordered another cocktail.

"I kind of like losing control."

He took off his sunglasses and looked in my brown eyes. I noticed his were green, which totally worked with his auburn hair. I held his stare, and I knew he wanted me.

There was a big splash in the pool as some goofball did a cannonball and he looked away. I introduced myself.

"My name is William."

"Hi, I'm Tedd. I don't think we've met before, and I thought I knew everybody in this town."

His voice was high and singsongy, and he needed to work on his gut, but he had a nice ass.

I replied, "I haven't lived here long. I'm a soldier; I just got out."

Could there really be a guy in Dallas who hasn't heard me use that line?

"Oh my God, are you serious? Like a real soldier, marching and saluting and war and stuff?"

"That's it."

"Jesus, I can't imagine. No wonder you're drinking. I mean, did you have to wear uniforms and go through basic training and all that?"

"Yes, I went through all that and more." I looked down a moment in modesty. "But tell me about you. What do you do?"

"I'm a photostylist. I bet you don't know what that is, do you? I set up photo shoots; everything below the neck is my responsibility."

He gestured toward my chest and abdomen when he said that. I could tell he wanted to touch me, and I flexed my abs slightly for his benefit.

He continued, "I do everything for the photo shoots but hair and makeup. In Dallas I do mostly catalogs and department stores."

"Sounds like a glamour job."

"Hardly. Next week we're doing winter coats for Dillards, outside downtown. It'll probably be a hundred degrees."

"Wow. You're working hard for the dream, huh?"

"Well, this isn't exactly my dream. I'd rather be on the other side of the camera."

"You want to be a fashion photographer?"

"No, not that. I like to think of myself as an artist. I'm flattering myself probably, but I'm trying to build a body of work as a serious photographer and hopefully get the attention of some galleries." I smiled at him as he put his hand on my shoulder and said, "Listen to me rattling on about my pipe dreams to someone I've just met. I'm sure I'm boring you to death."

"I'm not bored, I'm stimulated." I leaned toward him. "Maybe you could take my picture."

"Do you still have any of those uniforms?"

That was all it took. We never made it to the blue party. Later at my apartment, when we were finished, I was about to get out of bed when he suddenly grabbed my hand and pulled me over into a spooning position. What the fuck was he doing? Was he falling asleep? I didn't say he could stay over. He spoke without opening his eyes,

"That was really nice, William. You're a sweet guy. I thought all the guys at those parties were shallow, but you're different. Special. I'm glad I met you."

I get it. He likes a little sweet talk. Sure, I can do that.

"No, you're special."

Okay, that was about all I could come up with. I was better at dirty talk; besides, we were through and it was time for him to leave. He snuggled into me a bit more, and I counted the seconds until I could claim my arm was falling asleep and roll back over and remind him again of how early I had to get up. I guess he read my mind because shortly, he kissed me and went into the bathroom. He came out a few minutes later with his pants on. He pulled out his business card, wrote his mobile number on it, and handed it to me.

"Tedd with two *d*s," I said. "Did you fabulize your name a bit when you came out?"

"It's short for Teddy. My parents are so country they didn't even know it was supposed to be a nickname for Theodore, so Teddy's on my birth certificate. I just dropped the *y*. I got tired of the bear jokes."

I looked at his baby face and nearly hairless chest and said, "You're hardly a bear."

I opened a drawer by the bed and pulled out one of my preprinted cards with my first name and phone number. I gave it to him, secure in the knowledge that he would obey the cardinal rule of tricking: always exchange numbers and never use them.

The next day he called. I actually answered the phone, which I never do, so I was caught. He suggested what he called a "glamour date," which involved drinks and dinner, so I figured why not? I fucked him, why not let him buy me dinner? Besides, my friends have been telling me that I should be open to the idea of a relationship. In fact, just the other day at brunch with Joe and Michael, Joe said I should "get back in touch with that sweet guy from Alabama that you used to be, before you got all bitter. A bitter queen is such a cliché."

"First of all," I told Joe, "I'm not *from* Alabama; I was just forced into a brief military exile there before I escaped."

"Whatever, you know what I'm talking about."

"Secondly, I got bitter for a reason. I fell for every goofy line and was fucked over too many times."

Michael put down his mimosa and leaned over the table. "Girl, please. Spare me the dramatics. You were here maybe two months before you discovered the party circuit. You had, what, one boyfriend who dumped you? If you think that's being 'fucked over too many times,' then you need to walk a mile in my pumps."

"All I'm trying to say," said Joe, "is try a little change of scenery. Do some different things and give yourself a chance to meet some guys other than those walking eating disorders you party with. Maybe try dating."

"What do you mean try dating?" I said. "I date. I date more than anybody I know."

"Dragging some pretty boy home from a bar and kicking him out at three a.m. is not dating," said Michael.

Joe said, "There are still decent guys out there, just be open to it. Don't give up on relationships."

"Okay, okay, fine," I said. "I'll be open to it. Can we stop the intervention now?" I made a circular motion with a finger for the waiter to bring us more drinks. "Next thing you know, you'll be inviting me to one of your goddamn church socials."

So I said yes to Tedd. I called Joe and Michael and told them I had a date. They were thrilled and made me promise to call them the minute it was over.

I must say that Tedd went to a lot of trouble and arranged a lovely evening. We started with drinks at a glittery bar high atop a downtown building, looking out at the skyline. It's amazing how pretty Dallas is at night, considering how it looks by day. He ordered champagne cocktails for us and asked the singer to dedicate "Stars Fell on Alabama" to me since I used to live there. I hated Alabama, but it was a nice gesture. Next we had an elegant dinner at Milieu, which was the ultra-trendy restaurant of the moment. I don't know who he slept with to get the reservations, although I suppose that's more my style. The décor was minimalist in a Philippe Starck sort of way with a single calla lily on each table and waiters who looked like soap opera actors. It was all very chic, and despite myself, I enjoyed the conversation. He told me about his family and the small Texas town where he grew up. I told him about my military experiences and my decision to leave the army and come out. I found myself talking about things I hadn't shared with other people, like my compromises with myself as a closeted soldier, laughing at the fag jokes and not defending gay soldiers who were outed. I forgot the first-date talking points I had rehearsed and allowed myself to open up to him. It felt good. I haven't had another date like it.

After dinner, he drove me home and parked at the curb, and we walked to the door. When I opened it, he hesitated.

"Don't you want to come in?" I said.

"Yes, but not tonight. I want to take it slow."

"I think the take-it-slow option has passed. We had sex already, remember?"

"Oh, I remember, all right. The sex was great." He paused, looked at me, and brushed my hair off my forehead. I had a brief flash of Hubbell outside the Plaza. "Next time, I want to make love."

I said nothing. He kissed me and got back into his car. I stood there, frozen to the sidewalk as he drove off. Did he just turn down sex? With me? Did he just tell me he loves me? This is our first date and he's already using the *L* word? I had Joe on my cell phone before I moved off the sidewalk.

"I asked him to come in and he said no. *No!*"

"Do you mean to tell me you had a date with an actual gentleman? This must be a first for you."

"I'm serious. We've already had sex, so it's not like he's

saving it for marriage. I mean, I showered, I worked out this afternoon, my pecs are perky, what kind of guy says no to sex?"

"The kind of guy who realizes how special you are and wants to build something, that's who. He's an endangered species, a nice guy. Tedd sounds terrific."

"Tedd Terrific just said he loves me."

There was a pause, then Joe said, "Hang on; I'm getting Michael on the line." Michael picked up on the first ring and Joe said, "Start from the beginning. Tell me exactly what he said."

"He said he didn't want to come in with me because he doesn't want to just have sex. He wants to make love."

Michael sucked in his breath. "That's so beautiful! I'm so jealous. Oh my God, it's just like Harry Hamlin and that guy from the Rookies."

"William," said Joe, "calm down. He did not just declare his love for you. He just wants the sex to be special. This guy sounds like a prince."

"Seriously," said Michael, "you are so lucky. He clearly feels a connection. Do you feel it?"

"I don't know. Maybe. This is only our first date, and I'm already confused. God, dating is hard. The Internet is so much easier."

"Stay away from Manhunt," said Michael. "Don't fuck this up, do you hear me? Do you know how long it's been since a decent guy walked into your life? Has a decent guy ever walked into your life? He was telling you that he thinks you're special and worth waiting for. I would love to have a man treat me that way; it's called respect. This is what we dream of. Don't freak out, okay? Now, when do we get to meet Mr. Wonderful?"

I didn't arrange a meeting with Joe, Michael, and Tedd just yet. All I needed was the three of them ganging up on me. They'd serve me my balls on a platter—in our lovely new pattern from Pottery Barn, of course. I wasn't quite ready to be domesticated.

The next day Tedd called again. *Shouldn't he give me a chance to call him occasionally?* I thought. He told me how much he enjoyed our date, then hit me with this:

"Listen, I'm invited to this party on Saturday; it's kind of a big photo shoot wrap thing, you know, from that Dillards job I told you about? Anyway, lots of my friends and people I work with will be there, and I'd love for you to meet them. I've already told everybody all about you, and they can't wait to see the mysterious William. Let's go!"

I stood there holding the phone, letting his words sink in. *Holy crap, he wants me to meet the friends. One date and he wants to be my instant boyfriend, and we haven't even "made love" yet. This is taking it slow? Calling me every day and parading me in front of his friends? Shit, what the hell has Joe gotten me into? I need to nip this in the bud.*

"Tedd, listen, you're such a nice guy."

"Thanks. So are you."

I paused and he filled the silence.

"What? Do you not want to go to the party?"

"It's not the party. It's us. We should talk."

"Wait, wait, what are you saying? Is it about last night? My not coming in? Is something wrong?"

His voice was getting higher and more anxious. I lost my nerve.

"It's nothing. Really." I paused. "I'm just so swamped at work. I need to go into the office on Saturday."

"Oh. Okay. Well, everyone will be disappointed and we'll miss you. I'll miss you. Are you sure everything's all right?"

"Yeah, yeah, everything's fine. Great. We just shouldn't plan on seeing each other this weekend."

"You're working all weekend?"

"Yeah, I've got a ton to do. I just can't commit to anything."

"Right. Sure. That's fine. I understand. You can't commit."

"Hey, wait, that's not what I meant."

"I know, I'm being bitchy and have no right to be. I'm sorry. We've only had one date and you have to work. Really, I understand."

We hung up and I felt like such a tool. Why should I feel bad? He was the pushy one, getting all clingy after one little date, and yet I did. I called him right back.

"Tedd, I don't have to work all weekend. I can carve out some time to go to your friends' party. I want to."

"William, it's all right. I understand you have to work."

"No, I want to."

"William, you don't have to. I didn't have any right to say what I did. Just get your work done."

"I want to go. What time should I pick you up?"

I liked the party at first and enjoyed meeting his friends. They were an artsy group, so different from the parties I was used to. Who knew there were gays who didn't work out? Tedd was the hottest guy there, and I was kind of proud to be seen with him.

Then the Dillard's model walked in. Had we hooked up? Probably not. I would remember someone that flawless. He looked kind of like a young Matt Lauer. He saw me, too, and we kept glancing at each other across the room. When Tedd went to the bathroom, he came over.

"You keep staring at me," he said.

"No, you're staring at me. Do we know each other?"

"No, but I'd like to. I didn't think I'd find somebody so hot at this dreary party." He looked around and rattled the ice in his drink, then looked back at me. "I see you're with someone. Too bad."

He slipped his card into my breast pocket, put his lips to my ear, and said, "Call me when you ditch the boyfriend."

Instinct took over. Without giving it a thought, I put my lips to his ear, my hand on the small of his back. "I don't have a boyfriend."

At that moment, Tedd appeared. He looked stricken, and Matt Lauer blended into the crowd. Tedd turned and walked straight out the door. It took me a moment to realize he was leaving me behind, and I followed, calling after him. He jumped in his car and drove away without saying a word.

I got home by cab. I couldn't very well ask one of his friends for a ride. I called Tedd as soon as I got home, and he didn't answer. I must have called ten times the next day, leaving messages each time, but he never answered and never returned my calls. Finally, the next night, I couldn't stand it any longer and I went to his house and knocked on his door. He answered and stood there.

"Tedd, I'm glad you answered the door. I didn't mean . . . really . . . all I did . . ."

Seeing Tedd in person made me forget everything I had rehearsed.

"All you did was hit on another guy the second I went to the bathroom."

I was surprised he was so angry. I suppose I shouldn't have been, but I was used to the calm, sweet Tedd. I hadn't seen this side of him.

"Tedd, it was nothing. Can't I come in? Let's talk about this."

"It was nothing? That's what you have to say to me?"

"Tedd, come on, it's not like we're boyfriends. We only had one date. I mean, you're a great guy and all, but he came on to me. I didn't do anything with him. He just gave me his number."

Tedd's face was red. "Is that really what you have to say to me? You think it's okay because you didn't throw him to the floor and have sex with him?"

"Tedd, calm down. I really think you're overreacting."

"Don't tell me how to react!"

His voice was cracking and I could tell he was about to cry, but he soldiered on. "You humiliated me. Do you really not understand that? I took you as my date, my *potential* boyfriend since you're so quick to remind me we're not boyfriends. I wanted you to meet my friends, and I wanted them to meet you. And what did you do? You were all over that bimbo model the second I walked away. You practically swallowed his ear. You couldn't control yourself, but you know what? I can control myself. I can save myself the further humiliation of dating you. Good-bye."

He shut the door.

✦

THAT WAS THREE years ago, and I didn't see or hear from Tedd again until last Tuesday when I stopped by a restaurant for a quick dinner by myself. It was a casual sandwich-and-salads kind of place in the heart of the gay ghetto and popular with the boys. The hostess seated me in a booth; I ordered a glass of wine and busied myself with my phone as if I had messages that needed my immediate attention. I was soon distracted by the table of butch lesbians next to me, laughing loudly over platters of onion rings, reveling in their lack of body-image issues. That last bit may be projection on my part, but it must be nice to be a part of a community that values plus-size instead of waif model. You see, after four years of civilian life, my army-fit body isn't what it once was, and those visible abs had long since disappeared. I recognized Tedd the moment he walked in, even though he'd changed. *Damn, he's looking good*, I thought. He's lost all the weight I've gained, and he's obviously been working out. I had almost picked up the phone to call him so many times, but never quite did. I had fantasized about him forgiving me, dashing over to my house, and falling into my arms, saving me from a loveless bachelorhood. Now, here he was in the same room. As I was contemplating all of this, a hot muscle queen walked in, went straight to Tedd, and planted a big kiss right on his mouth in front of God and everybody. Impressive. The boy's done well for himself. Then Tedd saw me. He said something quickly to the muscle queen and started walking toward me, and there I was alone in a restaurant in my fat jeans. Shit.

"Hi, William, it's Tedd. It's been a few years; what have you been up to?"

"Gosh, Tedd, hi. Um, I haven't been up to much, how about you?"

"Oh, you haven't heard? Well . . ."

He sat down next to me like we were best girlfriends. "Jonathan and I just went to Canada and got married!"

His voice went up three octaves when he said "married," and everybody in the restaurant turned. He waved his hand in front of my face as if he had a four-carat diamond instead of a simple gold band.

"How nice. Congratulations. Seriously. Congratulations."

Everybody in the restaurant went back to their meals except for the lesbians, who were obviously listening.

"He's the greatest guy in the world and so attentive, and let me tell you, he's packing some heat, know what I mean?"

Tedd winked as if I were loving this delicious secret.

"And just look at him, isn't he hot?"

We both looked in Jonathan's direction, and I agreed that he was indeed hot.

"We've delayed our honeymoon for a bit while we close on the place in Taos, but we're spending the month of June in Tuscany!"

Three octaves again.

"It'll be just heavenly, and he's arranged everything." He sighed and gazed lovingly at Jonathan. "And the timing is just perfect since my gallery show. Oh my, God did I tell you about my gallery show?"

"I heard about it. I wanted to come but . . ."

He wasn't listening to me and kept talking without pause. "Well, I had a show of my photography at the Uptown Gallery. It was so exciting, I can't begin to tell you. Anyway, it just closed and practically everything sold, so it's time to celebrate. Well, listen, it's been great catching up, gotta go. My lovah awaits."

He gave me a quick kiss on the cheek, and I grabbed his hand before he could get away. "I'm really glad you're happy, Tedd. I want you to be happy. You deserve a guy who treats you with respect."

"You're right about that. You can let go of my hand now."

My mind reeled. This was the moment I had thought about so often, but I wasn't prepared. "I just want you to be happy. I never stopped thinking about you."

He jerked his hand away. "What is this? You never stopped thinking about me? Are you fucking kidding me?

What sort of deranged step-nine bullshit is this? 'Hi, I'm William and I'm a sex addict.' Is that it?"

He threw up his hands and backed away from me. "You don't get to do this. I was done with you years ago. This is what I get for being nice and talking to you."

He got up and went back to Jonathan.

It took me a few moments to realize that all the lesbians were looking at me in silence. One of them passed the onion rings to me. "Take 'em, buddy, you need these more than we do."

I took the platter and sat there a while drinking wine and eating onion rings. I never looked back in Tedd's direction. When I finished, I went home and searched through my files until I found the step-nine letter I had written to Tedd a year and a half before and never mailed. Once again seeing Tedd in person made me forget everything I had rehearsed.

POOR RICHARD'S BAZAAR

RYAN FIELD

THAT SUMMER MILO Banks was a young man who was determined to have sex. He'd just finished high school, and he was starting college in the fall. Even though he wasn't sure who his first sexual partner would be, or how all this was going to transpire, he knew it was time to discover what he'd been missing since junior high school. His arms and his wide shoulders were muscular, thanks to four years of football practice. They tapered down to a thin washboard stomach and firm, narrow hips; his soft, delicate facial features created the perfect balance between rough and tender. And his thick, wavy hair was such a gentle shade of ash blond, it almost looked artificial. When he walked into a crowded room, young women would stop talking and stare. Then they would giggle and murmur things to one another. All he had to do was smile and nod and he could have any one of them. Mostly, though, he was more interested in their boyfriends.

Milo almost tripped on a narrow step when he walked into the quirky little gift shop in early June and asked a young man, "Do you need any part-time help this summer?" It was a touristy place on the river called Poor Richard's Bazaar, where people would linger on weekend afternoons in the candle section when there was nothing better to do. The name had something to do with *Poor Richard's Almanac*, but Milo wasn't sure why, and he really didn't care.

"Ah, well, I have been looking for a part-timer," the guy said, organizing spools of ribbon that were hanging behind the checkout counter. His deep voice sounded hollow and throaty; his movements were slow and precise. He was wearing a black T-shirt and tan shorts that day. When he reached to a shelf on the right for an employment application, you could see the outline of his penis swing back and forth. He was either wearing loose boxer shorts or no underwear at all.

Milo pressed his lips together and took a shallow breath when the guy handed the application to him and said, "Here, fill this out, man." Then the guy sat down on a stool and reached for a can of soda. His long, tanned legs were covered with a soft, light fleece. And his sandy blond hair had been shaved close; small silver rings looped through his earlobes; and his long, thick fingers reminded Milo of overstuffed sausages. When he glanced down, he saw a small tattoo of a bumblebee on his right ankle that made him want to go down on his knees and start licking.

He took the application and filled it out right there on the counter. Then he handed it back a moment later and said, "I'm free any hours, including weekends." He wanted to say, "I'm free to do anything you want me to do, sir." And he wasn't even sure if he was into other guys.

The guy reached for the application, glanced over it, and then said, "You're hired, Milo."

Milo's eyes grew large, and his head jerked back a couple of times. When the guy said his name out loud, it sounded sexy and exciting. People had been calling him by his name all his life, and he'd never experienced a pull in his groin. "Just like that," he said.

The guy laughed. It was a bottomless laugh from his gut, with a "tee-hehehe" sound. "You look honest, and I need someone right now. When can you start?"

"Anytime," Milo said. "I could start today if you want." He smiled and rubbed his palms together, then he bounced up and down on the balls of his feet.

The guy laughed again. "Come back tomorrow night," he said. "You can start out working four nights a week from six to nine. And my name's Ansel Berger. I'm the manager."

Milo reached out to shake his large hand. His palm was the size of a dinner plate, and his fingers were strong. "I'll see you tomorrow, Ansel." When he turned to leave, he had a feeling that Ansel was staring at him. But he didn't turn around to see.

The following night, Milo returned to the shop at six o'clock sharp, wearing a pair of faded jeans that hugged his round ass and a tight black polo shirt that showed off his round, defined chest muscles. He had thought about wearing shorts to work that night, but he didn't want to give the wrong impression too soon. When he walked into the shop, Ansel looked up from the counter and said, "Did you eat dinner yet?" There were white Chinese takeout cartons strewn across the counter, and there was a small piece of white rice stuck to the bottom of his chin.

Milo put his hands in his pockets and shrugged. "Yes. I ate." Then he pulled one hand from his pocket, pointed his index finger to his chin, and rubbed a few times to let Ansel know there was rice stuck to his chin.

But Ansel only leaned forward and squinted.

Milo smiled. "You have rice on your chin," he said. Then he rubbed his own chin again with his finger and said, "Here."

Ansel did the deep gut-laugh again, then he ran his hand along the wrong side of his chin and missed the rice. "Did I get it?" He was wearing baggy short pants again. His long, tanned legs looked darker that night. You could see from the way he was sitting, with his pants bunched up in his crotch, that he had a large pouch between his legs.

Milo nodded. "Nope." Then he reached forward and flicked the rice off Ansel's chin. It landed right between his legs.

Ansel picked the piece of rice from his crotch and laughed even louder. Then he tossed it into a trash can and said, "Perfect shot, man."

After that, Ansel gave him a detailed tour of the entire shop and showed him where things were located. It was a large shop, with many small nooks and alcoves filled with everything from angel collectibles to outdoor garden statues. You could buy anything there, from a hostess gift to a birthday present for your wife. They even sold unique pieces of hand-painted furniture, framed with hand-carved bamboo and Florentine gilt. And there was an outdoor garden area, too, which wrapped around the store, filled with outdoor patio furniture, ornate urns, and more garden statues. When the tour was over, he brought him back to the front desk and taught him how to ring up cash sales and process credit cards. Then he showed him how to wrap and package the gifts. Milo tried to pay attention to everything, but there was so much, and Ansel talked so fast. The only thing he could concentrate on was the way Ansel's powerful legs bowed slightly at the knee when he walked.

And the way his penis moved around in his pants when he turned to his side too fast. There was as much junk bouncing around between Ansel's legs as there was in the shop.

"I know it seems like a lot to learn in one night," he said, "but you'll catch on soon. And there's really no selling involved here. The customers know what they want. All you have to do is help them out once in a while, is all." He patted Milo on the back a couple of times and asked, "Do you have any questions?"

Milo smiled. "Not right now," he said, "but don't leave me alone just yet."

He wasn't trying to be funny. But Ansel did the gut-laugh and said, "I'll be here with you most of the time, man. Don't worry."

The shop wasn't busy that night, but an elderly woman stopped in to buy another large iron urn for her patio container garden. Milo took her outside to the garden area, helped her make a choice, and rang up the sale without a problem. He got a little confused with the credit card machine, but he basically did the entire sale all on his own. And though he was far from being a weakling, he pretended to need Ansel's help when it was time to carry the urn to the woman's car. "I'm going to need you to take charge here, boss," he said to Ansel. "You're a lot bigger and much stronger than I am." And when they went outside and Ansel lifted the urn with one hand, he said, "You make that look so easy. I would never have been able to carry that heavy urn on my own, man." The more helpless and delicate Milo pretended to be, the more Ansel was ready to offer his muscles. When they were about to close up shop at the end of the night, Ansel actually said to Milo, "From now on, whenever there is some heavy lifting to do, you'd better let me take charge and handle it; you might get hurt." Milo shook his head and agreed, then he lowered his eyes and smiled when Ansel held the door open for him.

By the end of that week, Milo and Ansel began to speak candidly about their lives. The foot traffic in the shop seemed to flow in spurts: there were either twenty people walking around or it was empty. And you could never predict when the spurts would come. So there was plenty of downtime to talk. It turned out that Ansel was actually the shop owner's son, twenty-seven years old and being groomed to take over the business one day. He'd made a few mistakes: a couple of arrests for drinking and driving that involved expensive legal fees. So he was working seven days a week to pay off his debts and start fresh again. And Milo told him that he was starting college in the fall and he needed the extra money to help with the expenses. So Ansel agreed to increase his hours to include Saturdays and Sundays. "Hell," he said, "you need the money and I need the help." Then he made a fist and pretended to punch him in the shoulder.

Monday was Milo's day off, but it was also payday. So early that morning he put on a tight pair of white shorts, a skimpy black tank top, and a heavy pair of black work boots with a three-inch heel. He shaved his legs twice a week; they were smooth and tan, and the higher heel made the muscles in his calves pop. It was a warm, humid day, with hazy sunshine and soft, thick air. His plan was to stop by the shop for his paycheck, but he didn't care about the money. He could have waited until Tuesday. He just wanted Ansel to see how he looked in tight shorts and heavy boots.

He parked up front in a tight spot, because he only planned to be there for a few minutes; just enough time to get his check and wiggle his ass a few times in Ansel's face. But he had some trouble getting his car into the parking space. The spot turned out to be tighter than he'd portended, and he wasn't a very good driver. When he pulled in, he misjudged the turn and hit one of the poles that held up a green-and-white awning over the garden statue area. The pole went down, half the awning fell on his car, and he wasn't sure how to back out without causing more damage. Ansel was outside that morning filling one of the water fountains with a garden hose. He dropped the hose, turned off the water, and jogged over to see why half of his awning had gone down. By the time he reached the front parking spaces and saw Milo turning the steering wheel back and forth, a huge smile formed on his serious face. Then he crossed toward the driver's window and rested his large hands on the door.

Milo looked up at him and smiled. Then he shook his head and said, "I guess you can see I'm not the best driver, especially when it comes to parking." He put the car in park and sighed. "I'll fix everything. I hope I didn't do any damage."

Ansel leaned forward and pulled the awning back so he could open the car door. "Calm down," he said. "It's cool; there's no damage. That pole was too close to the parking spot anyway. It could have happened to anyone. Are you okay?"

"I'm fine. Except now you think I'm a moron," Milo said, lowering his eyes to his lap.

"No way, man," he said, tapping the windshield. "Actually, I love this car. It's really cool." Milo had inherited a vintage 1987 red Mercedes convertible from his grandfather.

"It's older, but it has low miles and it never gives me any trouble," he said. When he looked up, he could see Ansel's hairy underarms.

Ansel opened the car door, then he looked inside and stared at Milo's naked legs for a second. "Why don't you get out, and I'll back the car out for you and park it in a safer place."

"Thanks for helping out like this," Milo said. Then he slowly spread his legs and got out of the car. But when he was standing next to Ansel, he said, "Hold on. I want to get a pack of gum in the console." He turned and bent all the way over the front seat. When he reached for the pack of gum, he knew Ansel was watching him. So he arched his back and spread his legs. And when he got back up again, Ansel was standing there with his hands in his pockets, unconsciously tugging his penis.

"I'll park it in the back, where it's easy to get out," Ansel said, lowering his eyes and turning his head much too quickly so Milo wouldn't notice that he'd been staring at his legs.

"Thanks," Milo said. "I'll fix the awning while you do that."

Ansel couldn't wait to get behind the wheel and drive the car. Milo watched him put it in gear and turn the wheel with one strong hand. His hairy legs were spread wide, and his knobby right knee rested against the gearshift. (It would have been so easy to just bend over and pull down his zipper.) Then he looked into the rearview mirror and backed it out with one smooth, fast turn. He made it all look so effortless and normal. He slipped it into drive, hit the gas pedal hard, and sped to the back parking lot with a determined expression on his handsome face. He drove like a man should drive, and Milo stood there and whistled back while the car disappeared around a bend.

While Ansel was gone, Milo fixed the awning and then went inside the shop to wait for him. He came loping through the back door and asked, "Did you have any trouble with the awning?" He was tall and lanky, but he was a big boy. When he walked on the old wooden floor, the room shook and outdoor wind chimes clinked together.

"No problem," Milo said. "I should have parked out back to begin with. I only stopped in to get my paycheck." Then he turned his back to him and bent over the counter to look for his paycheck on the shelf where Ansel had said it would be. He spread his legs and stood up on tiptoe, arching his back and lingering far longer than he should have. He wanted Ansel to walk up from behind and grab his ass; he was the older one.

"It's still in the drawer," Ansel said, crossing behind the counter. He opened the cash register and pulled out a white envelope with Milo's name written across the front. "Here you go," he said.

"Thanks," he said, turning to leave.

"I'll see you tomorrow night, then," Ansel said.

"See you at six o'clock sharp," he said, slowly crossing to the back door. In a mirror above a display rack filled with small lamp shades, he could see the expression on Ansel's face. He was watching his ass the entire time. His hands were in his pockets, and his lips were pursed together as if he was about to whistle.

The next night Milo showed up five minutes late. He told Ansel he got stuck behind a very slow car, but the real reason was because he couldn't find his tight, low-rise jeans. The ones that made his ass bubble out like a big, round peach. He apologized three times, and Ansel waved his arm and said, "It's cool, dude. It's only five minutes."

It was raining outside that night, and the shop was empty. They organized a few boxes of new items, took inventory on the wind chimes, and dusted the scented candle shelves. When no one walked into the shop by nine, Ansel said, "How about we close up early and go out for a drink? I'm buying."

"Sounds good," Milo said. "Let's go up to Apple Jacks. I'll drive, and then drop you off here for your car on the way home." Apple Jacks was a redneck country bar about three miles upriver, where locals drank beer from the bottle and ate deep-fried food. But it was close and familiar, and Milo knew a few of the bartenders, so he never paid for drinks.

When they were out in the parking lot, Milo said, "Just be patient with me driving. I drive slowly on wet roads. I'm not the best driver in the world."

Ansel hastened to say, "Then let me drive. I'm a great driver."

Milo hesitated and pressed lips together; his grandfather had always told him to never let anyone else drive his car. But maybe that was because his grandfather had never had a hot guy like Ansel ready to take control. So he handed him the keys and crossed to the other side of the car. "I'm glad you're driving. I really hate driving in the rain."

Though Ansel was a fast, aggressive driver, Milo trusted him completely. He knew how to avoid holes and cracks in the road without jerking the car once. And even though he drove with one hand, Milo knew he was in control the entire time. When he came to a stop, he pressed the brake pedal with care and eased the car slowly so nothing would move. Milo noticed that he sat with his long legs wide open, as if pressing them together might hurt his balls.

They talked for a few hours, sipping one drink each, partly because they both had to get up early the next day, and partly because Ansel had learned his lesson about drinking and driving. "I was without a license for a year," he said. "I don't want that to happen again. Trust me, I learned my lesson the hard way, dude."

Then it became an expected routine on Tuesday and Friday nights. They would close the store, go out for a drink, and talk for hours. By the end of July, Milo was so eager to get into Ansel's pants, he couldn't think about anything else. So on a hot Friday night when Ansel dropped him off next to his car, Milo asked, "Would you like to come over to my place tomorrow night and watch that new vampire series? I have it all on DVD and haven't had time to see it yet."

"Hell, yeah," he said. "What time?"

He was off that Saturday, but he knew Ansel would have to stay there and close up the store. So he said, "Anytime after nine. My parents are away for two weeks, and I have the house all to myself."

"Cool. I'll bring beer," Ansel said.

The next night, he knocked on Milo's door a few minutes past nine, with a six-pack dangling from his left hand. He was smiling so wide, you could see his gums. And when he put the beer down on the center island in the kitchen, he shoved his hands into the pockets of his short pants and said, "You look good."

Milo thanked him and put the cold beer in the refrigerator. Though it was supposed to be a casual night, he'd taken a long shower, shaved his entire body, and splashed himself with his best cologne. And he was wearing tight, black shorts; a loose, white tank top; and the black boots with the higher heel. His tanned legs were smooth and shiny, and the shorts were so tight the back seam rode up the crack of his buttocks. He made sure that when he bent over to put the beer in the refrigerator, he took his time.

When he stood up again, he asked, "Did you eat dinner tonight?"

Ansel smiled and rubbed his flat stomach. "Ah, well," he said, "I actually ate a whole pizza at around six. I had it delivered. I'm a growing boy."

"Are you still hungry?" Milo asked. "I stopped and picked up this great chocolate cake this afternoon." He was starved to death. He hadn't eaten a thing all day, because he wanted to be thin and ready for anything . . . in case Ansel decided to make a move that night.

"Cool," Ansel said, "but let's go start the DVDs first, and have some later."

"You grab a couple of beers," Milo said, "and I'll get the TV ready."

The family room was off the kitchen. The walls were a soft brown, the fireplace was beige stone, and there were two long, red leather sofas that flanked a large square coffee table. And there was a nice-size flat-screen TV above the mantel. The only lamp he'd turned on in the room was small and muted with a dark shade. Milo put the first DVD into the player, and Ansel sat down on the edge of one of the red sofas. He was holding both bottles of beer, and he wasn't sure where to put them. There were two red leather club chairs, too, but when Milo stepped back from the DVD player, he sat down on the same sofa as Ansel. "This is a comfortable, casual room," he said, "so feel free to put your beer down on the coffee table and your feet up wherever you want."

When Ansel reached over to place the beer on the table, Milo added, "And I can put on another light if you want. But I like to watch in the dark."

"Me, too," Ansel said. Then he kicked off his sneakers and lifted his hairy legs onto the sofa.

The vampire series started out slow, which prompted them to make fun of the characters. They laughed and joked and drank beer, just two good buds hanging out together. By the time they'd each had three bottles of beer, Ansel adjusted his position on the sofa and unbuttoned his pants. Then he asked, "Do you mind if I rest my feet on your lap?"

"Go ahead," Milo said. But his heart started to be at faster and he didn't take his eyes off the TV screen. When Ansel's white socks were on his naked lap, he could barely take a breath. And he was terrified to move, because he felt the beginning of an erection.

They sat that way for another ten minutes, until there was a really scary scene that made Milo's entire body jolt forward. He screamed so loud Ansel almost choked on his beer. "Fuck, man," Ansel said, "calm down." But he was laughing so hard, he had to hold his stomach.

"It's not funny," Milo said. "This show is getting creepy, and I've got to stay here alone all night. I have an active imagination."

Ansel smiled, and then he patted his lap. "Come over here and sit between my legs," he said. "I'll protect you from the monsters." Then he lifted his feet from Milo's lap, bent his legs at the knee, and spread them wide so Milo could sit between them.

Milo turned and crawled up the sofa on his knees. He spread his legs a little and arched his back on purpose. Then he sat down between Ansel's big strong legs and rested his back on Ansel's chest. There was another scary scene, and Milo jumped again. That's when Ansel wrapped his strong arms around Milo's shoulders and pulled him back. When he did this, Milo gently placed his palms on

Ansel's hairy knees for support. He'd never touched another man's knees like this; he ran his palms up and down slowly and squeezed them a few times without saying a word. But the lines had been crossed by then; he knew this was more than just another night with his buddy.

"That feels good, man," Ansel said, holding him tighter.

So he started to massage them, pressing the tips of his fingers into his firm leg muscles. They felt so strong and solid; he wanted to sink his teeth into them.

A few minutes later, Ansel said, "Sit up for a minute. I have to adjust my dick, thanks to you. It's hard as a rock, and it's pointing down; my balls are killing me."

Milo stared at the TV, but his eyes widened and his mouth fell open. Then he sat up while Ansel reached into his pants and pulled his erection up so it would point toward his stomach.

When his dick was in place, he pulled Milo back against his body and said, "Ah, that's much better. Nothing worse than smashed balls."

Milo took a deep breath and leaned forward. When Ansel started talking about his balls, he couldn't control his urges a moment longer. So he stuck out his tongue and started to lick Ansel's hairy thigh. He'd wanted to lick those thighs since the first day he'd seen them. They tasted salty; he knew Ansel hadn't showered all day.

"Dude, you are so fucking sexy," Ansel said. "I've wanted to get into your pants since the first day you walked into the shop." Then he bit his neck and started to suck.

Milo threw his head back and said, "Then I should probably take my pants off for you." He could feel Ansel's erection sticking into his back. He wanted to reach back and hold the big thing in the palm of his hand.

A moment later, they were kissing and sweating and licking. Pants, shirts, and dirty sweat socks flew all over the room until both were naked. Ansel naturally wound up on top, and Milo submitted to having his back pinned to the sofa. His legs went up fast, and he rested his ankles on Ansel's shoulders. And when Ansel spit on his erection to lubricate it, he closed his eyes tight and clenched Ansel's biceps. He knew what was going to happen and he suspected it was going to hurt, but he wanted this more than anything he'd ever wanted in his life and he was ready for the pain. To have this strong, wonderful man inside his body made his bottom lip quiver. When Ansel pressed the tip of his penis to Milo's soft pink opening, he said, "Just relax, baby. I'll make you love this, trust me." It went inside slowly; he took his time and waited for Milo's hole to open completely. And he didn't start to rock and pound and slam with full force until Milo's toes curled and his eyes rolled to the back of his head.

After that, they did it again twice in Milo's bedroom. And when Milo woke the next morning and realized that Ansel's erection was poking him in the stomach, he reached down and wrapped his fingers around it. His legs were sore, his hole was raw, but he couldn't get enough of it.

Ansel moaned and stretched out his long legs. "That feels really good, baby. Keep playing with it. Play with my balls, too."

He'd wanted to hear words like this from a man for so long, his body had ached. So he went under the covers, opened his mouth, and swallowed it to the back of his throat. It suddenly occurred to him that Ansel had been so eager to tag him, there hadn't been time for anything oral. He'd never had another man's penis in his mouth; it tasted salty and tangy: really good. Ansel moaned and pulled the covers off so he could watch. Milo's cheekbones indented and his head started to bob up and down. He'd watched how it was done in porn flicks; his instincts took control. He didn't gag once, and when Ansel exploded he closed his eyes and took it all. And that tasted even better.

When he lifted his head again, his lips were puffy and red. Ansel reached down and caressed his face. "Are you okay? I hope I didn't get too rough with you last night."

He looked down and saw bruises on the backs of his legs. But he smiled and said, "I may not be able to walk today, but I've never been better."

"Are you okay with what we're doing?" Ansel asked. "I kind of feel responsible. I'm a little older than you are. But I really care about you; this isn't just fun and games for me."

Milo grabbed Ansel's balls and started to massage them gently. "I'm glad it finally happened," he said. "I wish it had happened a week after I started working for you."

"I have to get up," Ansel said. "I don't want to be late for work."

"Let's take a shower," Milo said. "I'll wash your dick for you."

When Ansel left for work, he kissed him good-bye. But they had a huge fight a few days later. Milo showed up for his paycheck on a Monday afternoon wearing tight shorts and a skimpy tank top again. He thought Ansel would like it, but Ansel wound up punching a hole in the wall behind the counter when he saw how another male customer was staring at his round ass. The guy was literally rubbing his hands together and licking his lips. Well. Ansel threw the stool across the counter and shouted pejoratives: "What's fucking wrong with you? You're not supposed to dress like that now that you're with me. It looks like you're wagging your ass for other guys to see, like a little slut. I don't walk around like that; it makes you look trashy. In case you haven't noticed, you're not supposed to be showing that ass off to anyone but me, man. You look like a whore."

Milo clenched his fists and stormed out of the shop. He wasn't trying to tease other guys; he'd only wanted to look hot and sexy for Ansel. He pulled away from the shop with such speed, the back tires of his old Mercedes screeched. If Ansel wanted to have temper tantrums and throw furniture around, then he was going to do it without Milo in the room.

For the next two days, he called in sick for work by leaving messages on the voice mail after hours. But late Wednesday night there was a knock on his door and Ansel was standing on the porch with a six-pack of beer and a box of cheap chocolate cupcakes.

Milo opened the door and asked, "Are you here to scream at me for wearing the wrong clothes?" He was still mad as hell. "Or are you here to call me names?"

Ansel shook his head and stared down at the doormat. "No. I'm here to apologize. I was wrong and I acted like a jerk."

Milo pressed his lips together and took a shallow breath. Then he said, "Come on inside." He couldn't resist his soft, easy eyes.

Ansel crossed through the door and placed the beer and cupcakes on a hall chair. Then he grabbed Milo by the waist and pulled him into his body and said, "I'm sorry, baby. But it drove me crazy when that other guy was staring at your ass. I'm an idiot, I know . . . but I love you. I never felt like this before about anyone. And it makes me crazy to think that another guy wants to tag you the same way I do."

Milo sighed. He couldn't remain mad at him long. So he rested his head on his wide chest and said, "I just thought you'd like the way I looked in those shorts. I wasn't trying to attract other guys. I only wore them for you." He spoke with his innocent, soft voice. The one he used when he wanted Ansel to feel stronger and more powerful.

Ansel reached down and slipped his hand down his pants. Then he squeezed his ass and said, "I did like it. But so did that guy in the shop, and probably all the other guys you saw on the way over."

Milo shook his head. "C'mon. My ass isn't that great."

Ansel slipped his middle finger into the crack and started rubbing the pink hole. "Ah, well, yes it is," he whispered. Then he slowly started to work his finger inside.

Milo arched his back and spread his legs wider. He said, "I hope you meant what you said about being in love with me."

"Why?" Ansel asked, shoving his entire finger into Milo's hole.

He sighed. "Because I think I fell in love with *you* the first day I saw you."

OUT-ISLAND CRUISING

DAVID HOLLY

THE WHITE BEACH went on forever, and sand scalloped down to the green shallows kissed by the Atlantic waves. Shells dotted the beach. Washed-up horseshoe crabs and starfish expired beside plumes of wild sea oats. The sky was a mold of gelatinous blue punctuated with white puffs.

Yet, I was bummed; I was eighteen years old, and my future looked grim. The hawkish establishment was pointing its talons at me. The ambitions of powerful men threatened my survival. Nonconformists faced destruction, disgrace, prison, death, or worse.

Such were the dismal prospects clouding my thoughts when I spied the boy leaning against the coconut palm. The curving trunk's shadow obscured his face, but he looked to be my age. He was decked out in the same swimsuit, a Lycra Speedo bikini in a tropical print dominated with purple and green. He had been watching the fishing craft manned by the native Bahamians, but he turned in time to catch me staring at his crotch.

A designing grin twitched upon his wide mouth. "What's your bag, man?" he asked casually.

Balling his ass was my bag—or vice versa. However, the year was 1967, I'd graduated high school just a month earlier, and I'd only experienced sex with one other boy—my best friend, Rick. Rick and I had spent our senior year engaging in a little kissing and jerking each other off. We didn't go any further down that road unless you count the night Rick and I scored some mind-altering pot and ended up giving each other sixty nine side by side.

Rick had greater inhibitions about being gay, but he was also more wrecked. He forcibly undressed me and pushed me down on my bed. His lips touched the tip of my cock, and his tongue slipped around the hood. His warm mouth closed around my dick, and I felt him going down my shaft. As he took me deeper, his thick boner jutted toward my eyes.

Before I could think, I kissed the helmet of his dick. Rick was sucking harder and varying his pace. I squeezed his helmet with my lips as thrills rushed through my dickhead. I sucked his helmet and let my lips slide down his shaft. His cock was only halfway along my tongue when I tasted thick syrup. Rick moaned around my dick as he came in my mouth. My ripples throbbed down my cock, and the spasm shook me. I was coming in Rick's mouth and swallowing his spunk.

Sadly, we only scored that pot the one time.

By the time I boarded an airliner bound for Nassau, Rick was in basic training. He came from an air force family, and his old man had seen to it that Rick shipped off only days after we graduated from South Dade High School in Homestead, Florida. Whether Rick's old man suspected that his son was fruity, I never knew. Rick's old lady suspected, because she once remarked that she favored rearing a soldier to spawning a faggot. They wasted no time getting their son away from me. For Rick there was never a question of "coming out." Not in a 1960s agricultural town dominated by Homestead Air Force

Base. Not in a nation rioting about race, battling for gender equality, rending itself over military conscription, and gambling its soul in Asia.

Although my sense of loss and betrayal waxed heavily in my thoughts as I stood on that Nassau beach, the stranger lounging against the palm tree was stacked, and his hair was dark black, almost bluish black, and his face was downright pretty. His Speedo left nothing to the imagination: he had sprung a boner.

"Your dick is up," I remarked.

He glanced down, surprised at my forthright statement. My own cock was swelling. I surveyed the beach, but no one was near enough to see our erections.

"So is yours, man."

I was so close I could have touched his cock. "I'm Tom. I'm from Florida."

"I'm Dove," he said, placing his hand on my arm. "From Ohio."

"Dove? Is that your real name?"

"*We* don't use our given names."

A light dawned. "You're a resister?"

"I graduated high school before I had to register. Before the draft board caught up with me, I hitched a boat ride, made some connections, and changed my name. Are you registered, Tom?"

"They got me in high school," I admitted. "On the morning of my eighteenth birthday, the principal called me to his office. Some birthday present—a gung-ho school counselor was ready with the Selective Service registration form. But I have a plan." I drew a deep breath. "If they call me in for a physical, I'm going to claim I'm a fairy. They don't want homos in their army."

Dove surveyed me from toe to top. "Don't kid yourself, Tom," Dove said. "Last year a boy from my high school went to his draft physical wearing his sister's panties and cheer-leader outfit."

"What happened?"

"They drafted him and hazed the shit out of him in boot camp. He was killed his first week in Vietnam."

"What a bummer," I said, beset with helpless outrage. "It was a setup."

Dove nodded. "I'm glad you're a fairy, Tom. I'm one, too. My old lady told me it's because a cow kicked me in the head."

"Is that what causes it?" I asked, going along. "There's a lotta cattle in Homestead."

"Then we both got kicked," Dove said joyously. "Oh, Tom, we're gonna have such good times." He grabbed my shoulders and kissed my lips lightly. The kiss shot through me like a thunderbolt. My right hand slipped behind his head. His raven hair was thick and slightly coarse with a touch of sea salt. I met his lips hard.

We kissed until we spied approaching tourists. Our war-ring tongues had left our cocks throbbing. "This friggin' island is too crowded with establishment thinkers," Dove said, flicking my erection. "You gotta come to Funky Town where you'll be safe."

"You're not hiding out in Nassau?" I asked stupidly.

"Not a chance. New Providence is filthy with rich gam-blers and tourists, the bastards profiting from the war."

"So what are you doing here now?" I asked.

"I came to score some supplies," Dove said, picking up a faded T-shirt and ragged cutoff jeans. "I have a little boat."

My heart broke to see Dove's bulging swimsuit disappear into the denim. However, his cutoffs were tight and showed his moon-shaped ass to its best advantage. After he dressed, I found the sea grape bush where I'd doffed my cutoffs and sandals.

✦

POSH TOURIST HOTELS hugged the beach, and beyond them lurked the casinos. The part of town where I'd been staying was quite different. Dove and I passed aged wooden houses brightly painted in primary colors, then faded into pastel tints. Many were hard to see behind the overgrown foliage blowing in blossom or bract: Royal Poinciana, jacaranda, trumpet vines, poinsettia, frangipani, hibiscus, bougainvillea, and croton. Some houses bore gris-gris charms. On one porch, three solemn children wore their clothes inside out. Their mother had recently died, so relatives dressed them to fool the mother's ghost when she returned to claim her children.

The scent of night-blooming jasmine still hanging heavy in the morning air, we walked to the guesthouse where I had spent the night. I had blown Florida with only the threads on my back and a duffel bag containing a few toiletries and my swimsuit. I grabbed my bag.

Dove was waiting around the corner. "Is it cool?" he asked anxiously. He had warned me that my landlady was a known police informer.

"She's satisfied. She screwed me out of five bucks."

Dove motioned me to follow. He had an enticing ass that I would have followed anywhere. We hurried down a shady street, lined on both sides with Royal Poinciana, which the natives called flamboyant trees.

"Don't freak out over anything you hear," Dove suggested. "We're going to church."

"Hanging with JC and the boys wasn't what I had in mind."

"That's where we score food we can't grow, toilet paper, medical supplies, and shit."

"Do they know we're draft dodgers?" I asked.

"Man, don't say draft dodger," he whispered, glancing around. "They know."

We turned down a street dotted with neat vegetable gardens and flower beds surrounding blue timber-frame houses with pastel pink, yellow, or green shutters and window frames. The yards were fenced with white pickets and trellises covered by bougainvillea with red, orange, purple, or yellow papery bracts.

The Island Gospel Church sat far from the Paradise Island casinos, tourist hotels, and golf courses. This rustic fabrication opened to the outside air on the leeward side, and bougainvillea with green-and-white variegated foliage and soft pink bracts climbed its whitewashed wooden slats. A woman dressed in a bright print island dress and sporting the incongruous headgear of a nun's habit rounded the corner.

"Hi, Sister Inez," Dove said.

"We were starting to worry," she said, her voice wary. She shot me a dubious look. I made to introduce myself, but Dove interrupted.

"This is Elf," he said, whipping a nickname out of his ass.

"Did anybody send you, Elf?" Sister Inez asked. Until that moment, I had not fully comprehended that I had lucked into the underground railroad for draft resisters.

"No," I said. "I just graduated high school. I don't want the government to send me off to kill men, women, children, and their household pets."

My answer satisfied Sister Inez. "I'm glad you're here, Elf. You can help with the supplies." She turned to lead us into the pastor's office.

"She's a real Catholic nun?" I whispered. "This doesn't look like a Catholic church."

"It's an Assembly of God," Sister Inez answered. She had fantastic ears. "Christians work together in the field—those with social conscience."

A tall, sandy-headed man of forty blew in. He looked us over before shaking hands with Dove and me. I had the distinct sense that he read us right down to our concealed swimsuits.

Sister Inez introduced me.

"Elf, I'm Jim Hunt. Call me Brother Jim." A chameleon ran up the leg of Brother Jim's khaki pants. He carefully cupped his hands, caught the reptile, and gently placed it on the branch of a red-blossomed hibiscus bush that was pushing its tendrils through the open window.

"Brother Jim, these boys shouldn't stay long," Sister Inez urged.

"You're right," he said, slapping his forehead. "Ike and Julius have loaded the Skuzz Bucket, but Sister Grace wants the boys to sample her key lime pie before they leave."

Sister Grace turned out to be Brother Jim's wife. While Dove and I were forking down two huge slices of her pie and washing the pie down with cold milk, she told us she was a Quaker. I wondered if she had influenced her husband, who was ordained by one of the more conservative Pentecostal churches, toward the peace movement. Whatever the case, these people changed my opinion of Christians. I'd been brought up in the Florida Bible Belt and had always considered Christians to be intolerant, racist, and downright mean. Brother Jim, Sister Inez, and Sister Grace were entirely different.

The Skuzz Bucket turned out to be a rusty Datsun truck. Dove and I climbed into the back for the short ride to the shore. We had to squeeze between a bunch of boxes filled with canned food, sacks of rice and noodles, toilet paper, and items of personal hygiene.

"Why was Sister Inez wiggin' out when she saw me?" I whispered.

"If the Bahamian fuzz caught the Christians aiding us, they'd get kicked out of the Bahamas."

"Do you think Brother Jim knows about us?" I asked.

"He knows we're evading the draft."

"I don't mean that."

"You're asking whether he knows you want my cock?"

"Yeah, among other things." I copped a feel of his butt. Dove stuck his ass out and gave it a wiggle.

"Brother Jim knows everything," Dove said. "Not that he gives a shit. He thinks that sin is sin, so our sucking cock is no worse than siphoning gas out of somebody's car. He cares about the harm people do. He doesn't think that people should kill—not for country, anything."

"Are we going to do that?" I asked.

"Siphon gas?"

"Suck cock."

His lascivious grin was brighter than the weird hot light of the Bahamian sun. "Have you ever sucked one?" he asked back.

I told him about my experiences with Rick, including the time we went down on each other. "Have you sucked cock, Dove?"

"I've done it all, Elf. I got laid at thirteen," Dove confessed.

"My Uncle Ralph, who was twenty, put the move on me. I was ready—I'd been teasing the horny bastard for months."

The Skuzz Bucket slowed with a high-pitched squeal as the worn-out brakes engaged. The two black cats, Ike and Julius, jumped out, and Dove led us to a twenty-two foot sharpie anchored just offshore. *Far Out* was crudely painted on the stern. *Far Out* had a cabin that slept two, a tiller rather than a wheel, and three dull red sails. Once we finished stowing the cartons from the Skuzz Bucket, I shook hands with Brother Jim, Ike, and Julius, and climbed into the cockpit.

✦

WATCHING DOVE'S CUTOFFS lift his butt while he raised the sails was a treat. I managed to steer our craft away from shore, but my eyes remained fixed on Dove's buns straining the denim as he bent. The prospect of sex with him filled my thoughts as the sharpie lifted, and we hauled ass over the surface. That I was committing the federal offense of draft dodging barely troubled my mind. Once we were underway, Dove pulled off his cutoffs and worked in his Speedo.

"Outta sight!" I commented. Keeping one hand on the tiller, I skimmed off my shorts and T-shirt. When he had the sails catching the wind, Dove patted the inside of my thigh, checked the compass, made a course correction, and sat down beside me. I touched his cock and pressed my lips to his. He kissed me lightly but lifted my hand from his cock.

"I hate to bring you down, Elf, but I gotta steer," he cautioned, putting the seal on my new name. "You can navigate. When we reach Funky Town, you can ball my brains out."

"Let's grab a quickie now."

"You see how calm the water is?" he asked, pointing toward the sandy bottom twenty feet below. "That can change." The bottom dropped out as we slid over a blue hole. It was vivid reminder that if we crossed the outer banks where the extensive shelf upon which the Bahama chain ends so abruptly, we'd pass over a canyon wall plunging one mile into the deep. There giant mantas, sharks, swordfish, and sailfish did their fishy thing, and no shallow bottom calmed the white foaming waves of the dark Atlantic. High ocean waves filled with sea monsters were nothing I wanted to brave in a twenty-two-foot sharpie.

Dove tacked near to the wind. He handed me the nautical chart and showed me how to read the compass. New Providence was already out of sight. The lonely expanse of greenish water filled the curving horizon. I was shocked when Dove mentioned that our trip would take seven hours.

"We're not going into the Gulf Stream?" I asked nervously.

"The Stream is off that way," Dove said with a gesture. "We'll be staying within the waters protected by Eleuthera and Cat Island. Our biggest danger is a summer squall. They spring up in the afternoon, and one would be a real bummer."

I shivered in spite of the hot sun piercing the water. However, the bottom was only thirty feet deep below, and the water was a shade of blue-green found only in dreams.

"Are there many cats on Cat Island?" I wondered.

Dove laughed. "Captain Catt was a pirate who hid out on the island when he wasn't running down merchant ships, slaughtering their crews, and kidnapping their cabin boys."

"What did he do to the cabin boys?"

"The pirates of the Caribbean were a homosexual brotherhood," Dove said. "They swore vows of sodomy. Buttfucking made them loyal to one another."

"So the cabin boys got prodded."

"Having a tight virgin asshole was a lifesaver."

"Should we get boarded by pirates," I suggested, "I'm not your crew."

"You're a cabin boy," Dove finished.

As I daydreamed about pirates and cabin boys, we passed a small island, hardly more than a sandbar. Beneath us swam colorful parrotfish that ate the coral, butterfly fish, angelfish, a scrawled cowfish, and one magnificent queen triggerfish— a psychedelic denizen of the salt water. It was glistening gold with blue stripes, and beautiful filaments trailed from its fins. We passed so close above a spotted ray that I stroked its back, and the creature shivered with pleasure.

No humans inhabited the tiny sand-covered bars of coral limestone, some lush with coconut palms and mangroves. Off the leeward edge of one island, pink with nesting flocks of flamingoes, Dove asked me to take the tiller.

"You want *me* to steer?"

"I gotta take a whiz." He pulled down his Speedo and pissed over the side. Treated to my first view of his thick cock and his naked half-moons, I turned the tiller too far and sent us flying toward the island. Two sand sharks separated as we passed over them.

"Elf, man," Dove admonished grabbing for a handhold. "You gotta steer straight." In my excitement, I'd nearly dumped him overboard. The remainder of our voyage consisted of one long sailing lesson.

Late in the day, an island unnamed on our nautical chart appeared. It was composed of a creamy sand beach surrounding twin hills that rose over a hundred feet. On the windward side, the beach ended in a long row of Casuarina pines, which made a ghostly sound as the wind whispered through their feathery needles. Small doves pecked at something in the sand, their little heads bobbing like toys. Behind the pines lay a dense jungle, and again a shiver rippled up my sunburned back.

As we rounded the island, the glow of the late sun illuminated a half-moon beach, awake with rustling coconut palm fronds. Bluffs stood behind the beach, dotted with coral grottos and caves. Frangipani scented the air. Dove leaped from the boat. As I handed him the anchor, I saw seven weird aquatic creatures bearing down on him. I shrieked a warning, but Dove greeted the monsters with delight.

"Elf, meet the ladies," he urged. The *ladies* were wild pigs that had swum out to meet us. Dove patted each bristled back and promised goodies once we had hauled the supplies ashore. When I dropped into the water, the pigs surrounded me, friendly as dogs.

By the time Dove and I had brought the first cartons to the beach, Funky Town's Flower Children were there to help. Most of these dope-smoking hippies were American boys avoiding military service. A few were as gay as Dove and I, some liked both sexes, and the remainder grooved on chicks. Nevertheless, even though most of the chicks had come with their boyfriends, nobody in Funky Town was straight. The Flower Children were peaceful people who dug one another's thing. As one head said, "Sex is a gas, man. Mouth, tail, or twat, it's copasetic."

A bare-breasted chick in a bikini bottom laid a wooden bowl of fried breaded conch with squeezed lime and two joints on Dove and me. We lit up and nibbled the appetizers while the Flower Children carried the cartons up the hill to the village they called Funky Town. The wild pigs crowded around as we smoked. We shared our conch fritters with the ladies and with a friendly iguana that sat on my bare foot.

We smoked the joints and tossed the roaches as if Mary Jane grew all around us. It turned out that it did. As we trudged up the hill, I saw tall marijuana plants blowing in the trade winds. The inhabitants cultivated vegetables and herbs, too, but the marijuana plants enthralled me.

On the encircling bluff stood Funky Town, a ramshackle jumble of dwellings constructed of driftwood and palm fronds. Funky Town presented a haphazard appearance, though some of the huts boasted decks and towers. Poultry wandered freely among the dwellings. One freeloading rooster begged scraps throughout the meal.

Rough picnic tables formed a rude communal dining area. No walls surrounded the tables, but a high roof of bamboo and palm fronds protected the diners from the frequent tropical rains. Nearly fifty Flower Children crowded their asses together at the tables. Kerosene lamps provided light. Those who had the weekly kitchen rotation served celery stalks, green onions, red peppers, lobster salad, mutton snapper, yellowtail, rice, pigeon peas spiced with thyme, and coconut bread.

As the stars filled the sky, we cranked up cigar-sized joints while "Some Velvet Morning" rasped from a battery-operated radio, followed by "Itchycoo Park." I was sitting beside Dove, smoking and listening to music. Around me rose the mewing cries of Funky Towners gripped in sexual extremity. I turned toward Dove. Our lips met. My cock swelled, and when I placed my hand on Dove's crotch, I found him ready.

"What's your bag, man?" Dove whispered lovingly, his hand rubbing my cock.

"Fuck my horny ass, Dove," I said, and licked his ear. "Give me my first butt fuck." Willing to oblige, Dove displayed a lubricant concocted from coconut oil.

"I'll do you the way my Uncle Ralph fucked me the first time. Stand up, hold onto that coconut palm, and stick out your ass."

My heart was beating fast as I followed his instructions. "Keep your legs wide apart," Dove commanded. We were already naked, so Dove had only to slick my asshole with his finger. The coconut oil was slippery on my asshole. I pushed to let him in.

"You must want it, Elf," Dove whispered. "You're opening your ass."

"Yeah."

"Stick out your ass as far as you can. I'm gonna push in my cock."

"Do it, man."

I felt a tremendous pressure in my ass, so I pushed hard against it. I felt the fullness of his cock and gripped the palm tree for balance. Dove pushed all the way into me, delightfully, painlessly, and exuberantly.

"Fuck me," I said.

Dove drew back and pushed. He banged me slowly, he banged me swiftly, he kept the pace. I could only push back my ass to meet him, but each thrust was wonderful. I felt a deep sensation, not just the delicious feelings produced in my dilated asshole, but something so deep that I could not describe it.

"What a show," shrieked one delighted Flower Child. "Look at the boys fuck."

Dove reached around and grabbed my cock with his lubricated hand. He started jerking me off, giving me a first-rate hand job. Rick had jerked me that way, and Dove knew every trick. All too quickly, I was committed to orgasm.

"I'm gonna come in your ass, Elf."

"I'm coming, too, Dove."

Deep spasms shook me as Dove's tight fist flogged my dick. My muscles contracted, tightening my asshole as the pleasure milked jets of come out of my cock. I saw my spunk arc and splatter against the tree. It continued until I stood shaking with Dove's hands still holding my dick and ass.

"I love you, Elf," Dove murmured in my ear.

"What a fuckin' view!" the chick shouted again.

✦

THE HENS PROVIDED eggs for breakfast, and we had wonderful pancakes. Most of what we ate we grew on the island or caught in the sea. We never speared the ladies, for they were family, but once we had to trap a feral boar that had gone apeshit-crazy. It was a bum trip, but after we killed him, we smoked him for four days and he provided a lot of tasty pork. Lunch often consisted of macaroni-and-cheese and shellfish. Rock lobsters were plentiful, along with grouper, red snapper, and yellowtail, not to mention the random green turtle. Conch was a daily staple.

Dove was the official master of the ship, so I became his mate. Once a month Dove and I made the long sail up to Nassau to pick up supplies. We would spend one day sailing to New Providence Island, sleep in the boat's cabin at anchor, and the next morning we would walk to the Island Gospel Church, then make the return trip. Additionally, we made frequent voyages to other islands to obtain driftwood or to explore.

One night after we had secured fresh batteries for the radio, we dropped tabs of Yellow Sunshine. Donovan was singing "Hurdy Gurdy Man." A squall had passed earlier, leaving the sky starless black. One of the chicks was into boys doing other boys, so she talked me into balling her while Dove impaled me. Even tripping, I was more into Dove's dick filling my ass than I was into the girl.

"I'm coming in your ass, Elf," Dove moaned, humping my butt hard, which got me off.

"You're making me come, too," I breathed.

"What a gas," the chick howled into the dreaming darkness. That experience was the closest I ever came to heterosexuality, but it wasn't that close.

We celebrated every holiday, and though the Christians helped support us, we thought of ourselves as pagan. We held colorful and raucous parades on New Year's, Groundhog Day, May Day, All Hallows' Eve, Yule, and a host of other holidays including the solstices and equinoxes. The community turned out, dressing in costumes designed from donated clothing, shells, coconuts, and lost feathers. We played homemade bells, drums, and tambourines; everybody smoked a ton of pot; and each festival concluded with a cluster fuck in the surf. We declared Valentine's Day Free Love Day, and each Flower Child shared pleasure, but Dove and I were only into each other.

Funky Town lasted for two years after I arrived, supported by our efforts and those of the far-off Christians. The work was always light, the food was always tasty, and the sex was always spectacular. The community's orgiastic revels by moonlight or under the sun never grew old.

We heard rumors of U.S. federal marshals sending undercover spies to root out draft dodgers, and of U.S.

Coast Guard cutters circling remote islands. Without warning one afternoon, a single-engine airplane flew low over our island. Cream's "Tales of Brave Ulysses" was playing on our radio while Dove and I were balling in a hammock stretched between two coconut palms. I had already shot my semen into Dove's ass. We had changed positions, and I had pulled my legs up so he could fill me face-to-face when we heard the approaching engine.

"Don't stop, Dove," I demanded, and he drove into me. I clearly saw the low-flying pilot's stunned expression when he witnessed Dove's tanned ass slamming up and down and realized that he was seeing two boys fucking. Squeezing Dove's cock with my asshole, I flipped the pilot the bird.

"What's he doing?" Dove demanded. His cock was massaging my prostate just right on every stroke. I tightened my legs around his ass pulling him deeper into me.

"Keep humping, lover," I urged.

Between the pilot's first and second pass, the residents of Funky Town bolted into the jungle or concealed themselves in the coral grotto. Nevertheless, our palm-thatched shacks were clearly visible. From such a low altitude, the pilot could have counted the chickens that scratched around town. Terrified by the noise, the ladies tore into the marijuana patch and destroyed the crop. That plane signaled our last day in paradise.

✦

BROTHER JIM PROVIDED us with forged Canadian passports and arranged passage on a trawler that dropped us off on a bleak shoreline below Halifax. We traveled across Canada, assuming various identities until we pretended

Canadian citizenship. My given name disappeared, and I became a new man.

I did not return to the United States when President Carter pardoned the draft refugees, nor did I ever write to my family. My passport proved that I was a native Canadian citizen, and I saw no reason why anyone would ever question my origins. I attended college, secured a doctorate in history, and ended up teaching at a college in British Columbia.

I made one journey to Washington, D.C. There I scanned the Vietnam War Memorial for Rick's name, hoping against hope that it wouldn't be there. When I did find it, my vision fogged with the tears filling my eyes. Rick had been killed in action in early September while Dove and I were butt-fucking among scampering lizards on the out-island beach.

As for Dove, we drifted apart during our sojourn in Canada. We tried, but we had forged our love under the hot Bahamian sun and our passion could not hold in the colder climes. I still have my old Speedo, but its pattern has faded away and the cloth tears to the touch. Sometimes I lift it from the tissue paper and stare at it in wonder. Beneath it, I find my Florida driver's license and draft card. Then I think of Dove and remember our great days in Funky Town.

A CLADDAGH DESTINY

STEPHEN DEE

VENICE, ITALY

"HAVING EARNED HIMSELF the billionaire status that so many aspire to, the world's eyes are focused on Italian tycoon Pablo Argentine to see what his next venture will be." Isabella Casini glanced up from the newspaper she was reading, arching her eyebrows beneath the Dolce & Gabbana sunglasses. "Not to mention how many other firms he'll put out of business in the process. My, the papers love you!"

Pablo snorted, lowering his own sunglasses slightly so he could get a proper look at some of the tourists who milled about St. Marco Square. "Look at them," he sighed, "so eager to enjoy the beauty of Venice yet never realizing that they are standing on a virtual *Titanic* both physically and economically."

Henry Buttamore, the only non-Italian at the table, spoke up: "Surely you exaggerate," he said in almost fluent Italian.

Pablo eyed him skeptically. He wasn't sure yet what to make of his childhood friend Sergio Piro's new British boyfriend. "Tourism is the biggest source of income this city has, but answer me, what happens when the tourists go away after their day trip here? Very few come to Venice to stay more than a day. If the tourist season suffers, then it cripples the city. With global warming, the water is rising and the city is slowly sinking, and there is little to be done to save her."

Isabella reached for his arm. "I know you love this place, but let's move on to the reason I asked you to join us."

He smiled wryly. "I thought it was for my stimulating company," he said, stretching his strong legs out before him as he rolled up the sleeves of his dark shirt.

"Stop gearing yourself up for a fight," Sergio mildly commented. "She has your best interests at heart."

Isabella reached across to grab his hand. "I know the perfect young man to set you up with. He's a Dutch politician, reasonably well off, lives in Amsterdam, but has a villa in Florence that he regularly visits."

"No!"

"Pablo, you don't date, you meet guys all the time, yet beyond a casual acquaintance, nothing. You're thirty-six! Don't you think it's time you thought of settling down?"

His hand automatically went to the claddagh ring he wore on a chain around his neck. Sergio pretended not to notice the action, but suddenly Pablo was conscious of it and quickly withdrew his hand. The waiter—a slender, dark young man—came over and, trembling, placed another set of drinks in front of them. His eyes moved furtively over Pablo's strong, broad frame, resting on the dark eyes that stared back at him. Stumbling from having been caught looking, he moved quickly away.

"Why won't you agree to meet with him at least once?" Isabella continued.

"Yes." Henry nodded enthusiastically. "Sergio and I could come with you if you wish and make it a double date."

Pablo was about to laugh when he heard a familiar accent he hadn't heard in over four years. He automatically turned, seeing three tall young men walk across the square, laughing and talking at the top of their voices.

"Pablo?" Sergio questioned.

He turned to their surprised expressions, finding himself equally surprised to discover he had risen out of his chair. Frowning, he glanced back at the three lads, who had stopped and were looking back toward his direction.

"Caspian," one of them shouted, "hurry on."

Pablo felt his knees tremble, and a cold sweat break across his forehead. It couldn't be . . . and yet how many other young men had that name?

Sergio, having also heard the name, had risen out of his chair. "Pablo," he gasped.

A slender young man with pale skin and rich, dark red hair came into view, his beautiful features obscured by the giant ice cream cone he was trying to eat. But Pablo knew the features by heart, and within moments was maneuvering his way among the tables, leaving his friends in stunned silence.

Licking his lips, he walked right behind the young man, his hand tentatively moving out. "Caspian . . ." he breathed.

The young man froze in midstep, and the ice cream slipped to the ground. Slowly he turned his aqua green eyes, large in his face as they met his, and suddenly for both of them the memories came tumbling back. . . .

✦

DO YOU EVER feel when a door closes behind you that your path has been set, that nothing you do in the moments that follow can sway you from meeting your destiny?

As an imaginative (and bored) young man, I get that feeling a lot, almost every time a door closes. From an early age I learned to live in a world of my own imagining. In it I would uncover some government conspiracy or traverse vast plains of unexplored territory while being chased by vampires or flesh-eating koalas. Always thrown into the mix would be a handsome stranger in the form of Indiana Jones-meets-Sean Connery's James Bond. He'd shield me from unseen predators while practicing a mystical and ancient form of martial arts and make love to me by fire-light without breaking a sweat. Somehow it would all end happily ever after. I was a big believer in that. I'd tame his roaming, roving bachelor ways and we'd live in a cottage with a rose garden by the sea. I wouldn't have a clue how to look after the roses, but then this is a fantasy, so they'd always be perfect. Every morning after drinking our tomato juice (yuck) we'd walk hand in hand along the beach while our dogs would race on ahead, delighted with the life they had found themselves with. We would be a typical Mills and Mills or Boon and Boon family.

Reality for me was quite different and very normal. I origi-nated/conceived—or as mother would insist, the stork brought me—into a loving, secure family. Okay, when I started borrowing my sister's cleansers, toners, and moistur-izers, there was the occasional bit of friction! But otherwise we are the typical suburban household of moderate means. My only bit of notoriety besides being gay was being chris-tened Caspian after my mother overindulged in *The Chroni-cles of Narnia* while I was forming over eight months (didn't quite make the nine). I grew from a little wee bundle of three pounds and four ounces to the slender five-foot-nine frame I now possess. My eyes are dark green, accentuating my auburn hair and pale, freckleless skin (I have to mention that because a lot of redheads suffer—and I emphasize the suffer part—from freckles). My first boyfriend had called me beautiful almost every day, my second had used the phrase "unusually attractive," the third had been more interested in my best friend, Louis, and the fourth was so far back in the closet his sentences were strung together like verbal diarrhea, falling apart before they left his mouth. So I was left with uncertainty about my looks—ginger pubes just weren't everyone's cup of tea!

I worked in travel and tourism in a small Dublin-based firm and was quite content in my position. Did I aspire to a life different from the one I was living? Well, I guess on some level most people do. Did I believe that something would happen to change my entire world? No, not outside of fantasies. I believed I could see exactly the shape that my life would take: I'd move from boyfriend to boyfriend, always finding faults, always making excuses to not commit for fear of loss, and I would never leave my job and be constantly in debt due to the annual summer holidays I would venture on with my friends.

However, destiny, fate, that big plan that's mapped out for us all, had a lot more curves to my shape than I realized and that form taken was like something right out of my fantasies. . . .

It began when I agreed to go on a short break in the south of France with my friend Helena and her new girlfriend, Crystal. I would be the third wheel (and mediator should things go wrong); it wasn't a position I was looking forward to, but the need to get away had outweighed any concerns I may have had. So with minor delays in Heathrow airport, we arrived in the small French airport of

Perpignan. Our destination was nestled on uneven slopes in the midst of the Pyrenees, a mountain range that provides the border between France and Spain—a village called Tautavel.

Narrow streets merge with narrow streets, climbing steadily into the hills. Houses of generally three floors with their various shades of yellow paint, brown shutters, and old stone line the streets. It has a quiet, almost sleepy atmosphere, as the town takes part in the general Spanish tradition of siestas. At night, Tautavel becomes almost silent save for the wind, which can be heard rising over the mountain like waves crashing on a distant shore, or the occasional bark from a dog frightened by something moving in the night shadows. Rising behind the town is a large rock face, lit up and casting more shadows. It was quite a contrast having come from the city of Perpignan that was less than a twenty-minute drive over the hills. With my flaming red hair and pale skin, I was instantly recognizable as someone who did not belong. I was a visitor, a stranger who for a few days would merge my life with the people of this town.

I was unaware as I settled into the lazy days ahead that I was not the only stranger staying in the town and that my quiet break would turn into a story right out of my fantasies. . . .

◆

I WOKE, AS it would seem I would do every morning while staying in the French village, to glorious sunshine and a wafting smell of pipe, a smell that wasn't unpleasant and stirred the senses to revel in a relaxed atmosphere of timelessness. Yawning and hearing movement downstairs, I quickly dressed and pushed open the shutters on my window. Across the road an old woman sweeping the path outside her door glanced up at me. I smiled but received no acknowledgment. It was my third day in the village, and I had come across the woman's path at least twice in every one of those days and she had yet to respond to my pleasantries. Amused, I descended the stairs.

"Morning, girls," I said to my friends as I walked into the kitchen and began cutting sandwiches.

"Morning," they responded in sync.

"How far up the road is the gorge?" I asked.

Helena shook her head. "We're not going to the gorge today."

"I know you're not. I'm going alone."

She frowned, glancing at Crystal, then back to me. "Don't you want to come into Perpignan with us?"

"No," I murmured, placing sandwiches and a bottle of water into a small rucksack. "I'm going to go back to the gorge and take some pictures."

"Well, if you wait till the evening, we'll go with you. It will be nice and cool then."

I zipped my bag shut. "No, thanks, you lovebirds go to the city and I'll see you back at the cottage later."

"I don't think you should be wandering around alone," Crystal halfheartedly interjected.

"No, you shouldn't!" Helena cried. "You only have a small amount of French, and it's a strange landscape. Anything could happen!"

"Okay, girls, look, I'm not a child. I'll have my phone with me in case I get into trouble. No more arguments."

I swept past Helena, meeting Crystal's relieved gaze. I knew that she wanted to spend some time with Helena on her own so she could determine whether or not they had a future together, whereas Helena seemed to be holding onto me as if I were a lifeline. I had tried to explain to Crystal that it was Helena's first relationship and she was just nervous, but I could see her patience was wearing thin.

Opening the cottage door, I stepped out into the midday sunshine, instantly breaking out into a light sweat. Redheads weren't built to survive high temperatures. I walked slowly through the village, avoiding the curious gazes of the locals by pulling a pair of dark shades over my eyes. Once past the hinterland restaurants, I quickened my pace along the relatively flat valley road until soon gently sloping fields of grapevines rose steadily; they embraced the rocky mountain terrain that surrounded me. Ahead, another part of the enclosed mountain valley reached for the heavens, and it was between a break in those hills that the gorge had been forged. Leaving the main road, I descended along a small dirt track till the sudden burst of trees dispersed, revealing a glistening lake, and from the crack in the mountains a river flowed filling the lake with clear, fresh water.

No one else appeared to be at the gorge, and I gladly removed my rucksack from my sweat-stained T-shirt, though having anticipated that, I changed into a spare crisp white T-shirt that matched the three-quarter-length white shorts I wore. Kicking off my sandals, I stepped out into the cooling fresh water. I stretched my arms up, basking in the beautiful day and breathing in the scents of pine that floated in the air.

A sudden splash sent my heart racing, and I glanced up toward the deeper end of the gorge. On a flat outcrop of rock I spotted a bundle of clothes. Suddenly the water in front of me erupted as a bronzed body burst through the surface. I stumbled back and almost lost my balance.

He stood waist deep in the water about five meters away from me, his broad shoulders glistening with sparkles of water, the dark hair on his chest clinging to his well-toned body. Running his hand through his thick black hair, he grinned at me.

"*Bonjour*," he called.

"Hello," I stammered, blushing. Then, seeing him frown, I remembered where I was. "Oh, I mean *salut*. No that's informal, shit . . . *Bonjour*!"

His white teeth flashed once more. "I speak fluent English and while it would probably be amusing listening to you stumble over your words, I won't put you through that."

I smiled back. "I'm Caspian."

He moved toward me, more of his body coming into view. He wore dark swimming trunks that hugged his masculine form. I tried to avert my gaze as his hand gripped mine in a firm handshake. "As in Prince of Narnia?" he inquired.

I grimaced. "I think that's where the inspiration came from."

"I am Pablo."

My eyebrows arched. "That's not French, is it?"

"No, I am Italian. I am here on holiday, as I guess you are."

"Yes I'm staying in Tauteval."

His grin widened. "What a coincidence, me as well."

I blushed, suddenly knowing this wouldn't be our only encounter.

✦

PABLO SMILED BROADLY, feeling his stomach tighten. "You look beautiful."

Caspian's skin flooded that deep embarrassed red that so often happened and which Pablo found very appealing, especially as he remembered it briefly during sex.

Caspian moved into a stilted embrace. "My god, this is incredible, meeting you like this."

"I know, what brings you to Venice?"

"I've always wanted to come here, especially after you singing its praises all those years ago. It just took me a while, but you were right; I can't imagine a city ever coming close to this."

Pablo shook his head, closing his hands into a fist to stop himself from reaching out and running his hand down Caspian's face. "How long are you here for?"

"Five days. We've just traveled up from Florence and before that Rome, so we plan to tour a bit. You know how I like that."

Pablo smiled. "I remember our trip to Carcassonne and how I made love to you when we got back."

Caspian laughed nervously. "Yeah—" He paused, his smile fading as his gaze fell on the claddagh ring. "You kept it," he gasped.

"You gave it to me," Pablo said, noticing the sudden rapid movement of Caspian's eyelids as he tried to gain composure.

"I didn't think I meant that much to you," Caspian accused.

This time Pablo did reach out and gently cup his chin. "I didn't believe at the time that you did; you were a summer holiday fling, one of many and yet I have never forgotten you. I've traveled so much and always wished you were there with me. I'm sorry I hurt you; you need to know that."

"Caspian," his friends called.

"Please have dinner with me," Pablo pleaded. "Tonight. I'll meet you here at seven o' clock."

Caspian frowned. "I don't know, I can't deal with you, you're too—"

"Please, I'll be here waiting whether you come or not."

He nodded. "I'm not promising."

Pablo winced, hearing his own words thrown back at him. "I deserve that. I'll wait half an hour. . . ."

✦

I STRETCHED OUT on the flat rock, suddenly conscious of the Italian's gaze moving across the length of my slender frame. "What brought you to Tauteval?" I asked, reaching for more sun cream to slather on my pale skin. His eyes seemed intent on watching my actions as I lightly rubbed factor 50 into my skin.

"I needed a break. Tauteval was my family's summer destination growing up. We had an uncle living here whom we used stay with. That house is of course long gone, but I had good memories of this place and wanted to return."

I smiled, meeting his penetrating black eyes. "And has it lived up to the memory?" I asked.

He nodded, shifting position so he could lean on his side, and it seemed to me, inch closer to my side. I felt my skin heat up, and it had nothing to do with the sun. He reached out and gently began to rub a small clot of white sun cream that I hadn't smoothed out into my skin in a circular motion. "Tell me, Caspian, what goes through your mind when your skin reddens as it is now doing?"

I moved away from his touch, and he casually withdrew his hand. "You make me nervous," I stated, deciding honesty rather than games was the best policy.

The corners of his mouth turned upward. "I don't mean to make you nervous. I thought I was being friendly. In what way do I make you nervous?"

I sat up, frustrated, feeling suddenly like he was laughing at me. "It's getting late. I should be heading back for dinner."

His hand shot out and gripped my arm. I felt a slight tremor of fear as I suddenly realized how isolated I was. He seemed to sense me tense and let go. "Please have dinner with me tonight; there is a lovely restaurant just on the edge of town. I will meet you on the bridge at eight."

I felt my heart jolt. "Hhmm," I stammered, not even knowing why I was hesitating.

He leaned closer, his hands cupping my face. "And just," he whispered huskily, "so we are both clear on where we stand." His lips pressed softly against mine, his top lip pushing hard against my lower lip, his tongue moving against mine. My hand tentatively pressed against his chest and he moaned softly, which increased my daring exploration of his body. He pressed himself against my body, the straining desire in his dark Speedo very apparent. Our tongues clashed and he gently began sucking on mine, pulling me further into his mouth.

Gasping, I broke the kiss, my eyes meeting lustful dark ones. "We're clear," I murmured.

He laughed, a deep, throaty sound that made my legs feel weaker than they already did. "Then, my beautiful Irish prince, I will see you on the bridge at eight."

✦

ISABELLA CASINI MOVED through the large conservatory and out onto the wooden decking that overlooked the Venetian Lido where the lagoon met the sea. In the distance, she could see the beginnings of Venice. It was a spectacular view, one that could have only ever been commanded by a man as rich as Pablo. He sat quietly sipping on a cocktail Sergio had made up before he and Henry had left, promising to ring in the morning and find out how the dinner had gone. She sat opposite him, watching him carefully. He seemed ill at ease, excited yet nervous, apprehensive but energized.

"Who was that young man back in the square?" she asked. "I have never seen you like that before!"

He shrugged. "It is a long story."

She shifted position and set down her own drink. "I'm staying here for the moment, remember? I have time for a long story."

He rolled his eyes and sighed. "Last Christmas, you accused me of being coldhearted after I finished it with Giuseppe."

"You only gave it a month and broke up with him two days before Christmas," she interrupted.

He smiled, enjoying her defensive tone. "He was a sponger, Bella, only interested in what I could buy him. Don't get me wrong, he made up for it by being very adventurous in bed."

She flushed. "Fine. Get on with your story."

"Four years ago after Mama died, I went to the one place her memory was strongest, the French village of Tauteval. While I was there I met Caspian, the young man you saw today in St. Marco Square. I guess you could say I fell in love for the first time, yet at the time I couldn't see it, and I broke him. . . ."

◆

HELENA STEPPED BACK from the sizzling frying pan, grimacing as the oil still continued to spit threateningly at her.

"The oil is too hot, Heli, turn down the heat," I commented, glancing back to my reflection, pulling strands of my hair across other strands in a crisscross pattern. "Do you think the green shirt is too much?"

She inched closer to the pan, her gaze briefly sweeping toward me. "You look lovely. I can't believe we go to the middle of nowhere and you still manage to find a man."

"It's great," Crystal interjected, coming down the stairs after her shower, still in a bathrobe.

I smiled, knowing that bathrobe wouldn't be staying on long once I was out the door. "He's very enigmatic. I'm drawn to him yet nervous; he seems very experienced and I'm not sure if I'll know how to satisfy him, if," I started to stammer, "I . . . don't come home tonight."

"You'll know when you satisfy him, Caspian; it will be all over some part of your body."

"Crystal!" both Helena and I protested. Laughing, she slipped her arms around her girlfriend's waist. Taking one last look at myself in the mirror, I decided it was time to take my leave.

Nervously I wandered through the dimly lit village toward the sound of the river. He was already standing on the bridge when I rounded the corner, his gaze turned toward the darkening mountains beyond. Rubbing my palms on the light linen pants I wore, I tried to approach with confidence I wasn't feeling.

He was wearing dark slacks and a white T-shirt underneath a short-sleeved dark shirt. His broad, muscular frame was very evident in the tightness of his clothes. He leaned toward me and lightly kissed me on the mouth. "It's not far," he stated, leading the way up the hill.

The restaurant had low lighting and candles on every table. Nearly every table was full, and we didn't stand out like I imagined we would have if the restaurant had been empty. He ended up translating the menu for me as my poor French could only decipher every third or fourth word, and when the waiter came to take our order, he ordered for both of us, saving me any embarrassment.

"You look lovely," he commented, moving the candle to the side so it didn't stand between us. I blushed, hating the slow smile that crept across his face. "You could never be dishonest, could you? Your face would give you away!"

I shrugged. "If someone let wind go on the opposite end of a room, I'd go red and get even redder at the thoughts of people thinking it was me, making me in fact look more guilty. Fair skin is a curse."

He chuckled. "Great, if I need to break wind, then I'll just let it rip and blame the redhead."

I grinned back, allowing him to reach across the table and take my hand in his. A few cursory glances were thrown our way, but none lingered. "So, Caspian, tell me what you want."

I frowned, momentarily pondering the question. "I guess to be loved; isn't that what everyone wants?"

He looked startled by my answer and remained unsettled for the next twenty minutes as we delved into our starters. He had opted for the French snails in garlic butter. It was a lucky thing I liked garlic since I would probably end up getting personal with his breath. I had chosen a homemade French pâté, which melted into my mouth. He frowned and, placing his plate to one side, reached across to look at what dangled from the chain around my neck. "What kind of ring is that?"

"Claddagh. I can't wear rings on my fingers, so I wear it around my neck."

He studied it carefully. "I must get one. It is very lovely."

I reached around and unclasped the chain and handed it to him. He looked at it, puzzled. "It's yours," I murmured. He started to protest, but I placed it firmly in his hand. "It's the least I can do when you're paying for dinner. When you meet the one you fall in love with, then you must give it to him. A claddagh is not meant for just one person but to be shared between two hearts."

"Thank you, although I can't help wondering what you will do when you meet the man you fall in love with."

I smiled. "I have about a dozen of them; they are, after all, an Irish tradition."

"I will wear it like you do," he said, placing it around his neck and fastening it.

My heart began to race. . . .

✦

FIACHRA MONROE SAT down beside Caspian on the small wooden jetty behind their hotel. He took off his sandals and dangled his feet in the cool canal waters as Caspian was doing. Caspian smiled. "You know when a gondola passes, a trail of rubbish follows it? It's very sad, actually, but then when rubbish is collected by boat, some of it is bound to slip in."

Fiachra took his feet out of the water as a gondola passed, waving at the overexcited Asian tourists on board. "So have you decided if you are going to meet this guy or not?"

Caspian pursed his lips in indecision. "I don't know, and his name is Pablo, Pablo Argentine."

Fiachra's eyes widened. "The millionaire real estate tycoon?"

"Yep, the one and only. Of course I only found all that out after the fact."

"The fact?"

Caspian kicked some water into the air. "We were lovers for a short time—six days, exactly. There has never been another man who has excited and stimulated me the way he did. He was gentle, he was rough, he made me aware of my body in terms I never knew of. Somewhere in those six days I fell in love with him, and he knew it, too. He knew I would have done whatever it took to stay with him."

"What happened?"

Caspian laughed bitterly. "I don't know why he decided he had to hurt me, but he arranged a picnic at a gorge that we had met at previously. He was going to meet me on the bridge outside town, and we'd walk over there. He never showed, and I tried ringing him, and his phone rang out so I thought maybe I had it wrong and that we were going to meet at the gorge, so I walked over there." Caspian frowned at the memory. "He was there in the water fucking another guy. I knew as he saw me that he had meant it to happen that way. I think he didn't want any misunderstanding about what had happened between us; he didn't want me returning a lovesick puppy. I stared at him, and my world crumbled. I had shared so much with him, and I felt used. He started to apologize, that he wouldn't ever change, and I just walked away, defeated, my heart broken. He tried to talk to me afterward but the girls wouldn't let him near me. He even showed up at the airport, and the thing about it was he genuinely looked upset. He tried to give back the claddagh ring, but I threw it back at him. I told him it was a good thing we lived so far away from each other, that I would never have to see him again."

Fiachra put his arm around Caspian. "Yet here he is. Please tell me that you are not going to meet him after what he did to you."

Caspian stared across the canal at the opposite walkway. "He loved this place so much, it was in his voice when he spoke about it. He lives just outside Venice, somewhere by the coast. I knew all that, Fiachra, when I came here, so, you see, I think on some subconscious level I wanted to see him again, even," his voice broke slightly, "even . . . if just from a distance."

"Why?" Fiachra exclaimed. "How could you after what he did?"

Caspian pulled his legs out of the water. "Because he made me feel alive, and I haven't felt that way in four years, since I got on that plane and left him behind."

"Caspian—"

"Shh, Fiachra, I know I shouldn't go meet him; I just need to convince my heart of that. . . ."

✦

"WOW," I EXCLAIMED for the third time, gazing up at the walled cité of Carcassonne. "It's amazing."

He took my hand and led me up toward the main gates. "It's geared for tourism now, most of what was real is gone, much like your own Bunratty Castle and Folk Park."

"You've been to Ireland?" I questioned eagerly.

He nodded. "Yes, I started off up at the Giant's Causeway in Northern Ireland." They walked through the cobblestone entrance into the main part of the walled cité. "And finished my tour in a town called Cobh in the southeast."

I nodded, gazing in disappointment at the sudden cluster of shops. Tourist trap was right, although it still held a kind of charm. "I know Cobh," I said. "Well, I have relatives there. Imagine, we could have been there at the same time and never known each other."

He laughed. "You imagine the strangest of things. My mother liked Carcassonne. Every summer as children this was our day trip outside of Tauteval."

"Are you and your mother close?"

He let go of my hand. "We were. She died last month."

I was about to offer my condolences when he said he would get us an ice cream and disappeared into the shop. When he came out I felt the moment had gone to offer my sympathies so I kept quiet. We walked in among the twisting cobblestone streets, gazing in the windows of the medieval-decorated shops. I exclaimed my delight at a few trinkets in the windows, and each time I did, much to my chagrin, he bought them for me. It took us nearly an hour and half to drive back, and once there he drove us to his apartment.

He was kissing me before we even had his front door open; our clothes were gone by the time we had the bedroom door open, and from there I gave myself to his expert lovemaking.

Day three from the moment I met him dawned once again bright and sunny.

"I'm sorry about your mother," I said, pressing my naked body against his. "You should have mentioned it earlier."

He shifted in the bed so his arm slipped underneath my head. His breath was now hot on my cheek. "I wasn't going to mention it at all, but I seem to want to tell you things. Why is that? I'm usually a more private person."

I grinned. "Even with those you exchange bodily fluids with?"

"Especially those!"

I frowned. "Have you never been in love, Pablo?"

He shook his head, stiffening slightly. "And you?"

I shrugged, moving to gently nip his nipple. "I thought maybe once or twice, but who's to say what love is? Aren't there supposed to many degrees of love?"

His mouth sought mine, his hand tentatively leading me to his crotch. He was hard and warm in my hand. "That's what I know to be real," he whispered, moving on top of me, his mouth silencing any further conversation. . . .

✦

PABLO ARGENTINE WAS used to getting his own way; he was used to manipulating people, convincing them his way was the only correct one. He never succumbed to emotions that could weaken him, save for the moment his mother died. That had sent him on an emotional journey to memories of more innocent times and had led him to an encounter with a beautiful Irish redhead. From that moment on, he could never quite assess his feelings for Caspian. Had he actually fallen in love? Is that why he had been so callous toward him, because he didn't want the weakness, or had his emotions just been in overdrive after his mother's death? In those four years since Caspian had walked out of his life, he had thought of him at some point every day. Could you really be in love with someone after one week? The truth, as he had gradually discovered, was that he had fallen in love with Caspian, that was why he had hurt him so bad by arranging to have Caspian find him with another guy—because he wanted to hurt Caspian for making him fall in love. It had, as he had expected it to, driven Caspian away, but what he hadn't expected was a new onslaught of grief and loss. He didn't know where the empty feeling in the pit of his stomach came from and why it wouldn't go away.

Now that feeling was intensified as he paced up and down St. Marco Square. Lanterns had been lit, and several small bands of classical music began playing by different cafés. Would he blame him for not turning up; could he actually expect forgiveness? He walked toward the church and turned his gaze, casting it out across the dark waters of the lagoon and the bobbing tied-up gondolas as a slightly chilly evening breeze ruffled his shirt.

A slender figure became silhouetted against the horizon. He knew the shape perfectly and felt his heart begin to thud. Caspian walked uncertainly toward him. Around them the classical bands were reaching their crescendo. The waves from the high tide on the lagoon were splashing over the walkway. Slowly Pablo unlatched the claddagh ring and held it out. It seemed to catch the light from the stars as they began to appear in the sky.

Caspian frowned. "I don't . . ."

"You said once that I was to give this to the one I loved because a claddagh was meant for two shared hearts. I can't think of anyone I have ever loved aside from you. That week of my life affected the rest of it, and you weren't even here. Please give me a second chance and I will spend the rest of my days trying to make you happy."

Caspian felt his breath catch and, trembling, held out his hand. "Don't promise me anything yet, Pablo. Let's just wait and see what happens."

Pablo's hands closed around his as the orchestras reached their pinnacle to die down to rapturous applause. Two silhouettes moved slowly away, hand in hand, becoming swallowed by the dark Venetian lanes.

✦

CRYSTAL WANDERED INTO the kitchen, a letter in hand. "For you, Helena," she said, placing the Italian post-marked envelope into her girlfriend's hand.

Helena grinned. "Another letter from Caspian. God, in the two years he's been out there I could start a library!"

She tore open the envelope. Crystal turned on the oven to get it hot for the roast she was going to make. "What does he say?" She turned around when Helena didn't answer to find her girlfriend weeping quietly. "What's wrong?" Reaching, she took the letter from her hand.

✦

Dearest Helie and Crystal, you are cordially invited to the wedding of Pablo Argentine to moi, real invitation to follow shortly. It will be held in Canada with a further blessing at our home in Italy, all expenses paid so you can't refuse. He asked me last week on bended knee, my own legs gave way and, facing each other, I was reminded of the first time I saw him crashing out of the water in a place that isn't even on a map. I pondered on that and how we met again and realized it was always meant to be, that way. I was too young and idealistic when we first met. I would have driven me bananas, not to mention Pablo, but now the time is perfect. I get my happy ever after.

SOARING WITH A HAWK

KENN DAHLL

DAILY LIFE ON the American frontier at the beginning of the nineteenth century was at best tedious. Pa homesteaded our little farm twenty years ago. A year later he returned to Chicago and married Ma, a schoolteacher he'd been courting for two years. I'm the eldest of six siblings, born less than a year after the wedding. Pa and I, along with two of my brothers, built a nice place on the property. It's still a little cramped, and in nice weather I prefer to spend nights in the log cabin Pa originally built and in which the family lived until the farmhouse was built.

Privacy was a problem, especially since I and two of my three brothers have reached what Ma called "puberty," which she says accounts for our limited body hair and some pretty strange goings-on in our private parts. Pa gave us each a lecture on onanism and respecting girls, but until some of the events of this narrative, I was still not certain how it all worked. All I knew was that sometimes that part of me from which I pissed would become inflexibly rigid, and some mornings I awoke with it both hard and covered with a white sticky substance. I'd clean it up and never told Ma.

Before I turned eighteen, I had discovered that placing my hand on my male member felt pleasantly warm. I very slowly moved my palm up and down the hard shaft. The excess of skin which usually hung off the end permitted easy movement. Soon a juice leaked from where my piss usually flowed and my shaft became slippery, especially when I rubbed my palm over the bulbous tip. Only with great restraint did I refrain from yelling when a white creamy substance erupted from the little slit.

Once the weather warmed up, I slept in the cabin. It was a half mile from the farmhouse and had its own outhouse. I had the privacy to freely coax my juices to flow. My insatiable curiosity led me to taste them once. They were a blend of sweet and salty. I grew to savor the tangy flavor. My privacy ended after a year when Zeke, who had just turned seventeen, convinced Pa he should use the cabin, too. He was set up in the main room in the front section while I moved into the smaller, but more secluded, back room.

Early every Sunday morning the family got into the horse-drawn buggy and drove ten miles to attend church services. Because of the demands of the farm animals, Pa would stay behind until I was old enough. Then we took turns. The number of us alternating Sundays increased once Zeke could handle the chores alone. However, he got sweet on one of the Whitmore girls and often asked me to take his place. Sunday was the only day he could talk with her, as we were homeschooled by Ma. Since I wasn't interested in any of the local girls, I agreed, giving me two of every three Sundays to pursue my favorite activity.

One summer Sunday as I languidly lay under a large tree, bare-assed and leisurely stroking my hard shaft, I heard a twig snap. I stood and turned toward the sound to find myself face-to-face with an Indian youth. I wasn't afraid, as the natives in the area were peaceful. This particular brave was about my age. His long black hair was held back in braids, and he had less hair on his chest than the few stray blond strands I grew. He wore a buckskin loincloth which went between his legs; the front and back of the leather material hung over a cord that went around his waist. His high cheekbones and large black eyes gave him a dignified handsomeness. I was so caught up studying my visitor, I forgot I was more naked than him and that my penis was hard.

"Young white man has a warrior's lance," the Indian said with a glance at my privates.

"I wasn't expecting company," I said boldly, trying to rescue myself from the uncomfortable situation.

"Sorry, but not really sorry," he replied ambiguously. "My weapon too is ready for battle."

"What do you mean?" I asked, confused by his response.

"My English is not so good. Can I show you?"

"Yes," I said hesitatingly, not knowing what I was agreeing to.

The brave moved closer to me, so close that, as we were the same height, my rigid appendage was poking the front panel of his loincloth. I could feel his "weapon" through the leather, and it was indeed "ready." He placed his hands on my broad shoulders, then let them roam all over my upper body, which by then was quite muscular by dint of the hard farmwork. When he bent forward and ran his pink tongue over my tanned chest, I moaned softly. Then he licked my burgundy nipple, and my moaning became louder. My legs got weak, and the young brave lowered me onto a bed of soft grass, where he joined me.

Reclining next to me with our bodies touching from shoulder to hip, he surprised me by placing his lips against mine. Soft lips, insistently pressed against mine, caused a dizzying sensation in my feeble brain. Without thinking, I hugged him closer to me and pressed back on his lips. He hugged my body even closer, and his hands explored my back before they drifted down to cup my melonlike ass globes. Nobody but nobody ever touched me there since I was an infant.

I couldn't resist reaching down to feel his leather-clad butt cheeks. They were unexpectedly firm yet supple. My newfound friend grunted as I massaged his butt. He rolled over on top of me and sat up on my thighs. Then he reached to his waist and untied the cord on his leather garment, which fell open, uncovering his very large and hard organ, the same reddish brown as his skin. The tip of his shaft, however, was a deep burgundy, much deeper than even my nipples. Only a few black hairs were visible at the base of his shaft, and a few more adorned the bag with his male eggs, which hung down below his penis. There was some loose skin at the tip of his pole, but it didn't hang off the end like mine did, even when it was its most rigid.

The Indian lad smiled broadly, displaying remarkably white teeth as he held our two manly rods next to each other. His was longer than mine, about a hand's breadth in length, but not as fat. When he placed his hand around my member he couldn't touch his fingers with his thumb, as he demonstrated he could do with his own pole. He used both hands in the experiment and left the hand holding onto me in place as he reached between my thighs and fondled my ball sac. "Christ!" I yelled—the first expletive of my eighteen years. "Please let go or I will soil your hands."

"That is my plan," he replied cheerfully as he moved the one hand up and down my tool.

"I like to see the sheath on your weapon cover and uncover its top. I want to see what happens when your man-seed is expelled."

"Damn, that feels mighty fine!" I wanted to show him some pleasure, too, so I reached out and grasped his slender lance and fondled his hanging pouch.

"Yes, pretty white boy. That feels very good. Let us mingle our life fluids and become fast friends." For several minutes we held each other's privates. The only sounds other than the customary forest noises were our grunts and groans, which became louder and more frequent as our caresses turned to stroking and squeezing. To the accompaniment of a loud bird cry, we both sprayed forth our creamy gravy. Then, laughing like two little boys, we made our way to a small pond on the creek running through the property, dove in, and rinsed off. Sitting on a boulder in the sun to dry off, we exchanged names—Aaron and Soaring Hawk. "Nontribal people usually call me Hawk," he said. "I like it."

"Then Hawk it is. I like it too, and I like you. Will you visit me again?"

"I want to share my body with you and enjoy yours many more times," Hawk replied.

Two weeks later he was at the cabin as soon as Pa and the rest of the family were out of sight down the dirt road. We kissed and hugged. However, when I reached to stroke his weapon, Hawk held my hand back. "No, this time I give your lance the gift of many tongues." He squatted on the ground, took hold of my rigid male member, and licked at the tip.

"Good God!" I swore. "What are you doing?"

"Tasting of your life force." He flicked his tongue over the sensitive tip and along the sides. He even prodded beneath my loose foreskin. I was dancing from the multitude of sensations, and sweat poured down my hairless chest and from my underarms.

"God damn!" I yelled when his mouth covered the tip of my shaft. "Holy shit!" was my response as more and more of its hardness disappeared between his luscious crimson lips. I stared in amazement when his chin rested against my ball sac. My entire member was not just in his mouth, it descended into his throat. Hawk applied a sucking pressure and pulled his lips back until only the tip of my tool remained in his mouth. Then he dropped his lips back down to the few blond hairs I had at the base of my rod. Before he repeated this too many times I couldn't hold back the torrent of juices bubbling up from my balls and flowing into his throat. I could barely breathe let alone speak as I retracted my shaft from his mouth and collapsed on the ground. The Indian brave sat next to me and held me tightly as I recovered from the earth-shaking experience.

Being eighteen, I recovered quickly and insisted I give him the same gift. Hawk leaned against a boulder. I knelt between his legs and tried my best to emulate his actions. Imperfect as I'm sure I was, I succeeded in drawing a geyser of his warm, tangy juice from his long, thin weapon. Pleased with my efforts, I kissed my native lover and we exchanged his seed from my mouth to his mouth and back several times. We repeated those oral adventures at the cabin for several Sundays, until the weather became too cold for Zeke and me to stay out there. Hawk and I then met in the barn, as using the bed in the main house could be too risky—stickiness, sweat, and other aromas considered.

Some weeks the snow was too heavy for the family to go into town. At one point I was forced to go six weeks without seeing Hawk. To make matters worse, Zeke, as a typical younger brother, shadowed my every move. Finally it was spring. Zeke and I moved back into the cabin. Jonas wanted to join us, but we convinced Pa he should grow a year older first. Then we had a little talk with the pest. We convinced the kid he would be a lot healthier, and intact, if he left us alone. "But I'm sixteen and I have to sleep in the same bed as a snot-nosed thirteen-year-old who snores and stinks."

"It's that or risk life and limb with us," Zeke told Jonas, holding a pitchfork at his younger brother's throat. Jonas saw the light, and the pain in the ass left us alone for a while.

Hawk appeared the first Sunday I was alone at the cabin, dressed only in his loincloth and moccasins—in the winter he wore deerskin leggings. After we hugged and kissed a while, Hawk announced, "I have a special gift. But first we must be purified." He showed me the herbal soap he was carrying as we went down to the pond. The water was cold, and I stood shivering in the sun with my member barely visible as Hawk soaped up my body, paying special attention to my privates and butt. When he was finished, he asked me to soap him up. We then hugged and together went back into the water to rinse off before lying down on a boulder in the warm sun to dry. Warm and dry, with hard shafts, we moved to our customary grassy lair. We reclined head to toe and took each other's members into our mouths. I fully expected we would remain in that position until we erupted. Hawk had other plans.

"It's time for your special gift," Hawk said, and he moved me onto my hands and knees.

He squatted between my thighs, placed his hands on my buttocks, and pulled them apart.

"What are you going to do?" I asked with a mix of apprehension and eagerness. Everything he'd suggested so far had proven to be exciting.

"I'm going to show you where else your body can enjoy another man's attention," Hawk replied. He then used his talented tongue to tingle my puckered shithole. I realized instantly why we had to be purified, as he was not just licking my ass; his tongue was poking into the tight pucker.

"Hot damn! Hell, that feels great!" I yelled for the whole world to hear. Hawk feasted on my tiny hole and pulled my rigid shaft downward, stroking it at the same time. I was confused and delighted at the new feeling his actions engendered. I had never thought of my butt giving me such pleasure.

No longer having a hair trigger, I enjoyed Hawk's pleasure-giving tongue for quite a while with no danger of losing my man-seed too soon. Eventually, my curiosity prevailed and I asked, "Can I try this on your hole?" Hawk said nothing but lay down on his back and raised his legs over his head, bringing his pucker up for easy licking—which I did with a vengeance. I tried to stroke Hawk's shaft as I laved and probed his pucker, but he slapped my hand away. "Not yet, please."

"Okay," I said. "But my tongue is getting sore and all I'm tasting is my own saliva, not your sweet juices."

"It is time for the second part of the special gift then. Place the tip of your lance where your mouth-snake was and push it into my secret cave."

I didn't think it was possible. My weapon was a lot bigger than the tiny opening in his butt. Nevertheless, I decided to give it a try. Hawk had never misled me before. I rose up on my knees, pressed my pole's tip against the puckered opening, and leaned forward, putting my weight onto his little hole. Amazingly enough, the pucker opened and my shaft slipped into a hot, tight haven.

"Oh! Ungh!" Hawk moaned, as I was sure the girth of my member was tearing his ass apart. But he didn't tell me to stop, so I kept up the steady forward and downward pressure until my balls were slapping against his buttocks.

"God damn! This is the best thing yet!" I hollered. "I must be fucking you! I didn't know two men could fuck."

"It's the best gift a man can give another if their souls are united as one."

"That's darn beautiful! But I'm enjoying your ass too much to get philosophical right now." Hawk chuckled and tightened his anal muscles. That caused my juices to flow more forcefully and in greater volume than ever before. When I could no longer hold myself upright, I collapsed on him with my lance still impaling his ass. It was then that I noticed Hawk's weapon had fired without him or me touching it! As I lay there panting, Hawk stroked my hair and kissed my forehead. At that moment I knew I loved him with my entire being. I told him so, and he responded that he felt the same way. We promised never to be apart from each other.

Two Sundays later, Hawk was back. "I want to give you the special gift," I told him. After we purified ourselves in the pond, I pleasured his ass pucker with my mouth and tongue as he had mine at our previous encounter, and then I offered myself to him willingly, nay, gratefully. He was gentle, yet it still hurt like hell at first. My love for Hawk and desire to please him overcame the pain, and soon his body glistened with sweat as his lengthy lance speared my tender hole. The pain in my gut became a divine fire as waves of pleasure swept over my body. With a shudder, my life juices blasted from my pee hole and covered my torso. The convulsions in my bowels caused Hawk's weapon to go off, and he filled me with his precious cream. As we lay on the grass with our limbs entwined and our chests heaving, we heard a soft moan from behind a clump of trees. Upon investigating we discovered Jonas, his coveralls at his ankles and his member throbbing and spewing forth in his hands. Unknown to me, he had claimed a stomachache and was left behind. The little shit had suspected something was going on and wanted to find out what. He spied on my rendezvous with Hawk, but his lust gave him away.

"What they hell are you doing?" I asked angrily.

"Nothing like what I saw you doing with that savage. You were fornicating and committing sodomy. If I told Pa, he'd beat you before turning you over to the authorities, who would throw you in jail until you're old and gray."

"He's not a savage! Besides, why would you turn us in?" I raised my hand to threaten him.

Hawk held my hand back and whispered in my ear, "Offer him a bribe to purchase some time to come up with a better plan."

"I'll give you some of the money I earned at the granary if you promise not to tell," I proposed to my younger brother.

"It's a deal," he answered.

"Good. The cash is hidden in the old root cellar. Let me get dressed and I'll meet you there." He pulled up his coveralls and headed behind the cabin to the infrequently used underground storage area.

"Quick!" I said to Hawk. "Go home and pack everything you need. He'll hold this over me for more and more money.

When I run out, he'll wait for the right moment and tell Pa. I'll pack up after I lock him in the cellar. There's a wedding after the service today, so the folks won't be back until tomorrow. Be back when the sun is over the treetops. On your way, think about how we can disappear without you being accused of kidnapping. That could start a war. You know there are some in the territory who would use any excuse to chase your people off the reservation in order to seize the land."

"I will take care of it. My tribe respects me as an apprentice shaman and will assist."

Hawk ran into the forest, and I went to take care of Jonas, who, as I expected, was already in the cellar searching for the cash, which was actually secreted elsewhere. I locked and bolted the door from the outside and left him to berate his own stupidity and ponder how his greed got him into the situation.

Just as I finished getting the animals settled and packing, Hawk rode up with an extra horse. "Everything is arranged. We will ride south in the stream until we can get out on a rock ledge and head west. To be sure, two braves are now riding northward to create a false trail. Your brother will unfortunately tell his tale for revenge, but that will also make it difficult to claim kidnapping."

"Why are they doing all this? Do they know about us?"

"Yes, I told them we had joined our bodies and souls for life. They understand. It is part of our tradition, especially for shamans."

"Where will we go?"

"On the shores of the western ocean is a branch of my people. We will be welcomed there."

Several arduous months later, we arrived at our destination. As Hawk had predicted, we were welcomed as a couple.

I learned their language and made myself useful teaching English. I also picked up much of what Hawk did as a shaman. After a year, when I was twenty, I was invited to be initiated into the tribe. "The first step is to be named," Hawk explained after I accepted. "You will be given a potion that will cause you to sleep and dream. When you awaken, you must describe all the details of your dream to the assembled elders and shamans. They will discern your name from the account. I dreamed of a hawk circling above the encampment. When I awoke and told my tale, one of the elders went out from the tent and observed a hawk, of the exact colors and size I had described, circling overhead. That is how I was named Soaring Hawk. In our tribe, bird names are the most revered and predict shamanistic powers for the individual."

When I was revived from my drug-induced sleep, I described a raven—a most unusual one. In size, shape, and sound it resembled an ordinary raven, but it was as white as newly fallen snow. In the sky around the tree where the raven was perched, a hawk flew in lazy circles. That caused quite a commotion. Hawk escorted me from the tent and scanned the sky with one of the elders. When they spotted a hawk like the one I described, they went back inside and I heard a lot of loud talking that I could not understand. Shortly thereafter, Hawk came out from the tent, hugged me, and led me back inside by the hand.

"Your name is White Raven," the chief announced. "In our tradition that is the most sacred of bird names. You and Soaring Hawk will be the most revered shamans ever. Your abilities will increase as your love for each other grows stronger. You will die in each other's arms and be forever together watching over the tribe." Hawk and I wept as we heard those prophetic words. That was many years ago.

Tonight, we both know, is the last we will be together in the flesh. We are now eighty and have outlived scores of elders, but our bodies are frail and our hearts weak. We will share our physical love one final time, then fall asleep, never to awaken. Our spirits will be forever joined in the world beyond the sky, so we are at peace.

"Come to me, White Raven. Let me offer you my special gift for the last time."

"Yes, Soaring Hawk. I come."

To Lucy
From
Maia
Penfold

THE
RED
BUDDHA

poems by

Maia Penfold

HCOLOM
Press

The Red Buddha by Maia Penfold
© 2010 Maia Penfold

ISBN: 978-0-9776783-3-4

Cover Design & Layout: *Chris Yeseta*

Photo credits:
   Page 15: *Cindy Krieble*
   Back Cover: *Leslie Clapson; taken on*
      Bainbridge Island, 2010
   Section I: *Larry Penfold*
   Section II: *Larry Penfold*
   Section III: *photographer unknown;*
      taken in Augustfehn, Germany, circa 1930
   Section IV: *John Goldak; taken in*
      Prince Albert, Saskatchewan, Canada

Hcolom Press
605 E. 5th Avenue
Ellensburg, Washington 98926

web page: http://www.hcolompress.com

email: dasleben@fairpoint.net